MW00354914

BEYOND
PREJUDICE

A NOVEL BY RASCHELLE WURZER

With Love,
Raschelle Wurzer

Beyond Prejudice
by Raschelle Wurzer

© Copyright 2011 Raschelle Wurzer. All rights reserved. No portion of this book may be reproduced by any means, electronic or mechanical, including photocopying, recording, or by any information storage retrieval system, without permission of the copyright's owner, except for the inclusion of brief quotations for a review.

ISBN: 978-1-935986-11-9

raschellewurzer@juno.com

http://raschellewurzer.blogspot.com

LIBERTY
U N I V E R S I T Y™
Press

Lynchburg, Va.

www.liberty.edu/libertyuniversitypress

To my husband, Daniel,

for inspiring me to discover the essence of true love.

TABLE OF CONTENTS

CHAPTER ONE

Take your worries to the Lord. He'll carry them for you. The command came to Elizabeth as if floating on the ocean breeze. If only she could apply those words to every situation in her life, and truly trust that God was in control. She walked alongside David on the San Francisco beach, longing to slip her hand in his as the sun began to sink beneath the western horizon. The amber rays sparkled as if adorned with a thousand diamonds. Elizabeth let out a sigh of contentment at such beauty and breathed a prayer of thanks.

O Lord, thank You. Thank You for being bigger than my concerns. You know how I struggle to trust You. Please help me to trust You completely, both now and forever. She thought of the tightening immigration laws that had made her fearful ever since she met David. She had learned to love him, and didn't want the rising unrest to destroy their relationship. His father had come to America years ago, as myriads of other aliens had done over the last fifty years, to carve out a more promising future for themselves. What if Asian immigrants were turned away in years to come? Or even worse, what if the government sent non-citizens back to their homelands? *Please help me to trust You.*

Elizabeth's contemplations were interrupted by a light touch on her shoulder. She turned to see David, his ebony, almond-shaped eyes fixed intently on her, as if he were trying to delve into her innermost soul. She had seen that look before, more in the past weeks than she ever had. What did it mean?

With his arm about her shoulder, David turned his attention to the waves, but Elizabeth could tell his thoughts were not on the vast ocean. They were far off. Where, she didn't know, and she thought for one fleeting moment it might be better that she didn't. To her, a man's mind was a strange instrument. Something she hadn't quite figured out in her nineteen years. Not now; maybe not ever.

Lately, David seemed preoccupied with news of Hitler's movement in the war overseas. He'd also talked more of his ambitions to become a missionary to his father's homeland—Japan. To Elizabeth, the mission field seemed a daunting place, filled with people who would rather be left alone to follow the religions and customs of their ancestors, than to be led to faith in Jesus Christ.

David let his arm drop from Elizabeth's shoulder and back to his side. A cold mantle of disappointment settled over her. She had come to love his touch. Immediately, she chided herself for the feelings she would have deemed foolish had she experienced them a year ago. Yet, the longing for David's affection remained. It was a relatively new feeling, but it came frequently and intensely, just the same. To her, it was becoming a natural part of their relationship.

"Elizabeth?" David's voice was barely audible above the rush of the incoming tide.

"Yes?"

He sighed. It was not a sigh of contentment as hers had been, but one which held undesirable weight. Finally, he spoke. "So–so much has happened."

"What do you mean?" Elizabeth turned to face him. Still he stared at the waves. She stood, watching him, his chest ebbing and flowing with hard, quick breaths.

"So much has happened with us." Motioning with his finger at the space between them, he continued. "Even though we've only known each other for several short months, I feel that I know you..." With his last words, he turned to face her, "...better than anyone else in my life." Now his voice became stronger. With each word he spoke, he seemed more self-assured. His familiar grin threatened to spread across his face.

"We've learned to trust one another. I want to continue that trust." His thumbs gently caressed the back of her hands. "I want that trust to grow as I share every day of my life with you, if you'll let me. Will you marry me?"

The words rang in Elizabeth's ears. Had David actually proposed? Had she heard him correctly? At first, she feared she might be dreaming, only to awaken and have the magical moment slip from her.

But no, it was too real to be a dream. The full moon shone brightly over the water. She could feel the ocean breeze running its fingers through her hair and the wetness of fresh tears she didn't realize had fallen.

David was silent now, patiently awaiting her answer. He let go of one of her hands, reaching up to carefully brush her tears away. Then he tilted her head up, and looked directly into her eyes. As if staring through to his transparent soul, Elizabeth could read the extent of his love. He was not forcing his way in, as so many others would have done, but was in every aspect a gentleman, risking rejection and allowing her time to respond.

One thing she so valued about her relationship with David was their shared faith in Jesus Christ. And that made all the difference in the world. She'd had other boyfriends, the majority of whom had not shared this faith. The end result was always heartache.

She knew she must answer him. It would be unfair to keep him waiting even a second longer than necessary. She owed that much to him, regardless. But she was unable to find her voice. So, still staring into his eyes, she simply nodded. Yes, she would be his bride. Yes, she would share her life with him. Yes, without a doubt. Yes. David's face brightened, and at this confirmation he dug into his pocket, retrieving a small wooden box. He gingerly clicked open the latch, setting the top to rest on its hinges.

Elizabeth drew in a quick breath. She had endlessly dreamed of the moment when the one she loved slipped a ring onto her finger, declaring never to be parted from her. She felt the coolness of the metal. This moment was real. A single diamond shimmered as she moved her finger back and forth. Elizabeth looked up at David, and this time his smile spread from ear to ear. Maybe this was part of what had preoccupied him during the past weeks; the weight of somehow, somewhere, proposing marriage to her. But it didn't matter anymore. He had proposed and she had accepted. Nothing could change that now. Her heart leapt as she jumped into his awaiting arms.

* * *

Elizabeth rushed down the sidewalk toward the newspaper office, her mind congested with the overwhelming plans for her March wedding, just short of six months away. Her pulse quickened with the thought. She was ready, wasn't she?

Elizabeth remembered when she met David last spring. She and a friend had been browsing through the library, contemplating which of Shakespeare's tragedies to read next, when–whack! A paper wad hit Elizabeth squarely in the back of her neck.

Who had thrown that thing? She whirled around, her gaze met by a young Japanese student with a now familiar grin. He'd given a wave, and then proceeded to introduce himself. What a ridiculous way to meet a girl! An easy friendship was quickly followed by courtship.

Arriving at her destination, Elizabeth shut the newspaper office door behind her and scanned the room for the receptionist, Margaret Owens, her close friend from grammar school. She spotted Maggie crouched behind the desk, thumbing through a drawer of thick files.

"Hello, Maggie," she called.

Maggie stood up from her cramped position, moving to greet her friend as she dusted off her navy skirt. "Why, Elizabeth Tyler! If it isn't the bride-to-be herself! How have you been? Oh, let me see that ring. My, it *is* pretty. You've got a good man, that David Mitsuko." Maggie finally paused to catch her breath.

"I've been wonderful, Maggie, thank you." Elizabeth tried to stifle a giggle at her friend's excitement. She slipped her hand into her purse. "Actually, I came by to give you the engagement announcement and a picture for the paper."

Snatching the picture, Maggie held it up to the light. "What a handsome couple you are. Wish it were me getting married." She dabbed at her eyes, and then cleared her throat. "Enough of that," she said, more to herself than to her companion.

"You'll have to give them personally to Mr. Wyner, Elizabeth. He's the new editor. Says he wants to go over every advertisement, announcement, article, before it's accepted for print." She rolled her eyes. "I'll get him for you."

A moment later, a petite gray-haired man appeared in the doorway. His glasses looked as if they would slip off his nose at any moment. Glancing in Elizabeth's direction, he crossed the room to where she stood. "Morning. Maggie says you've got an engagement announcement for me."

"Yes." Elizabeth handed him the items. "We'd like you to put it in next week's paper if you could." As Mr. Wyner surveyed the picture, his smile faded, nearly forming a frown. He scratched his head as if deep in thought.

"Is something wrong?" Elizabeth asked.

"Huh?" Mr. Wyner lifted his eyes from the picture to meet her gaze. "Uh, no...I'll, uh...have this in for next week." He gave a little wave as if to dispel any further inquiry, but the smile did not reappear. Shuffling toward his office, he turned away from them. "No problem."

No problem? It didn't seem quite that way.

* * *

Elizabeth only picked at her food that evening at supper. More interesting than the meatloaf on her plate was her Great Aunt Rose sitting across the table from her. The elderly woman had stayed with Elizabeth and her parents on more than one occasion when seeking refuge in California from the fall and winter months of her Midwestern home.

"I remember one early blizzard we had in October," her aunt was saying. "We had snow up to our knees by the end of the first night."

Elizabeth shuddered at the thought of the snow and freezing temperatures. She'd stay right here in San Francisco, thank you very much. No wonder Aunt Rose spent so much time here!

"Is David coming tonight, Elizabeth?" her mother asked.

Elizabeth put down her water glass. "No, I don't think so. He's busy studying tonight."

"Ah, yes," her father said, "I remember those days. And those all-nighters right before finals. My goodness." He stared across the table for a moment, and then continued. "David is a hard worker, Elizabeth. He'll be a good provider. I couldn't have done better for a future son-in-law."

Elizabeth smiled at his response, but wondered at the pinched look on Aunt Rose's face. Was her leg bothering her again? Catching Elizabeth's eyes on her, Aunt Rose set down her fork, and promptly excused herself from the table.

* * *

Later that evening, Elizabeth sat in the living room, her long-time friend Patti at her side, each of them pouring through a catalogue filled with the latest bridal fashions. Other planning books lay strewn across the floor. "What about this one?" Patti asked. She pointed to a lacy gown with a chapel-length train and tiny satin covered buttons down the length of the back.

Elizabeth sighed as she stood up to stoke the fireplace. "I don't know. They're all so beautiful."

Silence passed between the friends for several minutes before Patti spoke. "There's something I've wanted to ask you, Elizabeth."

"About what?" Elizabeth returned to her seat beside Patti.

"Well, about David."

"What about him?"

Patti fidgeted in her chair. "Are you sure about marrying him? Positively sure?"

Elizabeth nodded as she bit her lip. "Of course, that's why I said yes to his proposal. Why wouldn't I be sure? I know I love him."

"But–you–he–you both..." Patti sighed. "...you both are different."

Elizabeth crossed her arms. "How?" She thought she understood what Patti was driving at.

Patti took a deep breath, then plunged on. "He's Japanese," she said, "and you're not." She sighed as if in relief over her proclamation.

"That doesn't matter." Elizabeth tightened her crossed arms. "We love one another. That's all that counts."

Patti closed her eyes and nodded. "I know that, and I wouldn't hurt you for the world. I just want you to be prepared."

"Prepared for what?"

"The future. A family. Children who won't have your blonde hair and blue eyes, but dark hair and almond eyes. Children with Asian blood, just like their father."

Elizabeth's mind flashed back to her encounters with Mr. Wyner and Aunt Rose. So that was the reason for their odd behavior. They also doubted the match.

Elizabeth had always dreamt her daughters would inherit her own thick blonde tresses. A miniature me, she used to think. But now, reality sunk into her soul with each word Patti spoke. If she married David, they would be different: she and her children. Thoughts of the San Francisco school district recently trying to segregate its schools crept into Elizabeth's mind. If President Roosevelt hadn't canceled the order, her children may have to go to an institution of inferior instruction. Mr. Mitsuko, David's father, had faced picket lines when he had opened his Japanese dry goods store. It was his quiet courage alone that dispelled the disrespectful crowd. Asian children could be faced with picket lines at the public schools, should the segregation issue be drawn out again. Was that something she was willing to face?

Would other friends and relatives react with racist attitudes, just as Mr. Wyner and Aunt Rose had done? Elizabeth looked down at the ring on her finger. Could love alone overcome this prejudice?

CHAPTER TWO

Sleep was hard to come by that night for Elizabeth. What little slumber she got was interrupted by incessant nightmares. In between her tossing and turning, she had dreamt it was her wedding day. The pastor was speaking as she and David stood at the altar. "If there be any objection to this union, let us hear it now." To her horror, nearly every hand raised in protest, including her own! Elizabeth lay awake, recalling the dream, and others where she couldn't find her own children in a sea of Japanese faces. How absurd! It seemed as if the nightmares signified that their marriage really wasn't meant to be.

Elizabeth sat up and lifted her eyes to the ceiling tiles. "O Lord God, what am I to do?" The desperate words tumbled from her lips. Accompanied only by the wanderings of her mind, Elizabeth watched the early morning hours slowly tick by.

When the rest of the house began stirring, Elizabeth methodically readied herself for the Sunday morning service. Watching a sunrise had always been one of her favorite things. To look on as a new day unfolded, extending its arms to anyone who dared to enjoy it, always invigorated Elizabeth. Now she wished the day wouldn't begin, because today, as on every Sunday, she would see David, and she wasn't sure she could look at him without him sensing something was wrong and probing in an effort to relieve it. He strove for complete honesty in whatever situation arose and that had always been his way, and one of the things she admired him for. Right now honesty was what Elizabeth feared most.

Nevertheless, the morning progressed, and she met David outside the church as she did every Sunday. Once inside, they sang the familiar old hymns, but Elizabeth found herself only moving her lips to the words, and going through the motions of a typical Sunday morning.

She glanced across the sanctuary at Peter and Anna, a newlywed couple. Peter put an arm around Anna, as if he were protecting her and the baby she carried. Elizabeth wanted her own marriage to turn out like that. Even now, one year after their wedding, Peter and Anna were very much in love. Anyone in the room could testify that their love had not faded with the wedding bells. They looked as though they loved each other more now than before.

No one had objected to Peter and Anna's engagement. Not a single soul. Why should she and David's engagement be questioned, then? Of course, Peter and Anna were both Caucasian, and that seemed to make a big difference in society's view.

"Hey, are you feeling all right?" David whispered. Elizabeth nodded numbly, willing herself to look at him. His eyes showed concern.

Elizabeth thought it best to keep her feelings at bay, so she forced a smile. . David returned her smile. Did he sense the problems that could arise as a result of their upcoming marriage? Had he the slightest clue what they would be facing if they went through with their plans?

* * *

"I want to build you a house someday," David said as they neared the Mitsuko's house on their walk from church that day. Elizabeth glanced up from studying the sidewalk cracks. David stared ahead, as if envisioning the home he would one day construct.

"It should be in the country, miles from the city. Fresh air, lots of space." David breathed deeply at his description.

Elizabeth smiled as she listened, but her heart held his words in check. Would their someday come, or would he be building a house for another woman? Maybe a young bride with ebony tresses and dark, almond-shaped eyes?

David opened the back door of his parents' house, stepping aside to let Elizabeth enter first. "Wasn't that a wonderful sermon this morning?" Mr. Tyler was saying from the living room. It had become usual for the two families to dine together after church, taking time for fellowship.

"*Hai,*" Mrs. Mitsuko said. "Pastor John is not afraid to speak the truth."

As she and David sat down on the sofa, Elizabeth smiled at Mrs. Mitsuko's interjection of Japanese. After coming to the States, she had vowed to keep her Japanese heritage alive. "For my children's sake," she had said, "and for their children, too." Elizabeth thought of David's sister Marie, studying at a university in Tokyo, and wished she were there to share the afternoon with them. Marie had often been a confidante, and Elizabeth longed to spill her marriage concerns to her friend now.

One glance around the Mitsuko's living room would easily reveal a Japanese heritage. Thin, oriental-patterned rugs in crimson and royal blue covered the wooden floor. Matching cushions were placed in the center of the room around a low, rectangular table. It was there that Mr. and Mrs. Mitsuko and Mr. and Mrs. Tyler sat now. They looked relaxed and content in their seated positions.

At one end of the room sat a nineteenth century sofa, upholstered in brick red material with gold threads. "It is for my American friends," Mrs. Mitsuko had explained in reference to the seat, "for the ones who don't want to sit on the floor!" The sofa faced the room's only window. "Toward Japan," she had said.

David and Elizabeth sat on the sofa, their fingers interlocked. "Yes, his message was good this morning," Mrs. Tyler agreed. "His thoughts about Christ ministering to the Samaritan woman were most interesting. I had never heard an interpretation of the passage quite like that before."

Elizabeth turned her attention once more to the day's sermon. Christ ministering to the Samaritan woman? Had that been the sermon's topic? Elizabeth wrinkled her forehead while trying to recall any of the pastor's words. It was useless. She couldn't remember any part of the sermon. Hadn't she been paying attention at all?

Mr. Mitsuko, silent until now, cleared his throat. He was usually quiet, speaking only when his words were well thought-out. "It touched me when he talked of Jesus, as a Jew, associating with the Samaritan woman, regardless of her race, creed, or background." His eyes traveled about the room, then settled on David and Elizabeth. "It was not a matter of outward things, but of the heart—of what the Samaritan woman had to offer by choosing to live a life of righteousness."

The room was silent now, everyone engrossed in their own thoughts. Closing her eyes, Elizabeth could feel the powerful love in the atmosphere of the room. A love of people peacefully coexisting together, with each one helping the others. If only all of San

Francisco could look past race and outward appearance.

Elizabeth thought of her discussion with Patti. Surely Patti had been wrong. How could this marriage not be of God, despite their ethnic differences? Yet the gnawing pain in her heart continued, and with each minute of carrying it silently, a little more weight was added to the already burdensome load.

The minutes ticked by, but still no one spoke. Elizabeth took in a jagged breath. How could she endure these worries alone? How could she face the realization that it might be difficult, or even impossible, for her and David to marry–all because of people who did not fully understand Christ's acceptance of all races?

She felt David's fingers tighten around her own. Did he sense her unrest? Without warning, Elizabeth pulled her hand away. Glancing at David, she saw surprise, then hurt shadow his face. What on earth should she do now?

Resting her head in her hands, she began to cry silent tears at first, and then her tears gave way to sobs.

David was the first to comfort her. "What's wrong, Elizabeth?" He placed his hand on her shoulder. "Tell me what's bothering you."

She sniffed, violently shaking her head. David tried to embrace her, but she jerked away. She'd never resisted his affections before.

I will not entertain what cannot be, she thought.

"Dearie, what's troubling you?" Mrs. Mitsuko came to her side. Soon, everyone was crowded around her, coaxing her to pour out her troubles.

At last, Elizabeth spoke. "It–." She was cut off by a sob. After it passed, she tried to speak again. "It won't work."

"What won't work, honey?" Mr. Tyler asked.

"Us." She pointed to herself and David.

"What do you mean?" David raised his voice. Mr. Mitsuko laid a restraining hand on his son's shoulder.

"We're different. And–and everybody knows it. They don't like it," Elizabeth finished, fresh tears falling fast.

"This concern has come up suddenly, hasn't it, Elizabeth?" Mrs. Tyler said. "You knew about the racial differences in your relationship long before you thought about marriage. Why should it bother you now?"

"I don't know." Elizabeth's tears began to subside. "It's mainly because of the way people are reacting to news of our engagement."

"Who, for instance?" Mrs. Tyler prodded, her voice even and controlled.

"Well, Aunt Rose last night at dinner." Elizabeth sniffed. "The way she acted when we talked about David. She looked almost–almost disdainful, as if she disapproved. Then she left the room."

"I noticed that, too." Mrs. Tyler shifted in her seat. "But you can't let that bother you. Aunt Rose has been through many trials that could have left her bitter." She raised her hand. "It's no excuse, I know, but you must try to be as understanding as you possibly can."

"Did you know, Elizabeth," Mr. Tyler said, "that Aunt Rose's fiancé died only a few weeks before their wedding day?" Elizabeth shook her head, her eyes growing wide.

Her father continued. "She likely remembers what it is like to be young and in love. But she also knows the pain of losing that someone."

"Has anyone else said anything to you?" Mrs. Mitsuko questioned several moments later.

"Patti," Elizabeth said, "my friend. She meant well, I know, and wasn't trying to pry, but she asked me about how I would feel, my children not looking like me. She said there would be problems."

Mrs. Tyler chuckled. "Well, my dear, your children will most likely not have your blonde locks, but it wouldn't make you love them any less, would it?

"Of course it wouldn't." Elizabeth stared at her lap.

"As for marital obstacles," Mrs. Tyler said, "I don't know of one couple who hasn't had their differences and their disagreements. But you know, we're all stronger for it. And I think I'm safe in saying that a couple of the same ethnicity, if one of them has not accepted Christ as Lord and Savior, will have far more obstacles than you may face."

Elizabeth sat in silence. Mr. Mitsuko cleared his throat. "Have you ever thought what color we would see people in if we were blind?" His words were few, the meaning profound. What argument remained?

She looked at David, still seated beside her. He had remained quiet, letting her vent her concerns, and be comforted–not by him alone, but also by their parents.

"I'm sorry," Elizabeth whispered. She let him hug her then.

"Don't be," he said into her hair.

Yes, they could overcome the obstacles that plagued them. Elizabeth was sure of that now. Just as long as they were together, love would be enough.

CHAPTER THREE

The last days of autumn slipped into oblivion, as the mild Californian winter settled on San Francisco. It seemed like all other winters to most, but to Elizabeth, the season marked a newness. She felt as if she were on the brink of a fresh beginning that no one could take from her. Her future with David as her husband shone bright before her.

And now, amidst the mild winter of California, Elizabeth could barely contain the excitement that welled up within her. In the spring, Miss Elizabeth Tyler would become Mrs. David Mitsuko. It was as simple as that.

Elizabeth smiled, nearly giggling out loud in her merriment. Her steps became quicker along the pavement leading to the church, a shiver running down her spine. The bite of the early December breeze reminded her of idle tongues wagging in gossip. Perhaps now more than ever, she was the object of ridicule in her social circle. Through the past weeks, she had learned to tune out the ridiculous chatter of old women and young friends, who would just as soon have her marry a pigeon than an Asian. But it didn't matter now that she had learned to vent her concerns to her family and family-to-be, and let the Lord take care of idle gossip.

Elizabeth panted for breath as she approached the church steps where David stood waiting for her. "My, my." He said observing her breathless state. "You just couldn't wait to see me, could you? Did you run all the way from East Street?" Still unable to speak, Elizabeth silently took his arm and nodded toward the door. They would be late if they didn't get going.

David and Elizabeth slipped into the last pew just as first strains of the opening hymn filled the sanctuary. Today was unlike their regular Sunday worship. It was a special day for Peter and Anna and for their precious little one. A tiny, new one. Peter and Anna would dedicate their Anthony to the Lord today. The baby would hopefully belong to Christ and His service for his entire life, thanks in part to his God-fearing parents.

Pastor John gingerly took Anthony from Anna's arms. She leaned slightly on Peter, her strength not yet fully regained from the laborious pregnancy. But the serene look on her face would tell anyone in a second that it had all been worth it. All the pain and discomfort had been dissolved in a torrent of motherly love.

"Do you vow, Peter and Anna, to guide Anthony in the fear of the Lord, to train him to honor and obey God, and lead him to understand the salvation available to him through Jesus Christ?" Pastor John asked.

"We do," Peter and Anna replied. No hesitancy was found in their answer.

The pastor continued. "And do you, members of this congregation, vow to uphold the teachings of the church, and to guide Anthony in the ways of the Lord as far as it depends upon you?"

"We do," Elizabeth said in unison with the congregation. What a sacred moment it was, past generations promising the next to lead them in the light of the God of the universe. Yes, Elizabeth was sure this event had been orchestrated in heaven. Nothing so blessed could have derived from a sin-stained world alone. When would it be her turn to dedicate a little one? In His time, she was sure.

* * *

Elizabeth stepped outside the church entrance and into the sunshine. So the day had not turned out so dreary after all. Good. They could walk to the Mitsuko's. Elizabeth cherished her walks each Sunday with David. It was a time for just the two of them. In those moments together, there were no deadlines, assignments, frustrations. Time seemed to hold its breath as they walked the eight blocks and talked of nothing and everything.

David stepped up beside her. "Nice day for a walk," He said. She smiled, taking his arm. Maybe he enjoyed their time together as much as she did.

They strode in silence for the first few blocks. Of what David was thinking, she didn't know. Even so, it was enough to be together in the comfortable silence.

"How were classes this week?" David said a few moments later.

"Okay, I suppose. I should be finished with the secretarial course by Christmas."

David nodded and smiled. "I'm proud of you. I'm glad you'll be done before we get married."

Elizabeth looked up in surprise. He had always encouraged her endeavors, but had made it clear before that he wanted her to be a housewife after they were married. Elizabeth had every intention of making a home for him, yet her prior goals of going to college crept into her reasoning from time to time. Would he stop her from ever pursuing them?

When she made her decision to complete the secretarial course after graduating from secondary school, she had agonized over the decision, wondering if she might be overstepping the will of the Lord for her life at that time. Though she had always dreamed of going to college to pursue a career, the Lord had made it clear to her that her motives were founded on herself and not on Him when she prayed about her decision. A secretarial certificate could give her a marketable skill without having to possibly sacrifice getting married and having a family. Still, the decision had been a hard one.

"How are your studies coming?" Elizabeth asked.

"Good, but tiresome. This May is graduation."

"I am proud of you, Mr. Mitsuko. Graduating from Bible college. The mission field of Japan is in sight. I think you have heaven in your favor." David reached down, taking her hand in his.

"Hello, Mr. Wyner!" David called to the newspaper editor as they passed the office. Mr. Wyner only glanced their way, his dark features paling, his lips turning white.

David stopped in his tracks. "Are you okay, sir?" Mr. Wyner's jaw was set, his eyes looking as if they had been set on fire.

"Stay away," he hissed. Spinning on his heel, he slammed the office door behind him.

David and Elizabeth stood still for several seconds. Should they go after him?

"Do you think he's okay?" Elizabeth whispered, half afraid the man might come out again.

David shrugged. "He probably just had a late night out. He wasn't in church this morning."

Elizabeth thought back to the encounter she'd had with Mr. Wyner a few months prior. When she had given him their engagement announcement, he had seemed indignant. Was he trying to show further disapproval of their engagement now? Surely he wouldn't be so stubborn about something that didn't concern him.

Without further comment, they resumed their stroll up and down the steep San Franciscan sidewalks. As they crested the next hill, David looked to his left toward Dayton's Park. "Hey." He stopped. "Look."

Elizabeth's gaze traveled past his pointed finger in the direction of the park. She saw trees, their branches swaying in the breeze, slides, and swings. "What?" she asked.

"It's empty. There's no kids."

Elizabeth surveyed the landscape once more. Sure enough, there wasn't a single child in sight. On any other Sunday after the church service, the park would be swarming with boys and girls, and mothers and fathers trying to patrol playtime.

"Kind of weird, isn't it?" Elizabeth glanced around.

David shrugged. "Maybe not. They're all probably at Bob Somebody's birthday party."

Elizabeth nodded. Maybe so.

Several minutes later, David and Elizabeth stepped into the Mitsuko's house, greeted by the blaring of the radio. "Why is that so loud?" David called into the living room. A moment later, Mrs. Mitsuko hurried toward the door, her bare feet pattering until she reached the carpet. She lifted a tear stained face to her son.

"Mama?" David asked. "What's wrong?" Her only response was the quiver of her lip.

"Thank goodness you're here!" Mrs. Tyler opened her arms to her daughter. "I was afraid something may have happened to you, too!"

David and Elizabeth exchanged glances. What had gotten into their mothers? What was so dangerous about walking home from church?

David took a firm hold of his mother's shoulders. "Mama, tell me. What's wrong?"

"*Jiko desu!*"

"Tell me," Elizabeth said.

David's eyes remained fixed to his mother's face. "There's been an accident."

"Where? Who?"

"It was no accident." Mr. Mitsuko strode into the room, Mr. Tyler at his heels. "I'm glad you're home."

"Dad, what's going on? Everybody's acting crazy!"

Mr. Mitsuko motioned for the group to sit down. Elizabeth

eased herself onto the floor mat, David at her side. Mr. Mitsuko's expression was pinched, his countenance grave. Still, he maintained his composure. "There's been a foreign attack on the States." He slowly formed the words, then licked his lips.

"Where?" David rose from his position next to Elizabeth. "Who did it?" His father put his hands to his forehead, remaining silent.

"Pearl Harbor–in Hawaii," Mr. Tyler said. "They bombed the U.S. Pacific Fleet."

"Who's they?" David said.

Mr. Tyler hesitated and ran his fingers through his hair for a few seconds, as if weighing the impact of the information he was about to disclose. "The Japanese. They're the ones who bombed us. Thousands of American servicemen have been killed or injured."

Elizabeth closed her eyes against the horrific news. How could anyone do such a thing? Everyone knew that the two countries had strained relations, especially when dealing with immigration laws in the United States. The war in Europe had done nothing to ease the tensions. Even so, it hardly justified the extermination of thousands of innocent people.

The room grew silent as the radio broadcasts recounted the catastrophe over and over and over. Ships bursting into flames; bodies plunging into the watery depths in which the ships were anchored. When would this nightmare end? Mr. Mitsuko crossed the room to the radio, turning it off with a flick of his wrist. If only it were that easy to silence the effects of the attack. This disaster would likely tip the racial scales in favor of increased immigration control.

Elizabeth felt arms enfolding her. David's arms, strong and sure, that would never let her go. He would never want to let harm touch her. But what if it did, despite his efforts? What if further strains with Japan caused even more distress over their upcoming marriage? Would David feel the same about her then? Mrs. Mitsuko dabbed at her eyes, her husband consoling her.

What was to come because of this disaster?

* * *

"I'm having lunch with Maggie today," Elizabeth told David the next Saturday as they walked downtown. "Could you walk me to the newspaper office? I told her I'd meet her at 12:30."

"So what will you and Maggie have to talk about over lunch?" David asked.

Elizabeth giggled. "Well, most likely it will be her doing the talking. I'll just listen, nod, and agree. You should have seen her when I brought in our engagement announcement. She adores you, I'm sure."

David reached to open the office door. "You're not jealous that she adores me, are you?"

Elizabeth stepped inside. "Oh, of course I am!" She laughed. It was good to laugh, a way to forget Pearl Harbor and move on with life.

Not long ago, there had been prank air raid warnings. One report had claimed there were multiple planes circling the city, ready to deface whatever lay in the path of the inevitable bombs. No foreign aircraft had been found. Not a single plane. The tensions at home and overseas were worsening racial tensions. The rest of the world was making it hard to put the tragedy aside. Not only was there war overseas, but also war in San Francisco.

* * *

"Elizabeth!" Maggie's cheerful greeting dispelled the fog in Elizabeth's brain, helping her concentrate on the day before her. The Lord would watch out for them, foreign planes or not.

"Oh, you brought David. How special." She took one of each of their hands as if holding them out for inspection. "Ah, yes, such a handsome couple. Even better than the picture."

David gave Elizabeth a sideways glance. "Oh, don't mind me," Maggie said. "I'm known as a babbler. I just love folks, I guess."

"Maggie!" a voice thundered behind her. "This is a place of business, not a social gathering."

Elizabeth looked up to see Mr. Wyner, arms folded across his narrow chest, his eyes red and puffy. He leaned against the door frame, a scowl crawling across his lips.

For once, Maggie stumbled for words. "Uh, s-sir, I...I apolo-"

"And you!" Mr. Wyner pointed a long, thin index finger squarely at David's head. "What are you doing here, in my office?"

David gulped. "Well, sir, I just came to-"

"To what? Kill me, too? Kill me like your friends did my boy? While he was just doing his United States duty there in Hawaii, they just up and murdered him. It was just as if you did it yourself, you, you dirty Jap!"

Elizabeth's heart raced, her hands shaking. What would he do now? Gripping David's hand, she realized he was trembling too.

"Well?" Mr. Wyner said. "What do you have to say for yourself and your disgusting relatives?" He shook his fist in the air. "Answer me!" David made no attempt to answer, and Mr. Wyner's face reddened, the veins in his temples threatening to explode. "Get out!" he screamed, lunging for David. David stepped back, and Mr. Wyner's clenched fists missing him by inches. The lunge threw Mr. Wyner off balance and left him in a heap on the hard tile. He lay still, making no attempt to move.

David gently pushed Elizabeth toward the door, his eyes never leaving Mr. Wyner until the door had shut behind them. They swiftly walked several blocks before stopping for breath.

Elizabeth allowed the tears to come now, flowing swiftly down her flushed cheeks. "Oh, David! I was so scared. I thought he was going to hurt you."

David embraced her tightly. "I know." She felt the rapid thumping of his heart, his body still shaking. "I thought so, too."

CHAPTER FOUR

Elizabeth stared hard at the sequin she was attempting to sew on the white satin spread across her lap. How many had she sewn on today? A hundred, or more? Despite the tedious chore, Elizabeth smiled to herself. She had to finish sewing her wedding dress within the week. February was melting away, and March would make her wedding dreams a reality. Her parents' hushed voices drifted into the living room where she was working, the steady ticking of the grandfather clock keeping her stitches in time.

As she sewed, Elizabeth thought about the war, Japan, and Pearl Harbor. The war had already altered her life, she had to admit. After the bombings in Hawaii, some friends and neighbors had retaliated against all Japanese, even those who were American citizens. All names of friends and family members who had expressed disgust at the racial intermarriage had been crossed off the wedding invitation list.

A knock at the front door interrupted Elizabeth's thoughts. She hurried to cover the wedding dress with a nearby crocheted afghan as David opened the door. "David. I didn't expect you tonight."

He shut the door behind him. "I know. Where's your father?"

"In the kitchen." Elizabeth stared at David. He looked tired. "Is something wrong?"

"Just get him, Elizabeth."

Several moments later, she returned to the room, her father behind her. "I thought I heard your voice, David." Mr. Tyler crossed the room to where David stood.

David thrust a paper at him. "They've already taken Dad."

"What do you mean?" Mr. Tyler frowned and reached for the paper.

"Read it," David said. "It explains everything."

All was silent as Mr. Tyler read the paper. Elizabeth watched her father's expression as his frown grew deeper. The paper began to rustle as his hands shook and a gasp escaped his lips.

Carefully taking the paper from her father's hands, Elizabeth began to read. The legal jargon made her nervous, but what did it mean? What was the president saying? Elizabeth glanced up at David, his eyes fixed to her face.

"Keep reading," he said, "you'll understand."

Elizabeth scanned the remaining lines. What had David said? They had taken his father away? Who were they? Her heart felt cold as she realized Mr. Mitsuko had never become a United States citizen. "The government is evacuating Japanese immigrants?" she asked.

David sniffed as he took her chilled hands in his. "It's not just immigrants."

He rubbed his eyes. "It's not just immigrants. It's citizens, too." When she didn't respond, he sighed. "Elizabeth," he whispered, "they're evacuating me, too."

His words seemed shallow in the first few moments of their utterance, their meaning foreign. She had never heard of such a thing. Then slowly, as if being siphoned into her soul, the gravity of their situation hit her. Evacuated...taken away...to where?

Elizabeth's breath caught in her throat. Groping for a chair, she felt pressure constricting her chest. She had to think, and to find some way to make it all go away. This horrible nightmare must be erased from her life and the lives of those she loved. Finding nothing on which to lean, she let herself sink to the floor in a faint.

"Elizabeth!" The frantic voice calling her seemed distanced by the thoughts crushing her mind. Yet, even then, she knew it was David's voice.

"Honey, talk to us," another voice said, more composed than the first. Her father was calling. She must get up and face this. Slowly, she forced her eyelids open. There they were, David, her father, and now her mother huddled over her.

"Are you all right, Elizabeth?" Mrs. Tyler said. Elizabeth nodded silently. Her body was well enough. It was the pain of reality that seemed so unbearable.

* * *

The next afternoon, Elizabeth walked alone on the beach. The day was warm, the sun beckoning her out to the waves she had loved since she was a little girl. The azure water normally had a strange calming effect on her and she hoped to find it as true today as on any other occasion. Deep inside, her soul ached with a longing for the way things used to be, before Pearl Harbor. Yet, it had not been entirely peaceful then, either. Years before, a portion of society already viewed the Japanese as the lesser class. Then the world's war with Germany had started before the Japanese attack and had strained relations between Japan and America. The rising racism since Pearl Harbor threatened to shove aside the very core of all she held most dear.

Slipping off her shoes, Elizabeth wiggled her toes in the damp sand, still chilly this early in the year. Oh, to be a child playing in the sand at her mother's feet, distanced from the cares of the world by age and lack of understanding. To be a little girl, whose only cares of life are the proper architecture of a sand castle, and making certain that the sand was not too wet, nor too dry, and that her structure would not fall unless she wanted it to.

Squeezing her eyes shut, Elizabeth tried in vain to make the reality of her circumstances disappear. The waves roared in her ears, sending a shiver down her spine. The ocean was massive, bigger than anything she had ever seen. It was more powerful than the strongest man or machine, destroying whatever disturbed its path. And God had created it in one breath. Not only that, He had the power to calm this massive body of water, as He had done to the lake His disciples sailed on in the book of Mark.

Tears welled up in her eyes. She blinked, but the tears overflowed and rushed in torrents down her cheeks, her body shaking. Her mind was flooded with ideas of what would happen to them in the next months, weeks, even days. She would have to be evacuated with David after they were married. It was the only honorable thing to do. She loved him, and would rather be evacuated with her new husband, than forced to be married and estranged, even if it meant moving the wedding date up three months and sacrificing some of her previous plans.

Elizabeth sniffed, sinking to her knees in the wet sand. Today the beach would be an altar, for that is what she needed. The tide came in, drenching her skirt, but she paid no attention. Folding her hands, she began to pray.

"Dear Lord God, You know me even better than I know myself." She paused to wipe away several tears. "And You know my hurt just now. It must hurt You, too. I wonder why You don't calm the storm for me like You did so many years ago for Your followers. You have a plan, I'm sure, but I don't understand it. Please–please help me to trust You, both now and forever. I'm willing to go with David, Lord, I'm willing."

What did the Lord think of all this? One race putting down another, all in the name of war? What good could it possibly bring? She lifted her eyes to the waves once more, a sickening feeling filling the pit of her stomach. She could stay with David through the evacuation. It would be all right. Wouldn't it?

"Elizabeth."

Elizabeth whirled her head around at the sound of David's voice. How did he find her here?

He took a seat beside her on the damp sand. He sighed. "We need to talk about something."

What didn't need to be sorted out? Everything in life at present was rent apart by confusion and unrest. Elizabeth waited for him to go on. His eyes darted across the water as if in search of security. He looked down the beach once, twice. Finally, he turned toward her.

"What is it?" she asked.

He took in a shaky breath. "My dad has already been relocated." His eyes welled up with tears. Never had she seen David cry. She wished he wouldn't cry now. She couldn't stand to see him cry without crying herself. But as much as she wished otherwise, the tears readily spilled down his cheeks.

"Mama went to the county office to see where they had taken him," David said. "But all they said was that he was gone. We don't even know where!"

Elizabeth stared at him. The American government had taken Mr. Mitsuko and no one knew where? What had he done to threaten the country? Forty years prior, Mr. Mitsuko had come to America to start a new life. For what? Imprisonment by those he called neighbor and friend?

But now was not the time for questions and anger. Now was the time for comfort. Gently, she gathered David in her arms. So many times he had been the one to console, comfort, and protect. This time it was her turn.

He continued to sob, his tears wetting her sleeve. Let it all come out, my love, she thought. Let it all come out. David sniffed again, pulling himself to an upright position. "There's something else I need to tell you. All of us will be leaving soon."

"Oh, I know, David, but I'll be ready," Elizabeth said. "It doesn't matter that I can't have the large wedding we've planned. Just as long as we're safe and together, I'll be happy. I promise."

David stared at her. "What do you mean?" he asked. "Where are you going?"

Elizabeth frowned. "With you, of course, when you're relocated."

An odd look passed over David's face. What was he withholding? What did he mean, asking where she was going? They would certainly go together, wouldn't they?

"Elizabeth." David's eyes seemed to bore straight through her, peering into the thoughts of her mind and the anguish of her soul. "These past few weeks have been crazy. Everybody is taking sides and blaming one another. No one can even think clearly." He stopped, running his fingers through his hair. "No, that's not what I'm trying to say at all." He closed his eyes for a moment, as if in pain, and then slowly started again.

"We'll be leaving soon." His voice was barely above a whisper. His forefinger traced the outline of her cheek. "Only my family and me."

Elizabeth's hands shook. "What do you mean, David?"

He sighed. "You have to stay here. You can't come with me. It wouldn't be fair to you."

"But I don't want to be separated from you, especially just after we get married!" Elizabeth's voice rose with her proclamation. If there was one thing she was sure of, it was her own mind when it was made up. That was that. She got up to hurry away, but David grabbed her arm.

"Wait! Elizabeth, you're being unreasonable. I'm not about to marry you and desert you." The scowl on Elizabeth's face softened at his words. "It wouldn't be right to ask you to stop our wedding plans and get married in a quick ceremony. Not now, not while things are so uncertain. It wouldn't be fair. You deserve better than that."

Elizabeth's heart quickened. She knew what he was trying to say. He didn't want to blurt it out, not to her. She was sure he would give anything not to be the cause of yet another wound. "You–you mean we..." No, the realization was too painful already.

David gently reached down and touched Elizabeth's ring. "Let's wait," he whispered. It was half a command. Let's wait. How long would it be? A month, maybe more? Her bottom lip quivered. This couldn't be happening to her. Maybe it could happen to someone else halfway around the world in a country torn apart by civil conflict, but not to her here in sheltered California.

As if numbed by reality, Elizabeth nodded stiffly. They would wait. They would wait for a time not ruled by war and prejudice. That was all. Nothing could change the unthinkable situation. Nothing in the world.

"This doesn't mean things have changed between us, Elizabeth." He cradled her face in his hands. "I love you more now than I ever have. Don't forget that."

Elizabeth stood quietly, unable to even cry. The pain was too deep for tears. It gnawed silently at her heart, unseen by any passerby, but all the same quietly dispelling the world she once knew.

CHAPTER FIVE

Elizabeth gingerly stepped off the bottom stair and onto the cold basement floor. The darkness enveloped her as she groped around for the light, running her hand up and down the side of the wall until it contacted with the switch.

The far corner of the room wasn't bare as usual. Boxes now lined both walls, containing some of the treasures the Mitsuko family owned.

"Bring only what you can carry," the government official had instructed Mrs. Mitsuko. He'd given her tags with a series of numbers. The numbers were supposed to mean "Neena and David Mitsuko" as if they had been turned into a statistic that could easily be manipulated and calculated. Just a number. Weren't lives so much more than that? A story of character, independence, and love.

What belongings the Mitsuko's left behind had to be sold or stored. They preferred storage in the Tyler's basement to selling valuable items cheaply at the last minute.

Elizabeth turned her head toward the padded sound of light footsteps coming down the stairs. "Is anyone down here?" Mrs. Mitsuko descended from the stairway.

Elizabeth set down the box she'd been carrying. "Over here. Is that everything?"

Mrs. Mitsuko nodded as she opened a box. "Yes, my dear, thank you for your help." She began to pick through the carefully packed box. "Ah, here it is." She lifted a golden chain out of a small wooden box. A crucifix hung from the center.

Mrs. Mitsuko turned it over and over in her hands, examining each side. Even though her eyes remained transfixed on the piece of jewelry, she seemed to be remembering another time, another place. Maybe she was recalling a more pleasant time; one that had not been ravaged by the endless realities of war and the evacuation of loved ones.

A few moments lapsed before she spoke to Elizabeth. "Isn't it beautiful?" Elizabeth took the proffered necklace, watching the light from the overhead bulb strike its surface. "It was given to me by a missionary woman when I was still in Japan. She told me, 'Keep it. When you wear it, it will remind you of how near God is.'"

She reached to take the necklace back from Elizabeth. "I must take this necklace with me. It will help me trust God, even when I don't feel I can."

Elizabeth could only stare at the woman in disbelief. What faith she had! She was about to be sent from her home, exiled in her own country, without knowing where she was going or for how long, yet she still trusted God. Elizabeth wondered if she could have that kind of strength under similar circumstances. Would she continue to love and obey the Lord, or turn her back on Him, angry at His seemingly passive ways in such a situation?

"How can you trust God even now?" Elizabeth asked.

Mrs. Mitsuko fastened the chain around her neck. "Well, Elizabeth, I cannot. Not by myself." She took the young woman's hands in her own. "I can only trust when I confess to God that I can't do anything in my own strength. It is then that His grace abounds, and I am able to rest in His perfect plan."

Elizabeth fidgeted, unable to resign her will to the explanation of God allowing this horrible thing to happen. Why hadn't He stopped it? Why hadn't He made the hearts of the government officials soft toward the Japanese-Americans?

Mrs. Mitsuko took Elizabeth's face in her hands, and gazed into her eyes. "You must trust, my dear. You must let God finish the work He has begun in you." She released the clasp to her necklace, and secured the chain around Elizabeth's neck. "Here," she said, "I believe you will need this as a reminder."

Elizabeth touched the cross. David's mother truly trusted her Creator. Elizabeth wondered again if she had the capacity to have that same kind of trust. Without it, she feared she might fail to endure this hardship.

* * *

That evening after dinner, David and Elizabeth sat on the porch swing at the Tyler's as they had done many times before. Even so, each knew it was no usual evening. Elizabeth felt as if the wind was wrapping itself around her heart, twisting its grip tighter and tighter, with no restraining point. She took in a labored breath. Tomorrow was the day. The day when her world would no longer be the same. The day when thousands of people would be uprooted and sent away from their homes. Wherever that might end up being, no one knew. Tomorrow was the day she would say goodbye to David, and she had no idea how long he would be gone.

Elizabeth could torture herself no longer with the thought. She forced her hand to her ring finger, and slid off her engagement ring. She knew she must do this for both their sakes. Her voice quavered as she spoke. "David, you'll need money wherever you're going. I want you to take the ring back."

The creases in David's forehead deepened. "No-o, it's yours. I couldn't take it."

"I want you to take it. It's all I have to give you." Firmly but lovingly, she pried open his fist and placed the ring in the palm of his hand. For a moment, both stared at the ring, as though it held some mysterious power over them. Neither spoke. Words held a sort of emptiness lately, as if they were of no importance in comparison to the situation they faced.

David put his arms around Elizabeth and drew her close to him. How Elizabeth loved to be held by him! Even now, the strength of his arms offered comfort for her perplexed and anguished soul. She wished this night would never end–that tomorrow would never come. But she did not cry as she had done so many times before. There were simply no more tears to shed.

* * *

The next morning, Elizabeth awoke to a pounding on her bedroom door. "Elizabeth," her father called, "honey, the Mitsuko's are here." Elizabeth rolled over, hoping to get a few more minutes of rest. Her left thumb slid to her ring finger, ready to adjust her engagement ring. It had become a sort of ritual since her and David's engagement. But her finger was bare. In a fraction of a second, the depressing reality came flooding back to her. She wasn't engaged anymore. There was no wedding to plan. Those preparations were all gone now, dashed to pieces by government officials dictating executive orders.

Today was the day all the Japanese would be evacuated. Today she would have to say goodbye to the only man she had ever loved.

She sat up slowly and rubbed her sore, tired eyes. Her cheeks were warm, almost overheated. Methodically, she dressed and brushed her hair. The mere instinctive routine saw her through the morning's simple tasks.

Elizabeth gripped the bedroom doorknob, her knuckles turning white from the pressure. Her hand was still for a few moments, as if refusing to open the door would somehow stop this day from continuing.

"Oh, Lord God," she breathed, "how am I to face this?" Keeping her eyes squeezed shut, Elizabeth envisioned the ocean as she had seen it many times, vast and powerful. God had given her strength when she had sought Him at the water's edge in the midst of her grief. Surely He would meet her now, here in her room.

The doorknob groaned as she forced her fingers to turn it clockwise. Elizabeth made her way down the hall, stopping next to her parents at the entrance to the living room. There they were, Mrs. Mitsuko and David, bags piled neatly at the end of the sofa. Mrs. Mitsuko sat nearest, looking as if she had layered her clothing underneath her coat. It was strange with Mr. Mitsuko gone. His whereabouts were still unknown. Elizabeth hoped for the best, but couldn't help imagining the worst. What had happened to him? Where was he now? Was he alive and well?

In a few short minutes, they were ready to leave for the train station. They decided to walk, as the solace was greatly needed by all. Elizabeth studied David as they walked slightly behind the others. His eyes stared hard at the pavement.

"What are you thinking?" she asked.

David turned to her, giving her what he could manage of a smile. "I was thinking," he said, "about how much I'm going to miss you, however long we're gone." He paused for a moment before continuing. "I'll miss our walks after church every Sunday, and the time we spent with our families. I'll miss looking into your eyes and seeing your reactions when I talk to you."

He set down his bags, letting the others walk on, and turned to face Elizabeth. He drew her close to him and held her tightly for a few moments. Taking a step back, David tilted her head up, his eyes meeting hers.

Would things ever be the same, even if he came back soon? Could they pick up where they were about to leave off? Then, for a few seconds, the questions ceased as David gently kissed her. "I'll always love you, Elizabeth," he whispered. "Never forget that." She nodded silently, her tongue too numb to form words.

Just before reaching the train station, they crossed a river, long and narrow, that acted as a great chasm separating two worlds. One side was free, the other enslaved and occupied by confused masses. Armed guards were interspersed throughout the crowd surrounding the terminal. A little girl followed a sentry as he led her and her family to an assigned car. Was all of this disarray part of the great game of war?

The family was swallowed up in the multitude of Japanese people clutching what belongings they could carry. Elizabeth glanced around, spotting familiar faces amidst the throng. She shuddered, thinking of the great distress that must occupy the hearts of those upon the platform. They undoubtedly had stories of loss like her own.

Surveying the crowd a second time, Elizabeth saw Mrs. Yamumaka, her neighbor and her mother's friend. Mrs. Yamumaka had always been a vital part of their church. Vibrant and joyful, she had always extended a helping hand whenever she could. The color on the faces of those in need made no difference to the elderly woman. Her eyes now held a faraway look, a blank, white-washed stare. Her wrinkles seemed deeper now than Elizabeth had remembered. Dabbing at her eyes, Mrs. Yamumaka sniffed, her hand trembling slightly. Not far from her, a guard stood, arms at ready.

Everyone's bags were piled together, each piece of luggage identified by a tag which bore the number of the respective family. The passengers were boarding the train now. The guards kept the line moving quickly and smoothly. If they moved the evacuees at a steady pace, there would be less interference executing their orders.

Two men struggled to lift a stretcher into the window of one of the train cars. An elderly woman lay on it, her pallid face reflecting the disturbance in her heart. Even the sick were not exempt from evacuation.

Mrs. Tyler clung to Mrs. Mitsuko as they said their goodbyes. Together they bowed their heads for a last prayer together. Elizabeth knew the time had come, but her heart was still unwilling to accept the parting they must endure. Each second that ticked by was one second nearer their parting, slipping by without regard for the grieving that would ensue when their time together had run out. Tomorrow would come, without David to share it with her.

Once again, David turned to Elizabeth. This was it. She looked into his eyes, but could not bear the pain she found there. How could the government do this to them? They had nothing to do with Japan's attack on Pearl Harbor. Now their world was no longer the same. Their dreams of happily-ever-after had been postponed, or maybe even destroyed. No wedding now. No husband yet. All because of Pearl Harbor.

As David held her close, Elizabeth wished he would never let go. She hoped in vain that the seconds would stand still.

"Hey, you!" a guard called to David from across the platform. "Get moving, and leave the girl alone. You'll have plenty of time to get a Jap like yourself."

David's eyes met Elizabeth's as he turned his back toward the guard. This would have to be it. No more delaying. The time had come to say goodbye. Elizabeth shook her head. "No," she cried, "you can't go!"

"I love you." The tears spilled down his cheeks. He sniffed. "I'll write you when I can. I love you."

"I love you," Elizabeth returned, crying at the sight of David's tears. "How will I go on without you?"

He began to pull away. "Rely on God, Elizabeth, only God." He helped his mother onto the train, then climbed on himself.

"Daddy," Elizabeth breathed to Mr. Tyler, "don't let him go." Her father's arms reached around her as the train pulled out of the station, picking up speed with every revolution of the wheels, carrying David farther and farther away.

CHAPTER SIX

Elizabeth sat on the living room sofa, her eyes closed tightly, as Aunt Rose's voice drifted in from the kitchen.

"No, no," she said to Elizabeth's mother. "You always have to let the bread rise properly before baking it. It can't be rushed."

Elizabeth sighed as she listened to her mother's defense of her homemade bread. Who cared about that kind of stuff right now anyway? It was so trivial compared with everything else that was going on in her life.

Why did Aunt Rose have to come visit now? Of all times for her to come, right now was quite possibly the worst time. It had only been a week since Evacuation Day, and Elizabeth's heart was slow in mending. She was beginning to think that it wouldn't heal enough for her to function normally. The past seven days had been an endless barrage of scattered events, her grief clouding her memory of them almost completely.

"Elizabeth."

Elizabeth jolted at the sound of her name. Opening her eyes, she saw her great-aunt hovering over her. "Aren't you going to help your mother with the dishes?" Elizabeth opened her mouth to answer, but her mother peeked into the room, dishtowel in hand.

"It's all right, Aunt Rose," she said. "I've given Elizabeth the night off from dish duty. Why don't you two visit? I'll be there in a minute." Casting her mother a grateful glance, Elizabeth closed her eyes again, content to be lost in her thoughts rather than carry on a conversation.

"Young lady, are you sick?" Aunt Rose bit her lip as she squinted through grey eyes at Elizabeth.

Elizabeth shook her head. "I'm not physically sick."

"Well, what then? You certainly aren't acting like yourself."

"I'm just heartsick, I guess."

Her aunt's brow furrowed momentarily, as if she was confused. "Oh-h," she said finally. Gradually the creases faded. "Your young man left, didn't he? Left with all the other Japanese?"

Elizabeth nodded. Aunt Rose had been against the match from the start, she was sure of it. How could she offer consolation at a time like this?

"You know," she went on, "I never did approve of you going after an Asian man like that." She picked up her knitting as she sat down in the rocker across from Elizabeth. "It just didn't seem right to me somehow."

In no condition to receive criticism, Elizabeth looked out the window, trying to concentrate on the bird feeder outside instead of giving in to her tears once again.

"You're not crying are you, dear?" Aunt Rose peered over her reading glasses at Elizabeth.

Elizabeth turned toward her aunt, biting her lip hard to banish the onset of tears. But she said nothing in reply. Aunt Rose sighed as if regretting the atmosphere she had created. Depositing her knitting on the floor at her feet, she cautiously sat down beside Elizabeth. She repeated her regretful sigh before taking a breath.

"I'm sorry, Elizabeth. I had no right to scold you. Not now."

Elizabeth wondered at her aunt's response. Never had she heard her apologize to anyone. Before now, an apology had always indicated a weakness of character, or so Aunt Rose seemed to believe. Still, no words found their way to Elizabeth's lips.

"I remember what it was like." Aunt Rose gazed in front of her, as if a scene played before her. She smiled a sad smile as the tears welled up in her eyes. "My Tom was a lot like your David, I suppose. He was full of life and ambition, ready to take on the world. Or so he thought."

Shifting her position, Aunt Rose stared again at the empty space in front of her. "Then he lost his job at the bank. His career had been his life, and he had failed. In his own eyes, his manhood was diminished to shards."

Aunt Rose fell silent. Elizabeth thought of what her father had shared with her about Tom's death and wondered if she dared to prod for more information. A few moments later, she said, "What then?"

"He thought he had nothing else to live for. He said he loved me, but now I wonder if he truly could have. He took his own life, just six weeks before our wedding."

Elizabeth's breath caught in her throat. What an atrocity! She couldn't imagine the pain her aunt must have felt, and likely still felt. At least David was alive and well. And he knew that God, in His fullness, would provide and watch over him no matter what came. Had Tom had this same kind of hope? It didn't appear so.

"Aunt Rose?" Elizabeth said, almost in a whisper. "Did Tom know Jesus?"

Now the tears poured down Aunt Rose's cheeks. "I'm afraid he didn't."

Elizabeth reached over and hugged her aunt. Her father's side of the family had never been known for their outward expressions of affection, but that didn't matter now. "Jesus still cares for your hurt. And He's using you to help me get through mine."

Aunt Rose stared at her blankly for a few moments. "Maybe so," she said. "Maybe so."

* * *

The next week came and went much like the week before it. It seemed the cycle of pain, loss, joy, and suffering was never-ending. Elizabeth's strength was expended on the struggle of mentally staying ahead of her moods. One day she had been frustrated and crying; the next she had been confident that the Lord was working in the midst of her confusion for her good.

At the end of the third week since their parting, Elizabeth still had not received any news from David about where he was or how he was doing. What had become of him and the thousands of others like him?

* * *

Elizabeth sunk her hands into the sudsy dishwater, attacking a greasy breakfast skillet with the sponge. It helped her to stay busy these days, keeping her sane when she was tempted to incessantly dwell on her sorrows. Lately, she had entertained the thought of getting a job since she had completed her secretarial course. She had no idea when David would be back, and when he came, they would be planning a wedding again. Money would undoubtedly be needed. Especially considering that David would want to finish his last semester of college when he returned.

"Elizabeth," her mother called from the living room, "you have mail."

"What is it?" she asked, never losing a stroke with her sponge.
"It's a letter."

Elizabeth's hand stopped mid-stroke. "From who?"

"Um... I don't know, there's no return address."

Dropping the skillet back into the water, Elizabeth rushed to dry her hands. Could it be from David?

Once in the living room, she nearly grabbed the envelope from her mother. She stared at the penmanship that formed the words *Miss Elizabeth Tyler*. The h's hump was a little high and the i's remained undotted. Yes, it was David's handwriting.

Elizabeth's fingers shook as she tore a corner of the envelope and slid her finger through to the other side. She reached in her hand, pulling out a paper. Oh, what had he written? Unfolding the letter, she began reading slowly, savoring each word.

My dear Elizabeth,

How are you? It seems as if I have not seen you for years. Could it have only been a few short weeks? I think about you all the time, and wonder if there isn't some way to defy these ridiculous orders and come home to be with you. I wonder now why I didn't let you come. It would be so much more bearable with you here at my side, as my wife. But I must not think that way now, for I cannot change the past, nor would I truly want you to have to live here. It wouldn't be right.

Yet even through these trials, God continues to be my strength. He has shown me that He is preparing us, Elizabeth. We don't understand, I know, and our circumstances are unjust, but His Word is still true and God remains faithful to His Word. There are things in me that must be refined, and if suffering is the only way to do it, I pray our Lord will give me the endurance to walk through it.

Please pray for me, as I do for you, each and every day. Even here there is a mission field of souls, waiting to hear the message of Christ. How many there are that do not know Him!

Mother is doing all right. She misses Father terribly, though, and is probing for answers wherever she can about where he might be. I miss him, too, and wish his quiet words of wisdom could speak to me now. Mother may have a lead on his whereabouts. I'll let you know when we find out more.

Mother wants me to ask you if you have been wearing her cross. She said now would be a good time. She wants you to remember that her love is with you. Add mine to that as well.

I will receive any letters you write me at this address:

David Mitsuko
Manzanar Assembly Center
#17B - #1289
Manzanar, California

As you can see, we are still in California. I am grateful for that, though I am not sure where Manzanar is located.
Please write when you can. I long to hear from you.

All my love,
David

P.S. Don't worry about your ring. It is safe. You will wear it again someday soon.

Elizabeth lovingly caressed the paper, then reread David's words. He seemed far away. She was glad he was still in California, but the state was vast. Where was Manzanar? She crossed the room to the bookshelf, taking down the atlas. Turning to the index, she scanned the listings for Manzanar. How strange. It wasn't there. That made it even less believable that all of this wasn't some dreadful hoax.

Her ring was safe. Of that she was glad. He had probably taken it with him to Manzanar. Frowning, Elizabeth turned the letter over in her hands. David had said nothing of what was going on at the camp or what kind of house he lived in now. Had he purposely omitted that part? Seated at her bedroom desk, Elizabeth took out her stationery and began to write back.

Dearest David,

I was so excited to receive your letter today. I wanted to hear from you, and was worried about what might have happened from the time we said goodbye until now.

I am doing the best I can. Not the greatest, but I'm managing. I was able to talk with Aunt Rose quite openly on her last visit and that helped some. Even so, I will not pretend this separation is easy, as you already know it isn't. I plan to get a job in the near future which will help keep me occupied.

I wonder at the strength you seem to possess at a time like this. Your faith in God is steadfast and reflects the beliefs of your mother. I only wish I could be as strong as you are in your faith, and have your resolve to make a difference in the lives of those around you. What is it that I lack that I cannot claim this same kind of resolution?

You mother also has been a source of joy for me. You may extend to her my love as well. The cross is very precious to me.

Elizabeth paused her letter writing for a moment as she made her way to her jewelry box. The necklace hung on an inside hook. Carefully, she removed it and fastened it around her neck. "Lord, help me to trust in You more," she prayed. Sitting down at her desk she continued writing.

I am wearing it now. Please tell her that I will try to remember what she said, and follow her advice.

I wonder, too, why you didn't let me come with you. Why would you deny me the pleasure of being there with you? David, where are you living? Is the house comfortable? I am worried that you have omitted this information on purpose. Please tell me truthfully what it is like.

I miss you very much. Every day and every night I know there is something missing inside me with you away. A huge part of my life has been altered. I wait in eager anticipation for you to come home to me. Come soon.

> *I love you,*
> *Elizabeth*

* * *

"Elizabeth?" Mrs. Tyler came out on the porch, stopping short as she observed her daughter staring out into the yard. "Is something wrong?"

The long days often beckoned Elizabeth out to the veranda, but this time is was not the beautiful day which occupied her thoughts. Over the past week, a cloud of depression had settled over her. If David wasn't back now, after six weeks, when would he come? Would he come at all?

At her lack of response, Mrs. Tyler tried again. "Elizabeth?"

"Never mind." Elizabeth glanced up at her mother. "I'm okay."

Mrs. Tyler's face was pinched with concern, but she pressed the matter no further. "You have a letter from David." She laid an envelope on Elizabeth's lap.

Staring at the letter for a few moments, Elizabeth sat still. She didn't even bother to lift the letter from the folds of her skirt. Was hiding her pain better than expressing it? In one swift movement, she grabbed the letter and threw it to her feet. What was the use? David wasn't back yet.

Regardless of her anxiety, a minute later she snatched the letter back up from the wooden planks. Turning it over in her hands, she wondered at her own behavior. What was a broken heart capable of? Then she began to read, with the same sense of reverence as she had with the first letter.

My dear Elizabeth,

Thank you so much for your letter. You do not know how much it encouraged my spirit.

You wish me to tell you about where I am living now. Indeed, it is a strange place. More peculiar a place than I have ever seen. We don't have a house, but an apartment like every other family here. When we first arrived, we were told to fill cloth bags with straw for our mattresses. Then they took us to our apartments according to our family numbers. The apartment is small, only sixteen by twenty feet, but mother and I are able to have it to ourselves. I have heard that some small families were placed with strangers. I thank God we do not have those circumstances.

Looking down the dirt street that runs through the middle of camp, the buildings look identical, each row pin-straight. I would expect these kind of living conditions for trained military troops, but not for women and children. I feel as if we are living in army barracks.

Vegetation is sparse here, but mother is working on planting some flowers and vegetables near the outside of the apartment. She is determined to make it home for as long as we must stay here.

I see you wish to know all of what it is like here, and if it were not for your persistent spirit, I would spare you some of the following. But I've come to discover your character, and know you want me to be entirely truthful. So I will tell you everything.

I feel penned in at this place called Manzanar. Like a dumb animal that cannot care for itself. Around the entire camp is a fence. It is not a white picket fence that speaks of home, but one made of barbed wire designed to keep those in, prisoner, and those out, free, as if there were some distinction between one human being and another. It is not righteous, nor is it just. At the far corner of the camp, just inside the fence line, are guard towers monitored by armed sentries. It seems as if those childhood games of war, cowboys and Indians, are coming to pass before my eyes.

Elizabeth paused her reading for a moment. Through eyes blurred with tears, she saw that the next several lines of the letter had been crossed out by a heavy black marker. Strange. Who had done that? A moment later, she continued reading.

From this depiction, Manzanar must sound quite depressing. Surprisingly, there is still some good, even at a place like this. Many of the camp employees are Caucasian. Most are kind and helpful. I met one of the men when we were moving in, he asked if he could do anything for us. In a way, I think he was trying to apologize for the way things have turned out so far.

He made me think of you. Your caring ways and encouraging words could be used in a place like this. I know you were considering getting a job soon. My one request is that when I return and we are married, that you resign. Maybe the Lord would have you serve at one of these camps. Pray about it anyway, and see where the Lord leads. I know He will use you for His glory.

Remember how much I love you. I miss you. Write soon.

All my love,
David

Elizabeth clutched the pages to her chest. Would God have her go to a place like Manzanar? Could she handle it? A heaviness settled over her as she closed her eyes and began envisioning David at a place like the one he had described. Barbed wire. Armed guards. One tiny room to call home.

How could the government treat the only man she had ever loved like a caged animal? The answer was simple. They did not know the power that drove them, nor the mercy of the One who could save them.

With her eyes closed tight, she prayed a silent prayer. A prayer that words could not adequately express and groans could not utter. As she prayed, the heaviness lifted as a new presence filled her soul. Elizabeth could feel Him. Her Savior had come to hold her, comfort her, and guide her.

In that moment, she knew the path she must follow. Her Lord Jesus would go with her, every step of the way.

CHAPTER SEVEN

"So, you're really leaving?" Patti asked as she helped Elizabeth fold clothes in the Tyler's living room.

Elizabeth nodded, staring at the grey skirt she was packing.

"It won't be the same around here without you." Patti bit her lip. "I'm sorry if what I said about you and David wasn't what it should have been. I was only concerned."

"No, Patti." Elizabeth shook off the comment with a wave of her hand. "You didn't do anything wrong. It got me thinking. It was all for the best." She paused a moment, thinking of Patti's new boyfriend. "Besides, you'll have Ben to keep you company."

"That's not why you're leaving, is it? Because everyone gave you a hard time about David?"

Elizabeth smiled. "Of course not. I feel God is leading me to help these people. That's why I'm going." The next few moments were void of conversation.

"I have to admit, though." Elizabeth broke the silence. "I'm a little apprehensive. I've never been on my own before."

Patti nodded as Elizabeth placed another garment in the already overloaded trunk. "When do you leave?"

"Two weeks from tomorrow." Elizabeth thought back to the time she had decided to apply for camp employment eight months ago. The process had been slow and tedious, but the management had been in dire need of a secretary for an internment camp's project director in Poston, Arizona. From what she could see, working for an internment camp during wartime was not a sought-after position. The administration had probably been shorthanded from the start. Granted, the job didn't pay much and the living conditions were probably less than desirable, yet Elizabeth could feel that still small voice urging her forward.

The jangle of the telephone halted her train of thought. "Hello?"

"Yes," a booming voice said from the other end of the line. "Is Miss Elizabeth Tyler available?"

"This is Miss Tyler."

"Miss Tyler, this is Jake Collins from Poston, Arizona. I understand you'll be working for us as my secretary, starting the fifteenth."

"Yes, sir."

"I have a huge request," the thundering voice continued. "I need you to start immediately. This paperwork is getting out of hand. The government restrictions on this place are enormous. Could you be here, say, by the end of the week?"

Elizabeth's mind raced through her mental checklist of things to accomplish before she left for Poston. There was so much left to do. Still, it wouldn't be wise to get off on the wrong foot with her new employer.

I will be with you, My child. The words seemed to come straight from heaven.

Taking a deep breath, she lifted up a silent prayer. "I can try, Mr. Collins."

"Wonderful, that's all I ask. Is Friday too soon?"

Elizabeth's heart gave a leap. Friday. That was only three days away. "Friday's fine." The confidence of her affirmation surprised even herself.

"All right, see you soon."

The dial tone buzzed in Elizabeth's ear as she hung up the receiver.

* * *

The next two days were a blur as Elizabeth made last minute plans for her accelerated departure. She had signed her contract and mailed it to Mr. Collins. There was no backing out now. Poston needed her, and that's exactly where she intended to go.

The ride to the train station was longer than she had remembered. Elizabeth mentally noted each landmark as they passed by them. There was the Mitsuko's house with the front flower gardens drying to a crisp due to lack of care. Mrs. Mitsuko had always taken great pride in her flowers. Even now, she gardened in front of her little evacuee apartment.

"Mother?" Elizabeth said. "Will you promise me something?"

"Yes, of course, dear." Mrs. Tyler craned her neck from the front seat to look at Elizabeth. "What is it?"

Take care of Mrs. Mitsuko's flower garden. She'd hate to see it all dried up and full of weeds."

"I'll do what I can, Elizabeth," Mrs. Tyler said. "But it will be up to the new tenants whether or not they want it kept up."

Elizabeth met her mother's gaze. "What? New tenants?" How could someone just move in and take over after what had happened?

Mrs. Tyler nodded slowly. "They're moving in next week. The house couldn't stay empty indefinitely."

Elizabeth looked over her shoulder out the back window. Maybe it was best she was leaving now instead of later. She didn't know if she could bear to see someone else invading the domain of so many of her most precious memories. It was in the Mitsuko's living room where such beautiful fellowship had taken place on those lazy Sunday afternoons. It was there that all of them had encouraged her to trust God with her engagement to David and ignore others' opinions. Now it would be someone else's living room. The low-lying table would be gone, as would be the bright abstract carpets.

But the stream of memories did not fade as the car pulled into the train station. Instead, the thoughts quickened and worsened. This is where she had said goodbye to David. There was the exact platform. Passengers came and went now like they had always done. Business was as usual. It was as if that horrendous Evacuation Day had never happened. Did no one remember the look of betrayal on Mrs. Yamumaka's face while she dabbed at the tears that fell down her cheeks? What about the little Japanese girl following the armed guard to her assigned train car?

Then came the most painful memory of all. She remembered the hurt in David's eyes as he said goodbye. His dark brown eyes that had always lit up with every smile had then brimmed with unchecked tears.

Mr. Tyler stopped the car and opened the door for Elizabeth. Cautiously, she stepped out onto the platform, resenting her invasion of the sacred memories. She clutched her purse, her knuckles turning white. Could she go to Poston and make a difference, or would it just complicate matters? In one swift moment, her hand went to her heart and her fingers brushed over the delicate gold chain she wore around her neck. Mrs. Mitsuko's cross glittered in the sunshine at Elizabeth's touch.

Mrs. Mitsuko's words came back to her mind, as if floating on the breeze that playfully tossed her blonde curls. "You must trust, my child. You must," she had said. "Let God finish the work He has begun in you."

What was the Lord doing in her? She wished to scream the question at the train pulling into the station, but no sound came from her lips. Instead, she and her parents silently walked to where the train was stopping for boarding passengers.

"Be careful, Elizabeth." Her mother hugged her tightly. "Let God alone lead you and give you strength."

Her father's farewell was a silent one. Perhaps a voiced good-bye would have ejected the tears already brimming in his eyes.

Elizabeth climbed the stairs to her assigned car, handing over her ticket as she entered. Settling onto a window seat, she waved goodbye to her parents as the train cars tugged at one another, inching her toward Poston and an unknown future.

* * *

Elizabeth squinted as the afternoon sun poured through the train window, awakening her from her slumber. Her neck was sore thanks to her cramped position and she felt groggy as she tried her best to stretch in her seat.

Elizabeth quickly diverted her eyes from the penetrating gaze of a young man sitting across the aisle. Who was that? Had he been watching her sleep? She felt annoyed as she thought of what a sight she must be at the moment, hair tousled from her nap, her eyes heavy with recent sleep. It wasn't a time to meet strangers, that was for sure.

She turned her head to look out the window. They were entering Arizona. For a few seconds, rock walls sped past her window. The rocks soon disappeared, giving way to the vastness of the open desert, shrub brush scattered throughout the landscape. Jagged rocks protruded from the sandy earth.

Elizabeth turned away from the window. So far, her perception of Arizona was anything but comforting to her rising homesickness. Still, even through those feelings, she felt at peace. The peace would not leave her, nor would it let her turn back and go home. It was the peace that comes with following God's will. She fingered the cross necklace again, wishing Mrs. Mitsuko was with her now to give her wisdom and encouragement.

However, wishing did not make the woman appear in the

doorway of the train car. God alone would have to see her through. She knew that now. David and her parents, those who had given her strength in the past, were no longer near for guidance. Now she must choose the right way–God's way–and follow it through to the end.

She sighed and stretched once more. Hmm. That young man was looking at her again. She could feel his eyes on her face. After a minute, he glanced out the window toward the rocks, sand, and desert.

Elizabeth looked across the aisle. He seemed to be in his early twenties, his sandy brown hair slightly favoring one side. He was seated by a silver-haired man whose frame was much smaller than the young man beside him. Yet, he seemed to hold his head with a dignity that demanded respect. Elizabeth wondered who the older man was. What was his profession?

She started to turn her head back to the window, but her gaze was intercepted by the young man staring at her. He latched his eyes onto hers and smiled. His teeth were straight and white. For a few seconds, she wondered what to do. She searched the stranger's blue eyes that matched the color of the ocean water back in California.

Jerking her head toward the window in one swift movement, Elizabeth scolded herself for staring. She wouldn't stare at another young man if David were here. She couldn't do it now. That was that.

* * *

The sun had sunk completely out of sight when the train finally slowed at the end of its journey. Elizabeth climbed down the steps, grateful for the light, refreshing breeze.

"Elizabeth?" a female voice called. Elizabeth turned around to greet a woman several years older than herself. Her straight auburn hair fell nearly to her waist. Elizabeth nodded in affirmation of her name.

"I'm Anita." The woman extended her hand to Elizabeth. "The administration sent me to meet you." Elizabeth smiled and shook the proffered hand. "Actually, I'm your roommate as well. I also work in administration." Elizabeth nodded. At least she had a nice roommate. Maybe it wouldn't be so bad here after all.

Together they rode from the train station and out of town. After Elizabeth stared at the night's stars for what seemed to be an hour, they came to an unlit turnoff. Anita pulled onto the dirt road, which it wound its way for yet another few miles.

Taking her eyes off the sky, Elizabeth began studying the road. It had not been well maintained like the road they had turned off of several miles back. "Excuse me." Elizabeth pointed to the road stretching ahead of them. "Are you sure this is the right way? It looks deserted out here."

Anita nodded. "Oh, yes."

They rode in silence for a few more minutes before coming upon a driveway. It was blocked off by an iron gate. An armed guard came to the driver's side window. "It's just me, Private," Anita called through the open window, obviously recognizing the young solider. He squinted in the darkness.

"Okay, Anita," he said. "Just as long as there ain't no Japs trying to sneak back in with you, after a night out."

"No, no, not to worry." Anita inched the car forward. "It's just me and Miss Tyler, Mr. Collins' new secretary."

"She's Caucasian?" the private asked, still sounding a bit apprehensive at his lack of sight.

"Yes, she's Caucasian! Now just let us through. I'm tired and I'm sure Miss Tyler is, too."

The soldier backed away from the car door slowly and opened the gate, allowing them to pass. Anita pulled the car alongside a building just inside the gate. "Well, Elizabeth," she said, "welcome to Poston."

CHAPTER EIGHT

Elizabeth awoke the next morning to the bright Arizona sunshine spilling onto her pillow. She put her hand to her forehead for a brief moment. The night had been too short after the cumbersome train ride from San Francisco.

Slowly, her eyes adjusted to the light. The room wasn't so bad, she concluded after a skeptical gaze around the perimeter. Anita's bed sat directly across the room. Neither of the mattresses were stuffed with straw as David had described. Was that only done at Manzanar?

The bare white walls reminded Elizabeth of a hospital ward. She made a mental note to hang the pictures she'd brought as soon as possible. The wooden floor squeaked as she made her way across the room. Along with a night stand and bookshelf, a set of dresser drawers were at her disposal.

Elizabeth nearly jumped as the bedroom door swung open. "Morning." Anita entered the room, her hair wrapped in a bath towel. She looked at Elizabeth. "I'm sorry; I didn't mean to scare you."

Elizabeth shook her head. "It's okay. I'm just not used to sharing a room, I guess."

"Oh?" Anita fluffed the pillows on her bed. "Not even when you were little?"

"No," Elizabeth replied. "I'm an only child." Anita nodded and went back to making her bed.

Elizabeth looked around the room once more. Could it have been just yesterday that she had left California? A wave of homesickness threatened to descend on her.

"When does Mr. Collins want to see me?" she asked, hoping to dispel the feeling with a distraction.

Anita turned to face her. "He's in a meeting this morning. The earliest he can meet with you is after lunch."

"Oh, well, what should I do until then?"

Anita shrugged. "Check out Roasten if you like."

"Roasten?" Elizabeth frowned at the apparent connection.

Anita laughed. "That's what the evacuees call Poston Camp I. For starters, get dressed and come to breakfast with me."

Elizabeth nodded as she opened her suitcase. It looked like this would be an interesting day.

* * *

An hour later, Elizabeth found herself seated in the small employee dining room at the end of their block. Elizabeth looked around her at the others seated at the tables. They were all Caucasian. She stared at her scrambled eggs and toast for a minute. There was so much change swirling around her. It would definitely take awhile for it all to soak in and make sense. She began to eat, content to be silent and listen to the banter of the others.

"I don't even know why they're here," one man at the end of the table said. "It's just as well they be in their own homes, wherever they came from. They'll do no harm."

A burly man sitting across from the first snickered. "Yeah, right. Who knows how many catastrophes we've already bypassed because the Japs are here? I'll not take any chances, that's for sure."

The first man looked to his side. "What do you think, Caleb?" He leaned back, revealing a young man to his left. Caleb's sandy brown hair slightly favored one side, his eyes matching the color of the ocean on a sunny day. Elizabeth nearly choked on her eggs. It was the young man from the train. Just then, he looked up, latched his eyes onto hers, and smiled.

* * *

After breakfast, Elizabeth wandered around the camp. Was this camp so much better than the one David was in? Elizabeth saw no guard towers as he had described at Manzanar, but the community did have military guards around its perimeter. Elizabeth felt as if her life in San Francisco had existed in another lifetime. Surely it could not inhabit the same world as the internment camps.

She passed the administration offices, reading the sign on

one of the doors as she passed. It read, *Project Director*. Assuming it to be Mr. Collins' office, Elizabeth kept walking, soon finding herself out of the staff block and entering a section that held row upon row of identical buildings. Observing the perfectly spaced windows and doors, Elizabeth mentally compared the building to the pictures she had seen of army barracks. Without slowing her stride, she turned the corner to find a large square structure the size of a farmyard barn.

Outside the building, an elderly Japanese woman stood. She peered through a window and made motions to someone inside. A moment later, she turned from the window, a frown on her face.

Elizabeth moved toward the woman. "Can I help you?"

The woman jerked her head in the direction of the voice calling to her, but said nothing. Elizabeth tried again. "Do you need something?" The woman nodded, thrusting a baby's bottle toward her. "Only some milk," she replied in broken English. "Milk for my grandson, Toyo."

Elizabeth motioned to the door. "Is that the kitchen?"

The woman nodded again. "It is the mess hall, but they tell me I can't come in until it is time for lunch. They have locked the door."

Elizabeth frowned. Surely the kitchen help would give this woman what she needed if they knew it was for a child. She took the bottle from the woman and climbed the few steps to the building's entrance. She rapped on the door.

"I said we're closed!" a voice yelled from inside. Again, Elizabeth knocked. She would not give up so easily. A moment later the door swung open. A hefty woman filled the doorway. "Oh," she said when she saw Elizabeth standing on the step. "I thought it was that Jap woman again."

"I'm Elizabeth Tyler." Elizabeth extended her hand to the cook, ignoring the racist slang. The woman eyed her suspiciously as she shook her hand. "I need some milk for a baby." Elizabeth handed her the bottle.

"You have a baby?" the cook asked, cautiously taking the bottle.

"Uh, no." Where could she go with this? Obviously the woman had no inclination of helping her Japanese neighbor. "No," Elizabeth repeated, "but I have a friend who does." She shrugged her shoulders. "Why should it matter who it's for? A baby is a baby. Please, just get the milk."

Several minutes later, the cook reappeared holding the filled bottle and another quart of milk. "Here," she said. "I don't want to be bothered again."

When the cook had gone, Elizabeth gave the bottles to the Japanese woman. "Thank you very much. Toyo will be happy, now." Elizabeth nodded. "Tell me, Elizabeth," the woman continued, "why did you do it?"

Elizabeth shrugged. "Why not?"

The woman pointed to Elizabeth's gold chain. "You are a Christian, then?"

Elizabeth smiled at her simple words. "Yes, I am. And you?"

"Hai, I am Midori, your sister in the Lord." The Japanese word hung in the air between them. All at once, Elizabeth felt a severe longing for David and Mrs. Mitsuko and the way things used to be.

"Would you like to meet Toyo?" Midori asked. "Our apartment is not far."

Midori led the way down the dirt street, following it to the last block. She stopped when she reached a door labeled #13A and slowly opened it.

The apartment was tiny; only one room the size of her parent's living room back home. Splintery wooden boards covered the floors, dust and grime finding their way into the cracks. Two twin beds lined the north and east walls, the mattresses lumpy. Yes, these mattresses were stuffed with straw. A homemade curtain fell across the room's only window. Against the opposite wall sat a set of dresser drawers. A young Japanese girl, not more than ten years old, was crouched beside the dresser drawers. "Thank you, Aoi." Midori patted the girl's shoulder. "You can go, now."

Elizabeth jumped at the sound of a baby's shrill cry. She dropped her gaze, her eyes resting on the half open bottom dresser drawer. Midori scurried across the room and bent down. "Here, Toyo," she cooed, taking the baby in her arms, "no need to cry, Grandma's here now."

Elizabeth stared at the wrapped bundle. A baby in a dresser drawer? Where was his crib? Midori rocked the baby back and forth in her arms. Sitting down in a rocking chair, the room's only chair, Midori stuck the bottle into the baby's mouth. Soon the cries and sobs ceased, and all that could be heard was the baby's sucking and contented sighs.

Elizabeth gingerly stepped across the room to where the elderly woman sat. Looking down at the baby, she caught a glimpse of two round black eyes staring back at her. His hair was black as midnight–just like David's. Her mind wandered back to the conversation she had with her mother even before Pearl Harbor.

"And would you love your children any less if they did not

look like you?" her mother had asked. "It's quite likely they won't inherit your blonde locks."

Elizabeth stared down at Toyo again. How could anyone love him less for who he was on the outside? She reached down and patted the soft yellow blanket. Without a moment's hesitation, Toyo gripped her finger with his tiny fist, the even tinier knuckles turning white.

Her eyes misting over with tears, Elizabeth again thought of David. If only they could be together again.

"He knows you care for him already." Midori said, breaking the silence.

Elizabeth wiped at the corners of her eyes, hoping to dispel any evidence of her tears. "I hope so," she said. "He's a strong little fellow." Midori nodded as she lifted the baby up to her shoulder and gently patted his back.

"If you don't mind my asking," Elizabeth said, glad for having regained her composure. "Where is Toyo's crib?"

Midori closed her eyes for a second, as if remembering days gone past. "Only what we could carry." Her eyes remained closed. She clutched the baby tighter as she spoke. It was a full minute later that she relaxed her hold and opened her eyes. She looked at Elizabeth. "That is why we have no crib, my dear."

Elizabeth's mind flew back to Evacuation Day. David and Mrs. Mitsuko could only take what they could carry. The extent of their luggage had been a bag and a suitcase. They had worn many layers of clothing to conserve space.

A wave of guilt settled over Elizabeth as she remembered her own luggage on her recent voyage. She'd come with a travel bag and two heavy suitcases, and her trunk should arrive in the morning. No one had placed any stipulations on what she could bring.

"Where are Toyo's parents?" Elizabeth asked, wishing she wouldn't have voiced her thought the second the words came out of her mouth. "Never mind." She waved a hand in front of her face. "I shouldn't have asked. It's none of my business." What if Toyo had been separated from his parents during the relocation? Elizabeth didn't want to be the cause of yet another unhappy memory.

Midori pushed Elizabeth's comment aside. "No, no, there is no need to be sorry. Toyo's mother is my daughter. She lives here with me. Maybe you will meet her sometime."

Elizabeth nodded slowly as Midori stood up to put the sleeping baby back into his makeshift bed. What about his father? Elizabeth studied the round face of the child. His dark eyelashes were still wet with fresh tears. Glancing at Midori, she decided she wouldn't press the matter, at least not now.

"I should go." Elizabeth moved toward the apartment door. "Is there anything I can get for you? Anything I can do?" Elizabeth realized her voice must have sounded desperate. But she was not desperate to make sure that Midori's or even Toyo's needs were met. Rather, it was a plea to stifle the endless effects of Pearl Harbor.

CHAPTER NINE

Elizabeth stuffed her stationery and pen into her desk drawer at the sound of the office door. Mr. Collins must be back from lunch early. It wouldn't be right for him to catch her writing letters when she was supposed to be working, especially if they were love letters to a Japanese-American in an internment camp.

But instead of seeing her boss in the doorway, Elizabeth saw the young man from the train and the cafeteria on her first morning in Poston. Caleb, he had been called. "Good afternoon, Miss..." his voice trailed off, apparently waiting for her to introduce herself.

Elizabeth swept a curl from her forehead before she spoke. "I'm Elizabeth Tyler, Mr. Collins' secretary."

"Caleb Phelps." He extended a hand to her. "I guess you could call me 'Assistant Camp Director' like they tell me I am, but Caleb is fine, too." He smiled, revealing his perfectly straight, white teeth. "I came to see Mr. Collins." He glanced toward the office door in the far corner of the room. "Is he in?"

"No, he's not. He's at lunch." Elizabeth glanced at her wristwatch. "He should be back in a few minutes if you care to wait."

Caleb sank into a chair several feet from Elizabeth's desk. "I've got nothing but time." He had such a carefree attitude. She had always been one to see the more serious side of things. David used to have that carefree attitude, too, but all the events of the war had caused him to focus on stark reality instead. She missed their casual talk and his cheerful attitude. Looking up, she caught Caleb's eyes on her, his head resting on the back of the chair.

"Where are you from, if you don't mind my asking?" he said.

Elizabeth smiled at his friendliness. "Of course I don't mind.

I'm from San Francisco. I've lived there all my life. It's a neat place."

"San Francisco?" Caleb raised his head from its resting position. "And you came here? Why? It's certainly not as exciting as the big city."

Elizabeth adjusted her gaze to the picture hanging on the wall opposite her. It was a picture of the ocean, vast and mighty, unable to be conquered. She struggled not to let her thoughts go back to the last time she sat at the ocean's edge, but the memory appeared anyway. She was with David, as he gently tried to explain to her that she couldn't go with him to the internment camp. He wouldn't let her go, and would make sure she would be able to have the wedding she had always dreamed of, even if they had to wait out the war to make it happen. Her right hand crossed to her left, as if trying to adjust the engagement ring that had once graced her finger. If only things had been different.

"Elizabeth?" She jerked her head toward the sound of Caleb's voice. She must not reminisce like that.

"I'm sorry," Elizabeth hastily apologized. "You asked me why I came here? It wasn't for the excitement, of course." She smiled. "I tried to avoid excitement even in San Francisco."

Caleb chuckled. "A real city girl, huh?"

"Not really," Elizabeth went on. "I don't know how you feel about the Japanese, but I have to give you an honest answer. I came to Poston to make a positive difference for them, in spite of what has happened. I saw many of my friends and neighbors and those closest to me torn from their homes and loved ones. It wasn't right at all."

Caleb was silent for a moment, his expression neither affirming nor discrediting her statements. What was he thinking? How did he feel about the situation? His eyes searched her expression for a moment as if to procure a reason for her answer.

"That's quite a statement." He ran his fingers through his sandy hair. "I'll not pretend to be the philanthropist you seem to be, but I'm no militarist sympathizer, I can tell you that."

Elizabeth's gaze softened, satisfied with his reply. At least he wasn't opposed to the Japanese as some of the others at the camp were. That was something to be thankful for.

Heavy footsteps on the wooden steps announced Mr. Collins' return. The door swung open, banging against the wall to reveal a very red-faced Mr. Collins. He marched across the room, pausing before reaching his office door.

"If it's not one thing, it's another!" he thundered, spinning on his heel, directing his outburst to no one in particular. "They want everything, I tell you. 'We need better mattresses. We need baby cribs.' What do those Japs expect of me? I'm only one man trying to do his job, which happens to be keeping them out of trouble."

Caleb caught Elizabeth's eye for a moment as if to apologize for the outburst. "What happened, Mr. Collins?" he asked.

Mr. Collins snorted before replying. "Well, some old woman, Minordi, I think her name is, told me she needed a baby crib for her grandson and a better mattress for herself. Claims she has a bad back and can't sleep at night. What does she expect for free? This isn't exactly a fancy hotel, you know. I suppose now she'll want someone to escort her to mess hall. I'll not be doing her any favors, I can tell you that." With his final statement, Mr. Collins turned to enter his office.

Caleb caught Elizabeth's gaze once more. His eyes seemed to plead with her not to challenge the camp director's opinions or authority. Elizabeth's heart had quickened and her cheeks had grown hot as she listened to the man spew out racist comments. She had to say something, yet he was her superior. "Sir," she said with greater confidence than she felt.

Mr. Collins turned in her direction. "Yes, Miss Tyler?"

Stepping out from behind her desk, Elizabeth went on. "Sir, I hardly think that Midori had any ill intentions in stating her requests." Elizabeth was surprised at the evenness of her tone, despite her trembling hands. This speech could get her fired, and then how could she help the Japanese? Yet she could not keep silent in the face of such injustice. If indeed she intended to make a difference, she may have to contradict some people along the way.

When Mr. Collins made no reply to her comment, she continued. "A grandmother is naturally concerned about the welfare of her grandchild, just as a mother is concerned for her child, regardless of race or creed. And the elderly, also naturally, will have aches and pains unlike those younger than themselves. Surely you could respect Midori as your elder, Mr. Collins, whether or not you agree with her complaints?"

Mr. Collins' countenance seemed to soften at Elizabeth's words, yet he did not venture to apologize for his outburst. "I have but one suggestion for you, Miss Tyler," he said. "As young and naive as you may be, don't get too friendly with those Japs." He pointed his finger at her as if to accentuate his warning. "They are as unpredictable as can be. One old woman may be asking for a few conveniences today, but that doesn't mean the lot of them won't try to escape tomorrow or help their relatives back home to bomb us again. Just remember that." He walked to the office, shutting the door behind him.

Elizabeth sank into her chair, shocked and confused. Unpredictable? People like her David? What was Mr. Collins thinking? Obviously not of the souls beneath the yellow skin. David. How was he faring at Manzanar? Was he being treated as Midori was treated just now? The thought made her burn with rage, wishing she had something to take out her anger upon. Elizabeth bit her lip hard to blink back the tears that formed in her eyes.

Caleb reached out and gently touched her hand. Elizabeth looked up, but could only stare back at him. "I'm sorry," he said simply. "He kind of directed his anger at you."

Elizabeth dropped her gaze. "No. It's not that."

Caleb tilted her chin up, looking into her eyes. "Will you be all right?"

Elizabeth nodded. Caleb moved toward Mr. Collins' office door. "I better see him about what I came for." He offered a smile. Elizabeth managed a weak smile in return and nodded once more. "I'll see you at dinner."

* * *

Elizabeth glanced over the contents spread about her bed, making sure that she had omitted nothing. It had been several days since Mr. Collins' outburst and it was only now that she felt brave enough to carry out her plans to help Midori and her family. She admitted to herself that the small toiletry items, along with the baby blanket and powdered milk wasn't all that much to offer, but it was all she could discretely take to Midori, at least for now. She simply couldn't carry a new mattress and baby crib through camp and deposit them on the Japanese woman's doorstep. No doubt rumors would spread then, and she would likely lose her employment.

Gingerly, Elizabeth wrapped the lavender scented soap, lotion, and hair products for Midori and her daughter into the baby blanket, along with the powdered milk for Toyo. She prayed the small gifts would please the elderly woman and give her hope in the midst of her circumstances. Elizabeth looked about the room once more, then, satisfied that she had all she needed, locked the door behind her.

After rapping on Midori's apartment door, Elizabeth waited

anxiously. She had the right apartment, didn't she? Glancing about her, she half expected Mr. Collins to come around the corner, demanding to know what she was doing. Elizabeth jerked her head back in the direction of the squeaking door. Midori stood in the doorway, Toyo in her arms.

"Elizabeth!" She opened her arms as wide as her bundle would allow. "Come in."

Elizabeth stepped through the doorway, glancing about the room as she had done on her first visit. Nothing had changed. "What brings you here?" Midori asked. Elizabeth looked at her, snatching a hint of worry flashing across her dark eyes.

Elizabeth shifted her attention to the package she held. "I brought a few things." All of a sudden, she felt embarrassed at her tiny offering. After a moment, she handed the package to Midori, taking Toyo on her lap in exchange. Midori squinted, as if she didn't understand, but carefully unwrapped the bundle anyway. "I hope you can use them," Elizabeth said when Midori made no reply.

Looking up at Elizabeth, Midori's eyes moistened with tears. "Thank you, child." Her voice was low.

"I'm sorry it's not much."

Midori held up her hand. "No, child," came the low voice again, "it is very much indeed. You have given me, oh what shall I say?" She seemed to be searching for a specific English word. "You have given me great jubilation. Thank you." Midori reached out her arms to embrace her.

Elizabeth jumped at the sound of the apartment door. She turned her head to see a young Japanese woman not much older than herself standing in the doorway, staring at her. "Hannah," Midori greeted the woman, "come meet Elizabeth. She is Mr. Collins' secretary and a dear friend. She has brought some gifts for Toyo and for us."

The young woman's face did not soften from its wooden countenance. "Elizabeth, this is my daughter, Hannah, Toyo's mother," Midori explained. Elizabeth felt a wave of guilt sweep over her, aware that she still held the baby.

"It's good to meet you." Elizabeth extended one hand while balancing Toyo in the other. Hannah shook it, but made no greeting herself. Instead, she turned to her mother.

"I've just come to take you to supper," she said. "Are you ready?"

"In a minute, but you can go ahead. Here." Midori gently took Toyo out of Elizabeth's arms and handed him to Hannah. "Take him with you. I'll come shortly."

When Hannah had gone, Midori turned to Elizabeth. "I'm sorry for her unkindness." She dropped her eyes to the wooden floor boards.

Elizabeth was quick to respond. "Think nothing of it, Midori. We are all hurting in this war."

"You speak from experience with this hurt, I see." Midori took Elizabeth's hand. Elizabeth nodded, unsure what information she should disclose about her broken engagement.

"I'll not press you for answers, dear." Midori patted Elizabeth's arm. "Hannah is hurting for two reasons, and I think it is right for you to know." She cleared her throat. "Hannah's husband was taken to another relocation camp. He was a successful businessman and so was suspected as a spy."

An involuntary gasp slipped from Elizabeth's lips. "I'm so sorry." Though the words sounded pathetic, even to her own ears, she couldn't offer any other consolation. Hannah had to endure the same kind of pain as Mrs. Mitsuko, her husband being taken from her. Yet, Hannah, had a small child to care for as well.

"Another reason for her hurt," Midori said, "is meeting her replacement."

"Her replacement? What do you mean?"

"Hannah applied for your job. She needed the income badly, and her qualifications are adequate. She was informed that she had the job, but then Mr. Collins became camp director and informed her that she would have to seek employment elsewhere. His secretary, he said, must be Caucasian."

Elizabeth dropped her eyes to her lap. That seemed like something Mr. Collins would say. No wonder Hannah had seemed curt. "Do not blame yourself, Elizabeth," Midori said. "You are here for a reason, and you can help us more in that position than Hannah ever could." Elizabeth looked up at Midori and gave her what she could manage of a smile.

Glancing at her watch, Elizabeth decided it was time she be going. "I should go." She gave Midori a hug.

"You will come again?" Midori asked.

"Yes, next week, about the same time. Is there anything I can bring?"

Midori's eyes lit up. "Yes, there is one thing. When we left in such a hurry, I left my Bible behind. Is there any way you could find one for me to use?

Elizabeth smiled at her request. "I'll bring one for you to keep for your very own." She opened the door, cautiously looking about for anyone she knew. She turned back to Midori after assuring herself that the coast was clear. "I'll see you next week, then."

Elizabeth hurried to the end of the block and around the corner of the last apartment, nearly colliding with someone in her haste. A pile of papers scattered to the ground. "Oh, I'm sorry!" Elizabeth scurried to pick up the papers. A shadow fell across her face, and she looked up to see Caleb.

"Elizabeth?" he asked. "What are you doing..." his voice trailed off as he glanced around. All that was in sight was row upon row of evacuee apartments. "What are you doing here? Did Mr. Collins send you on an interesting errand?"

She began gathering the papers again. What should she say? She couldn't lie, nor could she be completely honest with him. Suppose he told Mr. Collins that she had befriended Midori? "Elizabeth?" Caleb took hold of her wrist. Elizabeth opened her mouth, but nothing came out. "Elizabeth, tell me," he commanded. "What are you doing over here?"

Elizabeth raised her chin in defiance as she had done when she was young, demonstrating her determination. "I can't." She shrugged her shoulders.

"You don't have to," Caleb said. "I already have a good idea. You came to Poston to make a positive difference, so you've said, and I find you around the evacuees' apartments. It's pretty obvious. You could lose your job for this, you know." Elizabeth paled. Would he tell Mr. Collins after all?

"But I don't want to see you go." Caleb picked up the last of the papers. "I won't tell."

Elizabeth let out a sigh of relief. "Thank you."

"Wait a minute!" Caleb's voice halted her from continuing on her way. "I won't tell under one condition."

"What?" Elizabeth was half afraid to know what that one condition might be.

"Dinner," he said. "Promise me you'll go to dinner with me sometime. We'll get out of camp, go somewhere nice. All right?"

"Dinner." Relief filled Elizabeth's voice. She smiled. "I guess I have no choice."

"Good." Caleb winked. "I thought you wouldn't deny my offer."

"I had better get going." Elizabeth inched her way forward.

Caleb nodded. "See you later."

Elizabeth hurried back to her room, shutting the door behind her, and sinking into the nearest chair. That had been a close call.

Too close. She looked down, and noticed an envelope lying on the floor. It was addressed to her. Elizabeth ripped open the envelope, and recognized the familiar writing.

My Dearest Elizabeth, the letter began. Yes, it was from David.

She gripped the letter to her chest. What had she just done? She had committed herself to go out to dinner with Caleb, to save her job and her reputation. What would David think?

CHAPTER TEN

My Dearest Elizabeth,

It looks as if God did indeed want you to serve in an internment camp. I know your heart, my love, and thought its contentment may be found in such a service right now. May God bless you for your sacrifices. Your mother forwarded me your change of address. She wrote a most encouraging letter, informing Mama that she and your father have taken ownership of our house and are keeping it up for our return. The new tenants failed to make a deposit, and so the place went up for sale. We can never thank your parents enough. We had been wondering what would become of our home.

Elizabeth sat back on her bed and breathed a sigh of relief. At least the Mitsuko's would have the familiarity of their former home once this interment situation was over. She had been concerned that the new tenants would let the gardens rot, and that they would have no regard for the lives that had been lived there. Thank God He had worked out the details. Elizabeth sighed. Should she be surprised that the God of the universe could take care of the Mitsuko's every need, and her own needs as well? Trusting God had not been simple lately. Though she seemed to be doing satisfactory work in her job and was now helping Midori and her family, there was still something missing. What was God's work for her in Poston? She continued reading.

God has chosen to use me at Manzanar in more ways than I could have ever imagined upon first arriving at this desolate place. God's presence lives here just as surely as it does in San Francisco. Do you remember me mentioning a kind Caucasian man that worked at the camp? Well, we have had several discussions since then, and he told me he is a Christian. Though his employment in maintenance at the camp does not allow him to socialize with the evacuees, he still encourages us in the Word of God. He came to work at Manzanar for some of the same reasons you went to Poston. He wanted to make a difference for the Japanese during this difficult time.

He has encouraged me to hold regular Bible studies at the rec hall twice per week for any evacuees wishing to attend. Many of them are still steeped in Shintoism and Buddhism and have no idea of their need of Jesus Christ. Last week we had one young boy give his life to the Lord. Praise God! Will, my maintenance friend, is supplying us with Bibles. It has been through this outreach to those of my own race that I have come to the full realization of God's calling on my life. Elizabeth, God has called me to preach the gospel to my native countrymen. I know we have spoken of this before, but now I am more convinced than ever that we are called to Japan. The Lord wants you to go with me. Perhaps He is training us for that work even now.

Again, Elizabeth paused to contemplate the full meaning of David's words. She had known that he had a heart for doing mission work in Japan and that he had been in training to fulfill the call on his life. But now, his words seemed different. They were laden with conviction that she had not known he possessed, until now. Surely God was preparing him for the work that had been laid upon his heart. Could something good actually be born out of the tragedy of the internment camps?

I received your last letter in a large envelope that I assume had held a package for me. Unfortunately, I did not receive what you sent. I am told that our mail is censored by the camp, although I don't understand why.

I must say goodbye for now, as the mess hall is about to close. I love you dearly. May God use you to your fullest potential in Christ. May we meet again soon. I miss you.

All my love,
David

Why hadn't her package arrived? Elizabeth had sent David the watch he had admired at *Kenning's*, a small San Franciscan jewelry shop. It was the same place David had gone to pick out her ring.

Walking past the shop one evening after business hours, he told her to pick whatever she liked best. They had done a lot of "wish shopping," so they called it. She had picked the ring, and he had picked the watch. Elizabeth fidgeted on her bed. She had wanted the watch to arrive in time for David's birthday, and now it was gone.

Elizabeth looked back at the lines stretched out on the paper. It seemed so long ago since she and David had been together. Her ears longed to hear his voice. Her arms longed to feel the warmth of his embrace, just once, in these long, lonely days.

Her thoughts returned to her earlier encounter with Caleb. It wouldn't hurt to have dinner with a business associate. After all, she hadn't any romantic intentions concerning Caleb, and neither should he. It would be all right. He would probably forget about her promise within the next few days anyway. She just wouldn't mention it again.

* * *

Elizabeth shuffled the papers around on her desk. Where was the file that Mr. Collins wanted? She had it just yesterday. Closing her eyes, she tried to remember if she had put it back in the locked filing cabinet before leaving the night before. She squinted her eyes tightly. No, it wasn't any use. She couldn't remember.

Elizabeth plopped into her chair, placing her head in her hands. "I should check for that file again." She rose from her chair and scanned through the files to O. Ona. It should be there.

But it wasn't. It didn't help that Mr. Colllins wanted the file to help convict a Japanese man of breaking into the office. He claimed he had all the evidence. Elizabeth thought Mr. Collins would be suspicious of anyone, even her. She hadn't heard anyone else talk of a break-in.

"Hey, what are you doing?" Elizabeth looked up as Caleb came through the door. She sighed. Hopefully he had come to see Mr. Collins and not to remind her of her commitment to go to dinner with him. When she didn't answer, he spoke again. "You look frustrated." He paused to study her face. "And tired. Are you okay?"

Elizabeth bit her lower lip. "I'm okay." She shrugged. "But I can't find a file Mr. Collins needs this morning. I had it out yesterday, but I can't remember where I put it." Caleb set down the bag he was carrying and moved toward the filing cabinet where she stood.

"Which one are you looking for?" he asked.

"Ono, Jon Ono."

"Ono, Ono," Caleb mumbled, running his index finger over the files. "Is this it?" He pulled out a file. Elizabeth grabbed the file and looked at the tab. *Ono, Jon*, it read. She put her hand to her chest.

"Thank you," she breathed. "I thought I'd lost it."

Caleb nodded slowly. "No problem." He paused a moment, rubbed his chin, then began again. "Elizabeth, I was wondering about something."

Elizabeth stopped in her stride to the desk. "Yes?" She lowered herself into her chair. Was he going to bring up going out to dinner with him? She held her breath, waiting for him to speak.

"I saw the office light on last night about midnight. Were you in here?"

His question surprised Elizabeth. Why would she be prowling around the office at such an hour? It wasn't as if she was a spy or anything. "No-o," she replied slowly, "I wasn't here. Why?" Caleb fidgeted on his perch at the end of Elizabeth's desk.

"Well," he said, "I just spoke with Mr. Collins. He said he and a security officer saw someone leave the office. I told him that maybe you were working on a project, but he said no, it was an evacuee. I thought I'd check with you, just to make sure."

Elizabeth frowned. Who would want to break into the office? She stared down at the file she still held in her hand. Jon Ono. Mr. Collins. It all fit together. This story of last night was probably the proof Mr. Collins had been bragging about yesterday. Yet how would he know about the evidence before the break-in actually occurred? It was absurd.

"Did he have a hunch who might be prowling around?" she asked.

"Some Jap– " Caleb began, then stopped short at the sound of his vocabulary. "Some Japanese by the name of Jon Ono. How he could pick him out in the dark, I'm not sure. He's one of the Japanese community leaders here. A sort of chief, I guess, with his people. Why did you need his file, anyway?"

"Mr. Collins told me yesterday he needed it to cinch a case against the man."

Caleb raised an eyebrow. "Yesterday, huh?"

Elizabeth nodded.

"Does that even make sense?" he asked. "Why would Mr. Collins ask for it yesterday? He didn't see him in the office until late last night."

"I wondered the same thing." Elizabeth shrugged. "It could only be one of two reasons," she said. "Either Mr. Collins has a profound gift of telling the future, or he's making all this up to convict an innocent man. I think his prejudice is that strong."

Caleb rose to his feet. "Now Elizabeth, you really don't think Mr. Collins would stoop to that level, do you?"

"I really don't know, Caleb," she replied softly. "But I do know that nothing in this war has been fair and just, up to this point. I'm ready to suspect anything."

* * *

"Child, are you feeling well?" Midori asked. She handed Elizabeth a cup of strong black tea. Elizabeth stared down at the cup, wrapping her fingers more securely around its warm surface. "You aren't acting like the Elizabeth I know."

Elizabeth looked up at Midori. Her words were kind and motherly. It was just what she needed right now. "I'm really not sure," she managed. "I haven't been sleeping well and I seem distracted at work. I couldn't find a file today that was right where it was supposed to be."

The words poured from her lips. "I'm agitated and restless. I want everything in the war to be over, but I can't see the end. I get angry with God and can't even pray. A lot of times I wonder why I'm here and not in San Francisco where I belong." Her words stopped as suddenly as they had begun. Elizabeth stared at Midori, trying to read her friend's thoughts. Midori blinked once, then twice.

"I'm sorry, Midori," Elizabeth apologized after a few awkward moments. "I didn't mean to be hurtful. I wouldn't exchange our friendship for anything. I wasn't thinking."

Midori slowly moved to where Elizabeth sat on the straw-stuffed mattress and lowered herself beside her, one hand stabilizing her back. "I am not angered, my friend," she said. "I only know that God wishes for you to cling to Him in these troubled times. Don't pull away from Him. He is your strength."

Tears stung Elizabeth's eyes as she looked at Midori. Her black eyes, just like Toyo's, reminded her of the one she had dared to love, so many months ago. Elizabeth blinked, not wanting to make a scene with her tears. She hadn't cried for David in weeks. Why did it come flooding back now? Though she had not cried, she had not slept either. The nights were lonely and cold.

The steam from her teacup warmed her face as she brought it to her lips. What had she done for God lately anyway? Had she placed Him on a shelf, like a used book for future reference, because of her pain? "My dear," Midori went on. "You have pulled away from me, and don't come to see me as you used to. Have I offended you by my words or actions?"

Elizabeth shook her head vigorously. "No, Midori. I didn't even notice I was avoiding you." She thought back on the previous weeks. She had avoided Caleb as well, going to meals later than usual, just before the cafeteria closed. Thinking it was because she didn't want to be bothered about a date, she hadn't really stopped to consider her motives. "I guess I have been avoiding nearly everyone, even God." Again she stared into the brown swirling liquid remaining in her cup.

"Is there something else causing your distress?" The tone of Midori's voice was soft, neither demanding an answer nor an explanation, but instead offering a listening ear. "You seem quite moved by the internment, even though you are Caucasian, and without Japanese relatives, to my knowledge. You have cared for me and my family at the risk of losing your employment. Please be truthful with me, Elizabeth. Is your Christian charity all that captivates your heart?"

Elizabeth drank in Midori's words. Had she been that transparent with her feelings? What if Midori knew she loved a Japanese man? Would she be offended? So many other friends and relatives had been appalled to learn of the relationship between her and David. She looked up at Midori once more. Criticism didn't dwell in her gaze. She only longed to understand and help her friend.

Should she tell Midori the truth? Was now the time? Her heart ached to spill out its story of love and tragedy.

"Speak, Elizabeth," Midori said, "or I fear the wanderings of your heart and mind will overtake you. I do not ask out of idle curiosity. I will only speak to God of the issue."

Yes, now was the time. Elizabeth drew in a long breath and let it out slowly. She must speak before she lost her courage. "Yes," she began. "Yes, Midori, there is more than Christian charity that captivates my heart and spurs me toward action on behalf of the Japanese." She paused, gathering her fragmented thoughts. Where should she start? There was so much waiting to pour out.

Elizabeth squeezed her eyes shut. She could see the train, the masses of people, the guard, David, and herself. "Hey, you!" the guard had called from across the platform. "Get moving, and leave the girl alone. You'll have plenty of time to get a Jap like yourself."

"No, you can't go!" she had cried, when David's arms threatened to let her go for what seemed would be the last time.

"I love you," David had replied. "Rely on God, Elizabeth, only God."

That was the source of Elizabeth's struggle. It hadn't been through God's strength that Elizabeth had been able to survive the past months. She was relying on herself and her own ability to mask her pain and live a life devoid of the memories of the past.

The tears came now. Built-up tears from weeks of numbed scars. With shaking hands, Elizabeth set her cup on the nearby table, nearing spilling its contents. Her hands now free, she wrapped them around her middle, willing the pain to cease. Next, sobs overtook her, great convulsing sobs that only come from a broken heart. Arms were wrapping around her now and holding her close. There was warmth and comfort in the embrace and someone to understand the pain.

Midori stroked her hair. When the tears had subsided, she spoke. "Tell me more. You do not cry for the Japanese alone."

Elizabeth sniffed, looking Midori in the eyes. "No," she said, "not for all the Japanese, but for one Japanese man." She studied the older woman's face and thought she appeared confused at the masked confession. Elizabeth reached into her purse that lay beside her. She pulled out the engagement photo she always carried with her and handed it to Midori. Midori stared at the picture, then stared at Elizabeth.

"I don't understand, child," she said after several moments of silence. "Who is this man?"

Once again, Elizabeth's eyes filled with tears. Just the reference to David made her heart long for him. "He was a very special part of my life, Midori. We were engaged." Elizabeth watched her friend's face reflect surprise, then soften as her lips turned up into a smile.

"A man, Elizabeth!" she exclaimed. "All this worry is over a man?" She kept smiling. "You must love him yet, no?"

Elizabeth nodded, wondering whether to laugh at Midori's relief or cry for her loss. "We were to be married last March. Then after Pearl Harbor..." her voice trailed off. There was no need for explanation. "You know. He had to leave. He didn't want me to be bound to him since he didn't know where he was going or how long he would be gone."

Midori reached over to hug Elizabeth. "Well, my dear," she said, "may I be the first at Poston to offer my sincerest congratulations."

"You're not upset, then?" Elizabeth asked.

"Upset, child? Over a soon-to-be-bride? Why do you ask such a silly question? I am honored you shared this news with me."

"Well, you know. Since I'm Caucasian and he's–"

"Listen to yourself, Elizabeth!" Midori scolded. "Have you come to think like the rest of them? You love the man, it's clear. You'll be married soon enough. I want no more of that talk, do you understand me?"

Elizabeth's eyes widened at the woman's response. Finally. Here was someone outside her and David's family circles who understood that racial lines did not have to determine her future with David. She felt her body relax as she wiped away the last of her tears. "Yes, ma'am." A smile crept across her lips. "I understand."

CHAPTER ELEVEN

There it was again, a rustling noise from somewhere outside. Elizabeth glanced at Anita, who was lying on her bed. Her breathing was heavy and even. What time was it anyway? Midnight or later? She groped in the darkness to retrieve her wristwatch on the nearby night stand. Tilting the face toward the window she could just make out the shadows of the clock's hands – ten till three.

It was another sleepless night. Though Midori's talk with her had helped immensely, late at night her mind began to wander and doubt and worry. She shut her eyes tight.

Her mind traveled to the noise outside. Was someone out there? Surely everyone would be in their apartments at this hour. But still. What if an evacuee was lurking in the shadows, bent on revenge? She had heard stories of vandalism and violence at other camps.

Light footsteps were now in the hallway, coming nearer her bedroom door. Elizabeth's breath caught in her throat. She dared not take another breath. What if they stopped at the door, or tried to get in? Should she wake Anita?

The steps stopped. A muffled knock sounded on the bedroom door.

"Elizabeth!" a voice whispered. "Elizabeth, wake up. It's me, Caleb. Open the door."

Both relief and confusion washed over Elizabeth. What in the world was he doing knocking on her door at this hour? Elizabeth stepped out of bed and quickly moved to put on her robe. In a matter of seconds, she cracked the door open and peeked out. There was Caleb, dressed as if he were on his way to work.

"What are you doing?" Elizabeth hugged her robe to her

middle. "Do you know what time it is?"

"Never mind that," he said. "This is important. How fast can you get dressed?"

"So now will you tell me what's going on?" Elizabeth asked as she stepped into the hallway a few minutes later. Getting dressed at three in the morning seemed absurd, let alone meeting a man at such an hour!

"Come outside." He grabbed her hand and pulled her toward the exit. "You'll see."

The night air chilled Elizabeth as she stepped outdoors. Caleb, still holding onto her hand, led her through the darkness to the end of the block, then turned in the direction of the administration office. "Where are we going?"

"Shhh."

As they neared the office, Elizabeth could see flickers of light through the window blinds. Caleb motioned for her to get behind him as he crept low. Elizabeth felt the siding of the mess hall, across the street from the administration office. It was cool to her touch and sent a chill down her spine. Why had Caleb brought her into this charade? Sure, she suspected Mr. Collins of foul play, but she hadn't any intentions of trying to prove it. She was no detective. She silently prayed they wouldn't be caught sneaking around. What would people think?

A figure moved inside the administration office, casting a brief shadow across the window. Despite her fears, Elizabeth was curious. Someone was inside, that was plain to see. Almost too plain. What thief would turn on a light to commit his crime?

"How did you know someone was in there?" she asked.

"I saw the light from my bedroom window, so I came to get you, just in case." His eyes remained fixed to the window.

"Why?"

"A witness."

Ever so slowly, they crept to the edge of the mess hall. "Okay," Caleb said. "We have to get across there fast." He pointed to the dirt street. "Follow me, but don't make a sound." He looked about him, then motioned to her that the coast was clear.

Once on the other side, they huddled against the administration building. "I'm going to try to see in." Caleb crept his way to the window, hunching close to the ground. The window was high enough so that he could stand underneath it without being seen. He stepped up on his tiptoes and cupped his hands against the glass.

In an instant, the room went dark. Someone moved toward

the door on the opposite side of the building. "Quick," Caleb whispered hoarsely, "the other side!" They moved as fast as they could around the building while still remaining hidden in the shadows. Getting to the end of the building, they peered around the corner. There was no one to be seen.

"Good evening, you two."

Elizabeth's heart jumped as she spun around, gripping Caleb's arm. Mr. Collins stared at them, a stack of files tucked under one arm. "Or should I say good morning? Out for a walk?"

"Sir." Caleb gasped, trying to catch his breath, "we thought someone might be prowling around in the office. I saw the light on from my bedroom window and went to get Elizabeth."

Mr. Collins nodded. "Of course. I saw it, too. By the time I got down here, they had left."

"Did you see who it was?" Caleb asked.

Mr. Collins nodded. "I'm pretty sure it was Ono again."

* * *

"Can I go over that page?" Midori pointed to the exercise in the grammar book spread across Elizabeth's lap.

"Of course." Elizabeth covered her mouth to disguise a yawn. Creeping around camp at three in the morning had seemed rather futile after their findings. Now all she had to show for it were tired, puffy eyes that ached for a break from the words that swam before her on the page. She readjusted her position, trying to focus on Midori's reading and the sandwich in front of her.

"What's the difference here?" Midori handed the book to Elizabeth, and pointed to the bottom of the page.

"Oh, yes." Elizabeth paused to let her eyes focus on the page. "'Their' is possessive, meaning ownership, 'they're' is a contraction for they are, and –" Elizabeth cut her sentence short when the office door swung open.

Mr. Collins stood in the door frame, first looking at Elizabeth, then at Midori, then back at Elizabeth. Finally, he spoke.

"What is this?" He indicated the scene before him by making circular motions with his right index finger.

"Sir," Elizabeth said, glad to have found her voice. "I've just been giving Midori a short English lesson over my lunch break."

"English lessons?" Mr. Collins arched his eyebrows. "To, who did you say?"

Elizabeth glanced at her friend. "To Midori, sir."

"Minordi." Mr. Collins rolled the incorrect pronunciation off his tongue. "Hmm..." He looked as if he were pondering the name. "Ah, yes, I remember," he said after several moments. Elizabeth thought he must have remembered Midori asking for a baby crib for Toyo and a better mattress for herself. She hoped he would remain calm, surprised that his temper hadn't got the best of him already.

"I must go." Midori quietly rose from her chair. Elizabeth wanted to stop her, but dared not, for fear that she would receive the brunt of Mr. Collin's anger. He remained silent as Midori made her way past him to the door.

Elizabeth's heart pounded. Surely Mr. Collins wouldn't let this incident pass. She feared he would explode at any second. What could she say in defense of herself? He could fire her and that would be the end of all her endeavors at Poston.

"Miss Tyler." Mr. Collins sauntered across the room and paused in front of Elizabeth's desk. "May I ask by what inclination you let the enemy in my office?" His voice remained even-toned, letting his words alone speak in his stead.

"Well." She licked her lips. "I'm a firm believer in all American residents speaking English fluently. Like you say, if they come to our country they should know the—"

"Don't mimic me, you Japanese sympathizer!" Mr. Collins yelled.

Elizabeth trembled, her fingers gripping her chair. Mr. Collins had never yelled at her before. Her eyes began to fill with tears, but she determined to hold them at bay, at least until she could release the torrent in private.

"What do you think we're running here, a charity school?" he exclaimed with a bit less volume. He leaned over the desk. "If I ever see or hear of you helping the enemy again, you can go home. I'll terminate your contract. Understand?"

Elizabeth nodded, dumbfounded. Mr. Collins marched to his office, slamming the door behind him. Elizabeth could still feel herself shaking. Glancing at the clock, she made her way to the door. She had to get out of there for the rest of her break and try to forget about what had happened.

"Elizabeth," Caleb called to her when she had made her way outside. He caught up to her stride. "Where are you off to?"

"I just need a little air, that's all." Her eyes wandered as she spoke.

"What's wrong?" he asked as they reached the administration block.

Elizabeth didn't answer, instead making her way up the stairs. She reached to turn the doorknob.

"Elizabeth," Caleb insisted, taking hold of her arm. "I heard Mr. Collins yelling at you. Are you okay?"

She nodded slowly. "Do you know what happened?"

"I can guess," Caleb said. "I saw your friend leave."

"Are you angry?" Elizabeth surprised herself by asking such a question. Why should she care what he thought about her actions?

He shook his head. "No, I'm more upset with you that you haven't come to dinner with me yet." Elizabeth smiled at his words, despite herself. "You haven't forgotten then?" he asked.

Elizabeth shook her head. "I've been busy." She excused herself.

"Busy doing what?" Caleb grinned. "Trying to catch a thief?"

Elizabeth turned serious. "What do you think about last night?"

Caleb thought a moment, then spoke. "I'll tell you over dinner."

"Caleb, seriously!" Elizabeth exclaimed, unsure how to handle his humor.

"I am serious," he said. "When can we go?"

Elizabeth hesitated.

"What's wrong?"

Elizabeth looked into his ocean blue eyes, determined to remain steadfast in her decision. "I don't think I can go."

"Why not?"

She shrugged. "I was seeing someone before the war. We put everything on hold, but we still have plans to be together, someday." She said the words almost wistfully.

Caleb stared at her a moment. "I understand." Letting go of her arm, he stepped back. "I'll see you later."

Elizabeth stood on the step and watched him go. He didn't seem angry, that was good. But still, she almost wished she could have said yes to him. Why, she wasn't sure. She sighed deeply. She just couldn't win in these games of love in war.

"God, I don't get it," she whispered as she let herself into her room. "It hurts not to be with the one I love, and it's tempting to be with the one I don't love because I'm lonely. Please help me to trust You."

Touching the gold cross that hung around her neck, Elizabeth thought of Mrs. Mitsuko. Her faith was unmovable, even in the midst of terrible adversity. What had she said those months ago? Elizabeth closed her eyes as she remembered the words.

"You must trust, my child. You must. Let God finish the work He has begun in you." She had taken the gold cross from her neck and given it to Elizabeth. "I believe you will need a reminder." Yes, a reminder of the love of God that had been shown through a friend, and a symbol of the grace she had already been granted though the cross. Elizabeth closed her eyes and prayed, "Lord, I surrender my will to Yours."

CHAPTER TWELVE

Elizabeth stared at the letter in her hands. Maybe this would get her mind off things for awhile. She hadn't seen Caleb for the last few days. Wondering if she had offended him, she considered going to his office to speak to him, but decided against it. Another encounter might only make matters worse and hurt their friendship even further. Had Caleb paid attention to her out of romantic intentions alone? Regardless of the situation, Elizabeth did not want to lose his friendship. Still, she decided to remain silent for the time being.

Elizabeth tore open the envelope and discovered that the script handwriting belonged to Marie, David's sister. For the past year, she had been studying at a university in Tokyo. She had been in Japan at the time of Pearl Harbor and the relocation, unable to come home. The American government must have suspected her, too. When would it ever end? Adjusting her position on the end of her bed, Elizabeth began reading.

Dear Elizabeth,

I am so glad to have located you! I was dying to contact you, knowing the months must be especially hard on you, as I know they have been hard on David. I have written him and Mama, and they seem to be doing well, despite their circumstances. I miss them terribly and long to come home, yet I know that home right now is not what I remember it to be.

David informed me that you both decided to pause your wedding plans. How hard that must be! From a woman's perspective, I can imagine the hurt you must feel, though your decision was mutual.

Please understand one thing, though, Elizabeth. My brother loves you dearly. With all his heart he longs to hold you in his arms and call you his wife. Of that I am sure. If I were in your situation, I know I would doubt that the love a man once had for me was the same after so much tragedy. I can tell you, David's love for you is still strong. Perhaps it is even stronger now than it was before. Please don't lose heart.

Since my studies at the university concluded in May, I have had to find other living accommodations. Thank God I do have relatives in Japan! My father's uncle and his wife welcomed me into their home. I am so thankful. I don't know what I would have done without their offer.

Being in Japan helps me grasp more of what mother and father left behind when they became Christians. My aunt and uncle were also here when the missionary came all those years ago and told my parents about the redemptive grace of Christ. Mama said that they, too, had accepted what they were taught, but as time went on and they stayed in Japan, they fell back into the cultural pagan worship. To this day, they still embrace Shintoism.

My heart aches for them to know the love of Christ, just as it aches for all the university students. The students are very learned in their fields, and are dedicated to their studies far more seriously than many American students, yet their souls are destined for hell because they do not know our Savior. David told me a long time ago that he wanted to become a missionary to Japan. I wondered at his reasoning at the time, but now know that preachers of the truth are desperately needed here. If God has called David to Japan, Elizabeth, He has called you as well.

Elizabeth looked up from the page. Had God called her to Japan? She had accepted the fact that David had a spiritual burden for the Japanese, and that he intended to do mission work in Japan, but had she really accepted this calling for herself? An ominous shadow crossed her heart. In her mind's eye, looming before her was a country filled with thousands of Japanese steeped in Eastern religions, oblivious to what Christ had done for them on the cross, worshiping the creation rather than the Creator.

Trust Me, came the response to her pondering. *Remember, you surrendered.* Surrender: giving up everything for a specific cause. Why would God call her to the Japanese, when she was Caucasian? She loved her home and was comfortable in it. She was unsure of herself in strange places and had always been labeled a homebody. She was Caucasian, her skin and hair as pale as the sand on the beach. Her love for David was her only link to the "land of the rising sun." Why would God choose her? *My grace is sufficient to override weakness.*

Elizabeth sighed. She would have to trust her Lord, or drown in her own inadequacies.

* * *

Elizabeth stopped mid-stride as she walked past the office window on her way to work. What was that noise? It was early, and not many people were outside yet. She heard the shuffle of feet on the hard wood floor inside the building. Leaning closer, she listened.

"Don't ever do that again," said a husky voice. "Understand me? I have but one piece of advice for you, young man."

Where had she heard that phrase before? Mr. Collins, no doubt. She mentally identified the voice disguised by lack of volume.

"What are you doing?"

Elizabeth whirled around to face Caleb. Her heart calming at the sight of him, she placed her finger to her mouth. "Shh, someone's in there."

Caleb lowered his voice. "Who? Another burglar?"

"No, really." Elizabeth pointed to the office. "Something is going on in there."

A chair screeched across the floor, followed by a thud. Elizabeth's heart pounded. Was someone getting hurt? "I'll see what's going on," Caleb said. "Follow me."

In one swift movement, Caleb flung open the door, just as Mr. Collins' fist met a man's nose. Jerking his head upright, Mr. Collins stared at the pair. The young man lying on the floor was Japanese, and looked to be in his mid-thirties. He held his bleeding nose in his hands.

"Good morning, sir." Caleb addressed Mr. Collins, breaking the unbearable silence. He moved toward his superior, slowly but confidently. "Perhaps you'd like to come with me. I came to get you for the board meeting. I'm sure you'll have plenty to share with the trustees." The older man's eyes searched Caleb's face.

"Elizabeth." Caleb's eyes remained fixed to Mr. Collins. "Help this man mend himself while Mr. Collins and I are gone, but stay here until I get back."

Elizabeth nodded her agreement. "Okay." Her voice shook.

When they had gone, Elizabeth turned to the evacuee. He still held his nose, struggling to keep the blood from dripping on the floor. Grabbing a handkerchief from her desk drawer, she handed it to him. "Here," she said. "Apply lots of pressure." The man did as he was told, remaining silent.

"Do you speak English?" she asked cautiously. The man nodded, then held out his thumb and index finger about an inch apart.

"Little," he said, "Not as good as I want to."

"What is your name?" It would be to his credit that he was eager to learn English.

The man shifted the handkerchief from one hand to the other before responding. "Jon," he said. "Jon Ono." His voice was nasal from the blow of only a few minutes ago.

Elizabeth tried to stifle the gasp that escaped from her lips. This was the man that Mr. Collins was trying to convict of a crime? Look at how he had treated him!

Jon walked slowly to the door and reached for the knob.

"Maybe you should stay here until your nose stops bleeding," Elizabeth suggested, hoping to ask him more questions.

He shook his head. "No, I must go."

"Caleb might have some questions for you," she tried in a last attempt.

"He can come to my apartment." Jon's face was expressionless. "I'll be there. He knows where to find me. Just look at your records. It will tell everything–what my number is and where I came from. It's all there."

The door shut behind him. It's all there. As if one's whole existence could be confined to several forms and typewritten pages. Jon must feel like a prisoner. Did David feel the same way?

* * *

The few hours Caleb was gone felt like days to Elizabeth. No matter how hard she tried, she could not limit her thoughts to the shorthand that lay before her, waiting to be typed. At a quarter past eleven, Caleb arrived. He looked tired, as if he had already put in a hard day's work.

"What happened?" Elizabeth was unable to contain her curiosity.

Caleb plopped into a nearby chair and rested his feet up on her desk. "Do you really want to know?" He closed his eyes.

"Of course." She wondered at his question. Maybe she didn't

want to know what had happened at the board meeting. For all she knew, Mr. Collins may have gotten her fired.

"Well," Caleb began, opening his eyes to look at her. "I explained what we saw this morning and asked Mr. Collins to give a reason for his actions."

"It doesn't really matter, does it?" Elizabeth rose from her desk chair. "He used physical abuse. There's no excuse for that."

"Hold on." Caleb held up his hand. "Hear me out. Mr. Collins claimed that when he came in this morning, he found this man, Jon Ono, snooping around the office, just as he had claimed before. When he tried to take Jon to security, Mr. Collins said he got feisty and tried to get away. The only way for him to calm him down was to use physical force."

"You can't be serious!" Elizabeth exclaimed. "No one actually believed that story, did they?"

"Elizabeth," Caleb commanded. Elizabeth sat down, confused and shocked at Caleb's reaction. "We have no evidence either, except for what we saw. Don't assume conclusions."

Elizabeth cast her eyes to the floor. "I'm sorry," she said meekly.

"I understand your frustration." He sighed. "I'm just tired. I didn't mean to upset you."

Elizabeth looked up slowly. "Anything else?" she questioned.

"I requested that Jon Ono be brought in. He was, and said he was in the office early this morning, waiting for Mr. Collins."

"How did he get in?"

"He said the door was unlocked. Mr. Collins, of course, claimed the opposite."

"Did the board decide anything?"

Caleb nodded. "I didn't think the lock looked tampered with." He glanced in the direction of the door. Since it was Jon's word against Mr. Collins', they decided the only thing to do was to go on eyewitness account–which was us."

"So-o?"

"They told Mr. Collins he had twenty-four hours to resign or he would be dismissed." Caleb let out a sigh.

"Really?" Elizabeth was relieved, but completely surprised that the board would carry out a decision that would cause them to lose their project director.

"Really," Caleb said. "Jon was given a week's confinement to his apartment so his behavior could be monitored."

Elizabeth bit her tongue to keep from defending the Japanese man against any punishment. After all, Caleb was right. She didn't have complete evidence to say Jon was without any fault. Elizabeth fidgeted, wondering what this change would mean for her. Mr. Collins would have to be replaced, and soon, there was no doubt about that. But who would take his place? Would the next project director be worse to deal with?

"What are you thinking?"

"I was just wondering," she said, "who would take his place. Mr. Collins' job will have to be filled rather quickly. I was wondering who they would hire and what kind of person he would be."

She looked up then. Caleb grinned at her. "Did I say something humorous?" she said, finding it hard not to return the smile even though she didn't know its source.

He extended his hand to her. "Miss Tyler," he said, imitating Mr. Collins. "Meet your new boss."

* * *

"He really quit, then?" Midori sat next to Elizabeth in the apartment.

Elizabeth nodded as she swallowed the rest of her tea. "Yes, he did. I never expected it, though."

"You know, child," Midori said, "sometimes it is when we least expect a miracle that God performs one for His children."

A miracle? Elizabeth hadn't thought of the situation as the result of supernatural intervention. But what was the chance that she and Caleb would be able to witness the conflict between Mr. Collins and Jon Ono, and that they would come just in time? After thinking about it, yes, it did make sense that God had carefully planned the whole ordeal. God was alive and working, even in the midst of all that had happened.

Is that what it took to see God move in great and mysterious ways? Surrender?

"I think you're right, Midori," she replied. "In fact, I think that Caleb will be a more pliable director. He seems to care about the evacuees more than Mr. Collins ever could."

Midori nodded. After several moments of silence, she spoke. "Is that the young blondish fellow who I see you with sometimes?" Elizabeth nodded in affirmation. "And how are you, do you say, connected with him?"

Elizabeth shrugged. "We're friends. We've worked together on some projects. That's all."

Elizabeth studied Midori's face. The elderly woman didn't seem convinced of her answer. "There's nothing between us, if that's what you're wondering," Elizabeth interjected. "Nothing, well, romantic or anything." She contemplated the words flowing out of her mouth. Were they completely true?

Midori smiled a crooked smile. "And how did you know that is what I was thinking, young lady?"

"Well," Elizabeth stammered. "I just assumed, I guess."

Midori's smile faded. "I am thinking what you assume." She frowned as she continued. "I only ask you about such things because I have watched the two of you together. He finds you attractive."

Elizabeth squirmed inside. Why did they have to talk about this subject? It was of no importance now, anyway. Caleb knew that she was as good as engaged, and that was that.

"I'm not accusing you, child," Midori went on. "You cannot help that Christ shines through you and that others are drawn to you, even if the others are young men. I only want God's best for you and know that flattery can be oftentimes tempting."

"What do you mean?" Elizabeth questioned.

Midori readjusted herself on the bed. "In Japan I became a Christian," she said. "At the time, I was in a relationship with a Buddhist man. Before I knew Christ, I saw nothing wrong with what he believed or practiced, since I claimed no religion at all.

"Against his parents' wishes, he prepared to keep our relationship, even after I became a Christian. He told me one day, 'Midori, we are different, but we can make it work, I am sure of it. You have your ways, and I'll have mine.'"

"What did you say?" Elizabeth's voice was barely above a whisper.

"At first I didn't know what to say. I loved him dearly. I couldn't bear the thought of losing him. For a while, I let things go on, just as they were. But they did not stay the same for long. Our relationship worsened. As I began to study the Scriptures for myself, I realized that as a Christian, I could not marry an unbeliever. We would only tear one another apart, and our children as well. How confused they would have been with each parent claiming a different truth as God's law!"

Midori fell silent a moment and moved to the table to refill the teacups. She came back, resettled herself in her place on the bed, and handed Elizabeth her refilled cup. Midori took a sip of the hot liquid then closed her eyes as if remembering where she had left off in her story.

Midori opened her eyes. "I knew then that if I was to truly follow Jesus, as I claimed that I did, I could not remain in that relationship. So, the next afternoon, I went to him and told him what I must do and why."

"What did he do?" Elizabeth stared at Midori.

"He was angry," Midori replied. "He didn't understand, and his persuasive words nearly trapped me again, but I praise my Lord, He gave me the strength I needed to remain steadfast. It wasn't easy though, child, not at all. But it has been worth it.

"One year after making this decision, I met my husband, who is now deceased. He was Hannah's father, and a man of God. Thinking back, I know it was God's grace that kept me from making a grave mistake and settling for less than what He had for me. How unsatisfied I would have been!"

Elizabeth only nodded. She knew that God had destined her to spend the rest of her life with David, come what may. Even so, she had struggled. She had struggled not to be taken captive by Caleb's flattery and good-natured humor. Midori held the wisdom that could help see her through this trial.

"I am not condemning you." Midori studied Elizabeth's face. "I do not wish to harm our relationship in any way. I only speak these words to you because of my love for you. I love you as my own daughter, Elizabeth. I want God's best for your life."

CHAPTER THIRTEEN

Two months had passed since Elizabeth had last heard from David. No reply had come to the three letters she had sent in the last weeks. She craved some sort of contact with David to keep her heart strong for him. Weeks without word threatened to squelch what hope she had for their reunion.

As Caleb took over the responsibilities of camp director, Elizabeth discovered many details Mr. Collins had failed to take care of in their filing system. Records weren't up-to-date and there were many flaws in the camp's school system. Evacuee children were trying to enroll for classes at the camp, and yet many of their school transcripts hadn't reached the camp, slowing enrollment and causing children to fall behind in their studies. November was fast approaching, and still the camp did not have many needed school supplies.

"Caleb?" She glanced at him through his open office door. "Have we received the supplies for the grammar school yet? They've been crossed off the list, but I haven't seen them come in."

Caleb peered over her shoulder at the paper she held. Elizabeth sniffed, faintly smelling his cologne. "Is there an invoice?" he asked.

Elizabeth looked through the file. "Here it is." She handed it to him. "You signed for the supplies. Where are they being stored?"

Caleb scratched his head. "Oh, yeah, now I remember. There were some used desks and blackboards from Tucsan. I stored them in town. There wasn't room here."

"Caleb, these kids really need to get back to school. They're falling behind. We don't even have any textbooks, and lots of the kids could use some decent clothes. They couldn't bring much, you know, and children are inclined to grow, evacuation or otherwise."

Caleb nodded and sat down. "I know, Elizabeth, I know."

"Isn't there any kind of budget for these things?"

"Not really." Caleb shrugged. "I guess the government didn't plan this far ahead when they decided to evacuate. They probably figured that things would be settled down by now."

"Things are settled down here." Elizabeth crossed her arms and raised her eyebrows. "We haven't had many uprisings lately."

Caleb cracked a smile at her remark. "Okay, okay, little miss philanthropist, I'll see what I can do." Elizabeth returned his smile. "But," he said, "I'll need some help doing some figuring with the budget and deciding what we really do need. Are you up to the challenge?"

Elizabeth's smile widened. "Of course. That's what I'm here for."

"We'll discuss it over dinner, then," Caleb said. "Tonight."

Elizabeth's smile faded. All he really wanted was a date.

"It will be strictly business, of course," he added.

Elizabeth looked at him, studying his eyes, hoping to find some reason to trust him.

"I promise." His smile melted her resolve.

"Okay," she replied slowly, "but we'll eat in the cafeteria."

* * *

"Get in," Caleb urged, opening his car door for her.

"I thought we were eating in the cafeteria." Elizabeth planted her feet, refusing to budge from her stance on the pavement.

"Are you serious?" Caleb laughed. "We couldn't talk about improving anything for the evacuees around some of the administration in there. Besides, you need to get out of here for a while. I do too. It'll give fresh perspective to our plans." He opened the door wider. "Are you coming?"

Elizabeth slowly got in the car. He had said it would be strictly business. She hoped she could trust him. Caleb settled himself in the driver's seat and started the engine. The growl of the motor sent a shiver through her body. Was she nervous? About a business meeting over dinner with a friend? Elizabeth questioned her own intentions. What was she expecting anyway?

When they entered town, Caleb chose a family diner for their meeting place. Elizabeth let out a mental sigh of relief as he parked the car. At least he hadn't chosen a fancy restaurant where lots of couples would be present. She watched a family with three small children walk through the front door. Maybe it would be appropriate after all.

"How did you end up at Poston?" Elizabeth asked after they had been seated in a booth.

"I just finished my graduate training in business." Caleb took a drink from his water glass. "The assistant director job was open. It wasn't my first choice, being from Detroit and all, but it's worked out okay."

"Wow," Elizabeth thought of her own education in secretarial courses. "Graduate training is quite an accomplishment for someone so young."

Caleb shrugged. "I plan to go back to school for post-graduate studies once I have some experience behind me."

Elizabeth smiled and nodded. She wished she had that many accomplishments to her name. She certainly wouldn't be a secretary anymore, that's for sure. An editor, maybe, of a large corporation in New York City? Thinking of David, she tried to dismiss her pondering. God wanted them in Japan, not corporate America.

"What are you thinking?" Caleb rested his arms on the table. "Your mind is racing, I can tell."

She smiled again. "I was just thinking that I would like to get more schooling someday."

"Someday?" he said. "What do you mean, someday? Why not now?"

"Well," Elizabeth said slowly, "when the war's over, I'll probably get married, and have children. There might not be room for the corporate world."

Caleb looked at her intently. "Can't you have both?"

"Both?" she echoed. "I don't think so. David and I both agree that a mother's place is in the home."

"But you want both, don't you?" Caleb leaned closer.

Elizabeth nodded. "Some days more than others."

"Why won't he let you?" Caleb asked.

Why had he asked such a question? Elizabeth swallowed hard. "I-I don't think it's that he won't let me, but just that–"

"Are you sure?" Caleb interrupted, staring her in the eyes. "I've seen this story over and over in the universities I've gone to. A bright young woman, such as yourself, gets swept off her feet by some chauvinist who wants to keep her at home, catering to his every whim. A lot of men think that way. I don't know why. I certainly don't agree with it. I take a more modern view of things. Women in the business place will be just as influential as men in fifty years. Don't you think so?"

Elizabeth bit her lip. She had no idea what to say in reply to his statements. Was it true? Was David trying to control her? She thought back over the months they had been together. It certainly hadn't seemed that way.

"I'm sorry," Caleb apologized in response to her silence. "I didn't mean to assume that he, well, doesn't love you or anything like that." He reached over the table and patted her hand. "I just see great potential in you, Elizabeth. More in you than in most of the women I know. You've got what it takes to achieve great things. I believe in you."

"Really?"

"Really," he said. She smiled then, relieved that everything was resolved between them. "I love the way you smile." Caleb looked into her eyes once more.

Elizabeth felt her cheeks flush and glanced away. She spotted the waitress coming toward their table and was glad for the diversion.

* * *

"The stars are out tonight." Caleb looked out the window as they drove back to camp.

Elizabeth nodded, but made no verbal reply. She was disappointed in the way the night had turned out. Caleb's remarks about David restraining her capabilities made her uneasy. They hadn't even talked about improvements for the evacuees that much. She had tried to bring up the topic several times, but her efforts hadn't seemed to accomplish anything. "You're awfully quiet," Caleb commented as they drove up to the camp security gate.

"Just you and the young lady, Mr. Phelps?" the security guard asked when Caleb stopped the car.

"Yes, Private," Caleb answered. The guard waved them on without any further questions. Elizabeth recognized the private's voice as the one who had questioned Anita the night she arrived in Poston. She shuddered, remembering his suspicion about Anita harboring a Japanese person in the car. But then again, maybe he had just been flirting. Anita, Elizabeth had come to realize, often provoked such interest in men.

"What are you thinking about?" Caleb asked as he parked the car outside the administration building.

Why did he want to be a part of her thoughts? Elizabeth shrugged. "I was just hoping we could have accomplished more tonight. We really didn't talk much about camp improvements."

Caleb shut off the engine and leaned back in his seat. "I'll admit, I was distracted tonight. I wanted to get more done, too."

"Distracted?" Elizabeth asked. "By what?"

"Not by what, silly," he said, "by whom." He leaned toward her and brushed his fingers against her cheek. "You." He continued to gently caress her face. "You." He leaned closer. She could feel her heart beating faster. What should she do? She couldn't let him... His lips brushed hers.

Elizabeth pulled back slightly. "I can't, Caleb," she said softly. A hint of regret laced her voice.

It was his turn to pull away. He looked out the window. "I understand." Elizabeth sensed no anger in his words, she was grateful for that much. But still, why couldn't things be different?

Back in her room, Elizabeth was glad Anita had already gone to bed. What time was it anyway? She squinted at her watch. Ten-thirty. Had they been gone that long? It hadn't seemed like it. She thought back over the night's events. Despite her reservation about the meeting, she had enjoyed herself. It had been good to get out of camp for awhile and remember what real life was like, with no security guards and swarming masses of people kept in one place against their wills. How could two places be so close to one another, yet worlds apart?

She sighed, wondering if she could even remember what life had been like before the war. No curfews or cafeteria lines. No broken heart. Just David. Elizabeth's eyes filled with tears. Could she hold on much longer to the love that now appeared to be a faded dream? Could she remain faithful to him forever? Was he struggling the same way she was?

Elizabeth readied herself for bed, then clicked on her bedside lamp, hoping Anita wouldn't wake up. When the form across the room remained still, Elizabeth slid under the covers and reached for Marie's letter. She had carefully hidden it with all the letters from David in a box underneath her bed. She scanned the letter, groping for some thread of encouragement to latch onto.

Please don't lose heart, Marie had written. That was easier said than done. What if the Japanese had to live segregated for years to come?

Her eyes fell to the paragraph about David wanting to become a missionary. *If he's called, I'm called, Lord,* Elizabeth silently prayed. *But how can I be a missionary for You if I can't even trust You that You have everything under control? I try not to doubt.*

Remember, you surrendered, the words came. Oh, why had she? She punched her fist into her pillow.

Caleb would think it absurd to know that she was trying to follow God's plan for her life by surrendering her will to the Almighty's. Their conversation earlier that night had indicated nothing short of agnosticism. He openly rejected a supportive role of wives and mothers, and demonstrated extreme confidence in his own abilities, apart from God. He believed that education was his window to self-fulfillment. He was even so bold as to suggest that her chance at happiness was daunted by the lack of pursuing her personal aspirations in favor of marriage and children.

Clicking off the lamp, Elizabeth frowned into the darkness. Even if she weren't devoted to David at this time, it wouldn't be right to pursue Caleb with his present beliefs and state of mind. *I feel so fickle, Lord,* she prayed. *I know what Your Word commands about romantic relationships with unbelievers and You have shown me that David is who You want me to marry. We're to be missionaries. You told him so. Please be my strength in this weakness.*

Closing her eyes, Elizabeth was shocked at the scene that played before her. They were in the car, she and Caleb. He leaned slightly closer, his lips brushing hers. Stop it! Elizabeth chided herself. She couldn't think like that. Not now. Not ever.

CHAPTER FOURTEEN

Elizabeth set her dinner tray on the cafeteria table. What a day it had been! Lots of meetings had crowded out time to catch up on her own work, now piled high on her desk. She closed her eyes to say a brief prayer over her meal, but opened them again at the sound of footsteps coming near. It was Caleb. Knowing her own vulnerability, she half wished he wouldn't pay her any attention at all. Of course, he hadn't figured that out. Maybe he came near because he suspected her vulnerability.

Caleb strode up to the table, his tray in one hand and a pile of mail in the other. "I just picked up the mail." He held up the envelopes. "It looks like we've got some school transcripts finally." He indicated the return address on one envelope.

Elizabeth smiled, grateful that the conversation could be business-related. "Wonderful. We can start getting the students enrolled in classes, then."

Caleb nodded, sifting through the pile. "I think there was something for you, here," he said.

"For me?" she asked. "From who?"

"I don't know." He handed her an envelope. "I think it was supposed to go to your personal box, but got stuck in here by mistake."

Elizabeth studied the piece of mail in her hands. It was from David! Finally he had written. "It must be good news," Caleb mused, his mouth full. "Though I don't know how you know without opening it. You're smiling."

Looking up from the envelope, Elizabeth remembered she was not alone. She couldn't read the letter now with Caleb sitting there. Reading any personal letter in public would be bad enough, let alone reading a love letter from a Japanese man in front of all the administration. David's letter would simply have to wait.

"Aren't you going to open it?" Caleb asked as he watched her lay the letter beside her plate.

Elizabeth shook her head. "Not now." She wondered at his inquiry.

"It seems like good news," Caleb went on, "It's postmarked from California. From a family member, maybe?"

Anxious for a diversion, Elizabeth took in the room with a glance. How could she change the subject tactfully? "I like to read my mail privately," she vaguely explained, still looking around. "Oh, there's Anita." She motioned across the room at her roommate. "You know, we're roommates, but we hardly ever see each other. I think she's dating someone."

Caleb only nodded. He had stopped eating and was looking at her intently. "Are you okay?"

"Yes," Elizabeth answered quickly. "Why wouldn't I be?"

"I don't know." He looked down at her tray. "You just got pretty excited when I asked about your letter, that's all. If it's from your man, I've got no problem with that. We've already talked about it, you know."

Elizabeth's heart skipped a beat. If only it were just that. What would Caleb think of her being involved with a Japanese man? It doesn't matter! She chided herself. Caleb wasn't God. She wouldn't have to stand accountable to him for her love life, but the Creator of the universe Who had placed David in her life in the first place. Of that she was confident.

Taking a deep breath calmed her nerves somewhat. It would not help anything to get upset over such a trivial matter. She glanced at the wall clock. Twelve-fifty. "Oh, no," she groaned. She was supposed to meet with Midori at twelve-thirty. They had agreed to do some Bible study together.

She hastily stood up from her chair. Caleb laid a restraining hand on her arm. "Elizabeth," he said, almost pleadingly. "Don't be upset. I didn't mean to pry. Stay and eat."

She shook her head. "I'm not upset, Caleb. I just remembered I had to meet someone twenty minutes ago."

"A meeting?" he asked as she stepped away. "With who?"

"I can't say." She hurried toward the exit. Not here. Caleb might understand her meeting with Midori, but certainly no one else would. "I'll see you later."

* * *

"And how have you been, my dear?" Midori settled herself on a chair in the apartment.

Elizabeth sighed. How was she to answer the woman truthfully? "Up and down, I guess," she finally replied.

Midori squinted her eyes. "Up and down, you say. Does that mean good and bad?"

Elizabeth smiled at her interpretation of the phrase. "Yes, Midori. It means good and bad and in-between. I guess you could say confused."

Midori shook her head. "It is not godly, to be confused."

"What do you mean?" Elizabeth asked.

"Well," Midori began, "our Bible tells us that God extends peace to us, not confusion, if we'll only accept it. That means that anything that represents confusion or a lack of wisdom is not of God."

Elizabeth nodded slowly. If what Midori said was correct, would that also mean that it was ungodly for her to doubt by withholding her complete surrender from her Creator? In the affirmative, it would also mean that she was in sin with her doubt about God's control over her relationship with David. She tugged at the letter she had slipped into her purse just moments before, wondering what it contained.

She gingerly pulled the envelope out of its protective covering and smoothed her hand over its surface. "Is that from your David?" Midori asked. Elizabeth nodded again, not looking up.

"It's difficult, isn't it, my dear?" Midori said.

Raising her eyes, Elizabeth stared at her friend. "Yes." What more could be said? Yes, it was difficult to be separated from him. Yes, even traumatic at times, not hearing from him for weeks. Was he eating right and getting proper rest? How was he being treated? Did he lay awake at night, thinking of her? Was he thinking of her now, even at this very moment?

Both women turned at the sound of the apartment door opening. Hannah stood in the doorway, Toyo propped on one hip, his legs dangling from her hold. "Elizabeth," Hannah acknowledged her.

"Hello, Hannah," Elizabeth replied. It was an improvement that Hannah spoke to her. "It's good to see you."

Hannah took a few steps into the apartment and sat down on the floor with Toyo. "I'm not interrupting anything, am I?"

"No, no," Midori said. "Not at all. I think we are all family here. Is that right, Elizabeth?"

Elizabeth nodded her agreement. Hannah seemed receptive. It was better to encourage her attempts at civility.

"Toyo is growing fast," Elizabeth said, hoping to start a conversation with Hannah.

Hannah smiled at the reference to her son. "Yes, he is, but I'm afraid he will not have any clothes to fit him before long."

Elizabeth looked at the child. His pants did seem a bit short and his shirt a little tight around his chubby middle. She would get her paycheck this week. Maybe she could buy some things for him. "Would you mind if I got a few things for him?" Hopefully her boldness wouldn't turn Hannah away.

Hannah bit her lip without a word. Midori spoke when her daughter's silence persisted. "We don't expect you to, Elizabeth."

"Oh, I know," Elizabeth said. "I just want to."

Toyo watched a beetle skitter across the floor and attempted to catch it. Squeezing its middle, he brought it to his mouth. "Don't eat that, silly boy!" Hannah reprimanded, brushing the bug from his hand. Elizabeth covered her mouth, attempting to stifle her laughter at his performance. The last thing she wanted was to vex Hannah in her discipline. She looked at Hannah. She was watching her. A smile spread across her lips. "Don't provoke him," she teased.

Hannah's smiled faded after several moments. "I agree with mother," she said. "You don't have to buy anything for Toyo. I can't pay you back."

"I wouldn't expect you to," Elizabeth hurried to explain. "I've just got a soft spot for the little guy, that's all." She reached down to pick up the baby. Toyo looked at her as if trying to remember where and under what circumstances he had seen her. He grinned, apparently recalling a pleasant memory.

"Okay," Hannah replied simply. Elizabeth looked at her again, surprised that she had consented. Hannah looked down at the floor. "Thank you."

* * *

"I need to go to town sometime," Elizabeth announced to Caleb that afternoon. "I need to buy some things for a friend's little boy."

Caleb looked up from the paper he was reading at his desk. "Oh?"

"I won't use administrative money, of course," she was quick to interject. "This 'project of benevolence,' as you may be so inclined to call it, is completely personal. I'm just asking for a ride into town." Elizabeth thought better of her words once they had escaped her lips, wishing she had opted for a ride with Anita instead. Caleb wouldn't try to make it a romantic outing like last time, would he? She bit her lip, waiting for his reply.

Caleb took his time folding his newspaper. "I thought you wouldn't want to ride with me again," he said, "after last week and all." He didn't look up, but busied himself rubbing at a spot that marred the desk's surface. Elizabeth said nothing, unsure of his intentions. Was he apologizing to her or accusing her?

Looking up, Caleb said, "I'm sorry, Elizabeth. I didn't mean anything by it, I just wanted to let you know I–"

"Forget it." Elizabeth cut off his statement. She didn't wish to discuss his romantic intentions, lest she get caught up in them herself. "I can find another ride, it's all right."

"No, please," Caleb said, standing up from his chair. "I'd like to take you. It's no problem." After a few moments of pinched silence, he added, "When would you like to go?"

Elizabeth cleared her throat. "Um, whenever you're free. I'm in no big rush."

"Right after work, then?" he asked. "At five?"

Elizabeth nodded. "Sure, thanks, Caleb." The young man nodded in return, his gaze still resting on her face.

Closing his office door behind her, Elizabeth put a hand to her stomach. What were these sudden butterflies, flapping their wings at Caleb's promise to take her to town? Was she nervous over him giving her a ride? Sitting down at her desk, Elizabeth began typing. She could busy herself for now. It was better not to think about it.

It was nearing four-thirty before Elizabeth remembered the letter she had slipped in her purse. Some words from David would do her much good. Running her fingers over the address, she could almost hear David's words. "I love you, Elizabeth. That's not going to change." She sighed. How she wished he was here! She would take him to meet Midori and Hannah. He would insist on playing with Toyo. In spite of her trembling lip, she smiled a faint smile. David would make a good father.

She slid her finger beneath the envelope's tab. It had been so long since she had heard from him. She wished to savor each word the first time they were read. Undoubtedly, if she and David were separated much longer, this letter, along with the others, would be read and reread, many times over, as a means of comforting a longing heart.

"Are you ready?" Elizabeth jerked at the sound of Caleb's voice. His back was turned to her as he locked his office door. She shoved the letter back into her purse. It would have to wait–again. Hastily, she dabbed at her eyes and smoothed her hair.

"I thought we'd get a head start so we could get back at a decent time," Caleb explained, turning to face her. "I could stand to get some paperwork done before bed."

"Sure." She reached for her purse. "I'm ready."

Together, they walked to the parking lot. Caleb opened the passenger door for her, and she slid in. "That's an improvement," He said, walking to his side of the car. He shut the door behind him and started the engine. "At least I didn't have to coax you in this time."

Elizabeth returned his smile, but inside her stomach was churning. She couldn't figure him out. Did he still intend to pursue her?

* * *

Elizabeth patted the packages that lay beside her on the car seat. She was happy with her purchases for Toyo. Two complete outfits, a pair of shoes, and a new blanket would surely help Hannah provide for her son. How awful it would be, to have to withhold such necessities from one's own child!

"I'm glad you're helping them out." Caleb nodded toward the seat. Questioning his unexpected praise, she remained silent.

Caleb pulled off the pavement onto a dirt road. "Where are we going?" Elizabeth asked.

"I wanted to show you something." The path was narrow and winding. Elizabeth looked out the window. She saw nothing unusual. After a few minutes, they came to an opening in the road. Jagged red rock jutted a hundred feet in the air, water cascading down its surface and gathering in the reservoir below.

"It's beautiful." Elizabeth said, opening her car door the second Caleb parked. She walked up to the bank where sand had been deposited, the water gently lapping at the shore. Caleb walked up beside her. "It reminds me of home," she added.

Caleb turned to follow the water's edge. "I thought you'd like it." Elizabeth trailed behind him, thinking of David and their last visits to the beach. The sound of the falls roared in her ears as she neared the base of the massive rock. "I think this is about as far as we can go," Caleb said above the torrent. Elizabeth nodded, taking in one last look before turning around to climb down the incline.

When they had reached the bottom of the hill, Caleb pointed to two large rocks. "Care for a seat?" Nodding, she sat on the rock opposite him. "I know you wanted to talk about improvements at camp," he said. "Is now a good time?"

"Of course," Elizabeth said, happy for his interest in the subject.

"Any ideas off the top of your head?"

"Yes." She had already prepared a mental list.

"Do you have paper and a pen?"

Elizabeth dug a ballpoint pen out of her purse, then searched for something to write on. All she had was the unopened letter from David. The back of the envelope would have to do. Caleb reached for the pen and envelope. "You talk, I'll write," he said. Reluctantly, she handed him the items. Again, he had temporary possession of her letter. Hoping he wouldn't prod further about its contents, she hurried to begin dictating.

"I know the camp budget is limited." She tried to refocus her thoughts on the evacuees. "So, I thought we could do some local fund-raising for more school supplies. We have some supplies, but could use more."

"We've already got the local public schools to give us what they could," Caleb commented.

"I know," Elizabeth went on, "but I don't think we've tapped into all of our resources. What about local charities and churches? I know I could get support from my church back in San Francisco. It wouldn't cost the camp a dime, and we could even get the children involved. What do you think?"

"Are you a public speaker?" Caleb asked. "You're a quiet person."

Elizabeth nodded. "I can be. Especially when it comes to speaking about something that's worth the effort. My passions and convictions run deep."

Caleb smiled. "On that point I am totally convinced. You even had the audacity to challenge Mr. Collins' prejudice. I admit, I don't know that I could have done it."

"Of course you could have," Elizabeth interjected. "If it's something you believe in."

"No, really," he persisted. "I'm more of a conformist."

Elizabeth only nodded in reply. No doubt he had conformed to the world's ways in many aspects of his life.

"Okay." Caleb redirected their chatter. "What else?" One by one, Elizabeth named off the rest of her ideas. Raffles, letters to government officials and teacher education associations, along with petitioning university presidents were included in the list.

"That's your department." Elizabeth leaned forward.

"What?" Caleb seemed clearly surprised that his philanthropy went beyond list making.

"Contacting the universities," Elizabeth said bluntly. "You've had practice dealing with people like that. I haven't, otherwise I'd do it."

Caleb sighed. "All right, but I'll only do it to get you a hearing, then you're on your own."

Elizabeth nodded. "That's all I ask."

"Is that all?" Caleb looked up from his writing.

"I think so. We have a good start."

"You mean a good finish." He scribbled a last note on the envelope. "If all your ideas work, the kids will be better equipped than those at Harvard." Elizabeth smiled at his praise. At least he was being cooperative now. "We'd better go, it's getting dark. Here." He handed her the envelope and pen.

Elizabeth stuck them into her purse and looked around. The sun had already begun to set, its last rays reflecting on the water. She thought of the sunsets over the ocean back home. "Thanks for bringing me here," she said.

Caleb smiled. "I'm glad you liked it."

* * *

Elizabeth settled herself underneath the covers. Now she could read David's letter. Anita had left her a note, saying she would be out late. Elizabeth wondered at her being out late nearly every night. No doubt her lifestyle was unlike Elizabeth's own. She had found several beer bottles stuffed in the trash can yesterday morning. Shaking her head, Elizabeth pitied the girl. If heavy drinking was Anita's hope and future, it looked pretty grim. Maybe she should have tried to spend more time with Anita. Having a good Christian friend may have helped detour her roommate from unwholesome company.

Wishing to forget the situation, she opened the letter, her eyes scanning the lines of text. It began:

Elizabeth,

She stopped reading, frowning at the page. No *Dearest* as usual, just *Elizabeth*. As if he were writing a note to a fellow Bible student. She read on.

I know it's been quite a while since you heard from me. Things have been pretty hectic around here. Everyone is anxious to get on with their lives. Rumor has it that the military wants to start an all-Nisei unit. If that's true, they'll probably be searching among the camps for Japanese-American recruits. Weird, isn't it? There are a lot of mixed feelings about that. Some of the evacuees think if the government recruits in the camps, they will force complete American allegiance and the abolition of Japanese cultural allegiance.

Mama has had word from Dad that he is well and will hopefully be coming back to us by the first of the year. I couldn't bear to enlist if I knew that Mama would be alone.

Elizabeth's heart beat faster. Had David written *enlist*? She reread the sentence. Yes, enlist. Why would he do such a thing after all that had happened to him at the hands of the American government? How could he pledge such allegiance to a nation that corralled him and his relatives like restless cattle? How could she support him in this? What if he became a casualty of war, or worse?

Please don't be startled, but join with me in prayer concerning the matter. I have not made a final decision.

I've got to go now. Please write soon.

David

Breathing a sigh of relief, Elizabeth set the paper aside. What a scare he'd given her! At least his decision was still unsettled. God wouldn't put him in the military after all that had happened, she was sure of it. There was such a thing as sticking up for himself and his rights, without allowing others to treat him like an American citizen only when it was convenient. Elizabeth crossed her arms over her chest. David's letter was short and not even sweet. He hadn't even said so much as "I love you," or "I miss you."

Had the war changed him? Did he still love her as much as he did the day they had said goodbye? Elizabeth shook her head, trying to clear it of the unnerving thoughts. Had he found someone else? Someone like him? A Japanese woman? She rubbed her eyes. She couldn't allow herself to think that way. She still loved David, of that she was sure. He must have just been in a rush when he wrote her, that's all. As she stuffed the letter back into the envelope, her eyes fell on the list she and Caleb had made. She should concentrate on her goals for camp improvement until the internment was over. Then she would be able to peacefully think of David and their future together.

Her eyes scanned the list, making sure all her suggestions had been written down. She smiled to herself. Caleb had pretty decent handwriting for a man. Elizabeth's eyes froze on the last line. In the same script was written, "I love you." A heart encircled the words.

Elizabeth rubbed her eyes, then reread the sentence. It said exactly the same thing upon a second reading. There was no mistake that Caleb had written the words. She struggled to keep herself calm. What should she do? Caleb would probably expect some sort of reaction from her. He might even ask if she loved him.

An unwelcome, bitter excitement crept into Elizabeth's heart. Maybe Caleb's beliefs would change over time to reflect hers. Elizabeth couldn't bear the thought of dying an old maid if the evacuees were forced to live in the internment camp for years to come. Surely David would marry someone else if it ever came to that situation. He would probably want her to do the same. Yet, it was unlikely that the government would spend such an exorbitant amount of money to keep the camps going, especially after the war ended. Then there would be no reason to keep them in operation.

A shiver ran down Elizabeth's spine. How she wished there was someone near to hold her. When she tried to picture herself in David's arms, she kept seeing Caleb instead.

CHAPTER FIFTEEN

Elizabeth shivered as she rushed from her apartment to the administration office, her heavy breaths escaping her lips in tiny clouds. The early morning air was crisp and clear. Many evacuees were outside their apartments in large groups, huddled together around makeshift bonfires. Elizabeth sighed. Hadn't they had their heaters installed yet? She made a mental note to put that on her list of camp improvements. Japanese or not, they deserved to stay warm.

"It's cold out there," Elizabeth commented to Caleb as she hung up her jacket. He nodded.

"I'm sure you noticed the lack of heaters this morning."

Elizabeth crossed the room to her desk. "We have heat in our apartments, Caleb. Why shouldn't the evacuees?"

He held up his hand as if to block the barrage. "I'm not disagreeing. I just wanted to let you know that installation is in the works. Put your mind at ease."

The corners of Elizabeth's mouth curved upward in a slight smile. "Thank you."

"You're speaking at a women's group tonight?" Caleb asked.

"Yes," Elizabeth replied.

"Do you want me to take you?"

Elizabeth shook her head. "No, I'll walk. I'm only going to Miss King's house. She's the president of the women's ministry and she lives only a mile from here." She looked at Caleb. His brow was furrowed, his eyes squinting. "What is it?" she asked.

He sat down and cleared his throat. "The evacuees are restless. They've been complaining about food shortages and no heat. I know their complaints are legitimate, but I can only do so much. I don't control Poston, the government does."

Elizabeth nodded and continued to watch his countenance. There was something more, she was sure. "Two men were arrested for beating a suspected informer. Officials want to try them in an Arizona state court, but evacuees resent the government and think it unfair. They have petitioned me to sign a release for the men, but I refused. The workers claim they'll go on strike and a protest looks inevitable."

Caleb's gaze was intent, his voice serious, lacking his usual humor. "I just want you to be safe." He reached across the desk and took her hand. "Elizabeth, I–"

"Please, Caleb." Her voice revealed more emotion than she intended. She couldn't bear to hear him say that he loved her. Not when she was so vulnerable, hearing the bad news about camp and being frustrated with David. She was weaker in spirit than ever.

They both turned at the sound of the office door opening. Midori stood in the doorframe. "Elizabeth." Midori's eyes stared at the hardwood floor paneling. "There is no food left for breakfast. Do you have something for us?" She began to cry, her hands covering her face.

Elizabeth rushed over to her, enveloping her in her arms. "Of course, Midori," she said in soothing tones. "We'll get something. Don't worry. It will all be over soon."

"Will it, child?" Midori looked up, her lip quivering.

Elizabeth looked her straight in the eyes. Pain dwelt there. It was the pain she had seen in David's eyes just before he left San Francisco. It was the pain of prejudice.

"Yes," Elizabeth said firmly. "God said He would never abandon us in our need. He'll see us through."

* * *

"Thank you for the food." Hannah quietly cleared the apartment's tiny table. Elizabeth nodded. It was Caleb who had gone to the administrative cafeteria and retrieved eggs, toast, milk, and coffee for the small family. "I'm sorry you had to ask at all." Elizabeth thought of the other families that had undoubtedly been turned away from breakfast that morning. Were their children going hungry as well?

"Mama has been strong for a long time." Hannah glanced toward the bed. Midori lay atop the blankets, sound asleep. Her frustrating morning had taken its toll. With her family fed, she could finally relax. Hannah reached for a blanket and covered her mother. "I wonder at her strength sometimes."

"She's certainly been an encouragement to me," Elizabeth said. She looked at Hannah. "Trusting God has never been my strong suit."

Hannah looked down, silent. She did not seem to embrace this idea of a trustworthy heavenly Father. Elizabeth wondered if she should refrain from speaking about her faith. No, she decided, God had brought her to this place, and He wished to draw Hannah unto Himself. He loved her.

"Do you and your mother share the same faith?" Elizabeth asked.

Hannah shrugged. "I went to church when I was little, if that's what you mean."

Elizabeth shook her head. "No." She adjusted herself on her chair. "That's not exactly what I mean. Does Christ have your heart and your life as He has your mother's?"

Hannah stared hard at the floor. "I won't pretend to have surrendered to Him," she said at last.

"Why not?"

"You wouldn't understand." Hannah fumbled with her skirt. "I was going to do it, give my life to Christ, but He let them take him away from me. I can't do it now!"

Elizabeth thought of what Midori had told her about Hannah's husband being taken to another internment camp. They didn't know where he had been taken, and had only received a single letter stating his safe arrival. No return address had been provided. "He is your husband?" Elizabeth asked.

Hannah only nodded. Her gaze was blank, seemingly devoid of life itself.

"Could I pray for you?" Elizabeth asked.

After a pause, Hannah shook her head no. "I don't know that it would do much good."

* * *

"What you're asking for is donations, right?" Miss King poured herself another cup of coffee, glancing at Elizabeth as she spoke.

Elizabeth looked around the table. She had been surprised at the turnout her invitation invoked. Eleven women huddled around Miss King's kitchen table, sipping coffee and nibbling cookies while listening to her appeal for textbooks and chalkboards, pencils and paper. "Donations would be greatly appreciated." She made eye contact with Miss King. "That isn't the only way for us to get the school supplies we need, though. Poston has many talented children who I'm sure would be willing to perform a benefit concert, at the church if you wish, in return for donations."

Miss King nodded as she listened. "Will the children be allowed clearance to come to the church?" a woman across the table asked.

Closing her eyes for a moment, Elizabeth searched for the words to say. She hadn't exactly asked Caleb yet if the children could do a concert, but she was sure he wouldn't deny her request. Not if it would help execute some of their plans for camp improvement. "That would have to be arranged," she said.

"That's not the question," the elderly woman next to the first woman blurted out. Her thick Irish brogue made the words nearly unintelligible. "Do we want them to come? Will it be acceptable to the congregation?" Elizabeth nearly dropped the teacup she held in her hand. Acceptable? What did the woman mean? Surely the church was not prejudiced as well as the government.

"Mother." The first woman chided. "You shouldn't say such things."

"Well, it's true." The older woman leaned on her cane. "Everybody has some form of suspicion right now. Can the Japanese be trusted?"

Taking in a sharp breath, Elizabeth willed herself to be patient. How could a Christian in a women's ministry group say such things?

"Iva May," Miss King retorted. "Of course the children will be well-behaved. I have never heard you talk like that. Remember Whom you represent." Elizabeth breathed a sigh of relief at Miss King's response. At least she hadn't been the one to have to reprimand Iva May.

"I wasn't asking you," Iva said. "I was asking her." She pointed a bony finger at Elizabeth.

Elizabeth took her time formulating her response. "I doubt the children will misbehave," she said slowly, "though they may be excited for a little road trip. However, I don't think that we are discussing a matter of children's behavior at the moment, but that of color." The elderly woman tensed at the sound of the words. She thought of Mr. Mitsuko's words over a year ago. "Have you ever thought what color we would see people in if we were blind?" The room was silent. Looking around, Elizabeth noticed that each woman seemed absorbed in thought about her question.

"I have noticed your Irish accent." Elizabeth directed her words toward Iva once more. "Christ was not Irish. He was a descendent of David, an Israelite. Did He forsake you because you are Irish, or me, because I am Swedish?" Iva remained silent, her eyes diverting from Elizabeth's gaze.

Elizabeth directed her words toward the entire group. "I think you understand the needs of the evacuees. I will let you make your decision. Thank you for sharing your evening with me." The women began to get up, but Miss King motioned for them to sit back down.

"I speak for myself when I say this," she said, "but I will say it, nonetheless. I agree with everything Miss Tyler has said tonight. We owe it to the Japanese and to God to do our part in helping them. Will you support me in bringing this need before the elders of the church?" Her voice was authoritative. She looked at each woman, making eye contact. After a moment, several women nodded their affirmation.

"It's settled then, Miss Tyler," she said, taking Elizabeth's hand. "Thank you for coming."

"Will you need a ride back to camp?" Miss King asked, opening the door for Elizabeth after the other women had left.

"No, thank you." Elizabeth made her way down the porch steps. "There's enough sunlight left for me to walk back. Thank you so much for all you did tonight."

Miss King simply nodded. "I couldn't have done any less and been settled in my heart with my Creator."

Waving good-bye, Elizabeth quickened her step toward Poston. What an interesting meeting it had been! Though she had not been prepared to give an answer to racial comments, she believed the Lord had given her the words to say and had burdened Miss King's heart with love for the Japanese. Everything would work out to raise the needed funds for the children, she was sure of it. Now all she had to do was convince Caleb of the need for a benefit concert at Miss King's church.

Twenty minutes later, Elizabeth neared the Poston gate. The camp really did look like a prison from a distance, with identical housing surrounded by a fence and sentries standing guard.

The sun was sinking below the horizon when she reached the camp entrance. The buildings became great shadows and the people faceless forms. Everyone seemed to be out of their apartments tonight.

The rumble of angry voices reached Elizabeth's ears. She

stood still for a moment. "Miss Tyler?" the guard asked. Elizabeth nodded. He opened the gate for her, swiftly shutting it once she had entered.

"What's going on?" she asked him.

He nodded toward the crowd gathering near the rec hall. "You mean with all those Japs?" She abhorred his racist slang, but said nothing. "I'm not sure." He scratched his head. "I know they were all upset this morning, with nothing to eat and the cold. Don't think it would do much good to break into the mess hall, if that's what they aim on doing, though. If there's no food, there's no food."

Elizabeth made a few steps toward the administration office. She should find Caleb. He would know what was going on. Squinting toward the throng of people, Elizabeth could see two men unfolding a Japanese flag. Ripping the American flag from the flag pole ropes, they mounted the white field with a crimson circle, representing the "land of the rising sun." What did they think they were doing, tearing down the American flag? Most of the evacuees assembled were American citizens. Walking as far from the crowd as she could, she neared the administration building.

"Stop it, all of you!" a booming voice yelled at the crowd. In a moment, guards were surrounding the people. Elizabeth's heart began to race. *Oh, Lord,* she inwardly cried, *let no one get hurt.* She climbed the office stairs in two short steps and reached to turn the door knob. It was locked. What now? Backing down the stairs, she nearly collided with someone. Her hand went to her chest. The enveloping darkness made it impossible for her to see more than the faint outline of a Japanese man's profile.

"Where's the director?" he demanded.

Elizabeth's lip quavered. What did he want with Caleb? "I-I don't know," she managed. The man's voice seemed familiar.

"Aren't you his girl?" the gruff voice questioned.

Elizabeth violently shook her head in spite of the darkness. "No, I'm only his secretary."

The man took a step closer. Gripping the railing, she stepped back up the stair. In one swift moment he grabbed her wrist. "Tell me where he's at!" he yelled. "He put my brother away to be tried by some Caucasian court. I've got a score to settle with him." Elizabeth could contain her tears no longer, terrified she might be hurt. He twisted her wrist back, sending a stabbing pain up her arm. "Tell me!"

"Leave her alone," a voice yelled. The man turned, hastily letting go of Elizabeth's arm. "You're upset with me, not her."

"Caleb!" Elizabeth looked in the direction of the voice.

The evacuee lunged at the man before him, knocking Caleb off his feet. The two men wrestled on the ground a moment before Caleb regained his composure and jerked the man to his feet, holding him at arms' length. The evacuee swung his fist at Caleb in one last attempt at revenge. An instant after the blow to his jaw, Caleb returned the punch, sending the man sprawling on the ground.

Shaking with fright, Elizabeth stared at the motionless man. Was he conscious? "Sergeant!" Caleb called into the darkness. "Come get this man and take him to solitary confinement." The sergeant arrived only moments later, a flashlight in hand. He shined it on the still form. Kneeling down to examine the man, Caleb said, "Charge this man with female assault. I want the full measure of the law brought against him."

The sergeant nodded. "Can we identify him, sir?"

Caleb looked at the Japanese man a moment longer before replying. "Ono," he said. "Jon Ono."

An involuntary gasp escaped Elizabeth's lips. Could this man really be the one who had come to Mr. Collins' office the day the project director resigned? Had Mr. Collins been right that Jon had been the guilty party? Maybe Mr. Collins didn't have anything to do with it. She shook her head. No, Mr. Collins had seemed off-beat from the start. Surely he wasn't completely innocent. It appeared now that neither of them was.

In several moments' time, a few more guards arrived at the scene. They tended to the cut on Jon's face, the evidence of Caleb's fist. Jon regained his composure and sat up. "Think you've got everything under control, don't you?" he spat at Caleb.

Caleb laughed sarcastically. "When it comes to a woman's welfare, yes, I certainly hope I can be in control and protect her. This charge against you won't be erased."

Jon swore under his breath as he was led away. "This matter isn't settled!" he yelled.

It was completely dark now. The security guards had taken their flashlights. Elizabeth felt a shiver crawl down her spine, her body trembling, partially due to the chill of the weather, but mostly due to the fear in her heart. Was Poston a safe place to be anymore? She looked toward the rec hall. Everyone was going back to their apartments at the direction of the guards. Maybe it was all over.

"Elizabeth," Caleb said softly. She turned her head, unaware that he had come near her. "Did he hurt you?"

She sighed. "No-o, I don't think so." Her voice quavered, betraying her feigned composure.

Caleb was silent a moment as if measuring her words. "I'm not so sure you aren't," he said. "Do you want me to stay with you awhile?" Elizabeth said nothing. "Come on," he urged, leading her by the hand.

When they got to the administration apartments, he stopped. "Can we talk in my living room?" he asked. Elizabeth merely nodded. She had no idea that the camp director had an entire apartment to himself. He opened the door and led her inside. There was a small living room attached to an even smaller kitchenette. "Cozy, huh?" he said in mock pride. Despite the evening's events, Elizabeth smiled.

"Are you sure you're feeling well?" Caleb asked again after they had seated themselves on the sofa. Elizabeth could only stare at Caleb, still unable to speak. She closed her eyes. Putting her hands to her face, she began to sob.

"I'm sorry." She tried to wipe the tears away. "I don't mean to–"

"Never mind," Caleb said. "Don't apologize. You're entitled to tears after what you've been through tonight." He touched her wrist. "That Jap left a bruise on you!" His voice rose with each syllable.

"Caleb, please don't," she said. "Let's just put it behind us."

Caleb fidgeted in his seat. "That's not the point. He could have hurt you badly if I hadn't shown up. I could have killed him if he had." His eyes searched Elizabeth's for a moment. "I'm sorry," he said. "I don't mean to upset you." Ever so slowly, he slid his arm around her shoulder and drew her to his side. "I just care about you."

Elizabeth closed her eyes, letting herself be pulled into his embrace. She could feel his heartbeat and the rhythm of his breathing. At last she was sheltered from the world by one strong enough to weather its blows. His arms were protection and security. A retreat from the confusion and pain of war. A haven from a broken heart.

What would David think if he saw her now, letting another man hold her close? Surely he wouldn't approve. Yet, he had seemed distant and complacent in his only letter in months. He hadn't even said he loved her, but only referred to the very thing that had separated them–the war. He was even considering joining the military! How could he do it after all the pain the government had caused them? What if he enlisted and was killed while defending his country? What then? Would she die inside or pick herself up and get on with life? Loneliness still didn't appeal to her senses.

"Elizabeth?" Caleb broke the silence. "Did you get my note on the envelope the other day?"

She pulled herself away from him slightly. Thinking he had forgotten the incident, she hadn't been prepared to answer him. "Yes," she replied softly. "I got it."

"I meant it." He pulled away further to look at her. "Could it ever work out between us?" Searching his face, she could tell his words were genuine. He really did care for her. Without waiting for an answer, he began to stroke her cheek. "I love you, Elizabeth Tyler."

Fresh tears pooled in Elizabeth's eyes. How could she resist him? For months she had longed for arms to hold her and someone to love her. Here was her opportunity. Who knew when it would come again, with David or anyone else? Closing her eyes, she memorized the moment. Tears seeped out of her lids, falling to her lap. Perhaps they could make it work.

He kissed away a tear. She opened her eyes and met his gaze.

"Please give us a chance," he whispered. He propped her chin up with his hand, running his thumb over her lips. Tilting her head up, he brushed her lips with his, slowly back and forth. Elizabeth relaxed her body, leaning up against the couch. She was weak, unable to resist. He kissed her once, then twice.

Yes, she thought, *we can make it work.*

CHAPTER SIXTEEN

Elizabeth rolled over, squinting at the sunshine spilling through the window pane. Reluctant to get up, she squeezed her eyelids shut, hoping to get back to sleep. Footsteps sounded in the hallway. How late was it? A low voice called down the hall. "Merry Christmas, Anita!"

"Merry Christmas to you, too, Mr. Murdock." Anita's footsteps followed the voice.

Elizabeth sat up in an instant. Christmas Day! How had she forgotten? Bouncing out of bed, she thought of spending the day with Caleb. He had told her the night before of a surprise and wanted her to reserve a good part of the day to spend with him. Though she had promised to visit Midori, she agreed to Caleb's plans, postponing a visit to Midori until that evening.

She had no sooner finished readying herself for the day when a knock sounded at the door. "Are you up, sweetheart?" Caleb called in to her.

Elizabeth opened the door to greet him. "All except for some earrings." She returned his kiss.

"You don't need earrings." Caleb stepped into the room.

Elizabeth surveyed herself in her vanity mirror. "You don't think so?"

"Not with these." Caleb snapped open the lid on the velvet box he held.

Elizabeth whirled around. A sparkle caught her eye. In the box lay a necklace with a single diamond hanging from its gold chain with earrings to match.

"Caleb," she breathed. He gently turned her around to face the mirror. He unclasped the necklace already about her neck and handed it to her. She looked down at Mrs. Mitsuko's golden cross that now lay in her hand instead of hanging around her neck. It had been the last visible remembrance of David that she hadn't been able to give up. In wearing it, she still felt a glimmer of hope for the life they could have shared. Now it, too, had to be relinquished.

She reached up to touch the diamond. It danced in the sunlight, bouncing the rays off its surface.

"Do you like it?" Caleb asked.

Elizabeth nodded. "It's beautiful." She smiled.

"It looks great with your black dress," he commented.

Wincing at his remark, she remembered the last time she had worn the outfit. It had been her last date with David before Pearl Harbor, the night he had proposed.

"We'd better get going." Caleb turned toward the door. "Christmas Day won't wait." Taking in a deep breath, Elizabeth gathered her purse and coat. She would have to soon forget everything about David or it would drive her crazy. Maybe what she felt was guilt. She was dating one man when she was all but engaged to another. She pushed the thought from her mind. David had only written one letter in several months, and it had been completely devoid of romance. He had probably found someone else by now.

"Are you ready?" Caleb eyed her as if he could hear the thoughts playing through her mind. Elizabeth nodded. Fingering the diamond necklace, she resolved to enjoy the day.

* * *

"Where are we going?" Elizabeth asked after what seemed to be a lengthy drive.

Caleb glanced at her sideways, taking his eyes from the road for a moment. "Well, it was supposed to be a surprise, but I guess it's only fair to warn you now."

"Warn me?" Elizabeth asked. What had Caleb planned for the day?

"It's always thought to be a traumatic event to meet a boyfriend's family, am I correct?" He grinned and squeezed her hand.

"Your family is here?" Elizabeth was shocked at the thought of meeting his family. Did he think they were more serious than they actually were?

"Not my whole family. Just my mom and brother. They've

rented a house around here for the winter, wanting to get away from the Midwestern cold."

Nodding, she replied. "I have an aunt that does the same thing, only she always stays with my parents."

"Oh, how long does she stay?"

"At least two or three weeks." Caleb raised an eyebrow at her dour response. "She can be testy," she added.

"Well," Caleb said, "Mother isn't like that. She would rather have her own place where she can bring her housekeeper, companion, and cook. Let's just say she likes the comforts of home."

Elizabeth's eyes grew wide. "The comforts of home?" What kind of woman was Caleb's mother? "It sounds more like the comforts of a mansion."

Caleb chuckled. "You'll see, my dear."

A few minutes later, Caleb turned the car down a paved drive with overhead lights lining each side. The drive curved up a slight incline. When they had crested the hill, Elizabeth saw a brick mansion, the bay windows as high as they were wide. A long flight of cobblestone steps led to a set of great oak doors. As they neared the house, a man in a suit stepped out, his gloved hands folded, his countenance demure. In Elizabeth's estimation, his greying temples did not identify him as Caleb's brother.

Elizabeth swallowed hard before speaking. "Who's that?" She pointed in the direction of the house.

Caleb leaned over. "I'm not sure. He must be a new one."

"A new one?" she asked.

"Yeah." He studied her face. "Haven't you ever heard of a butler before?"

Elizabeth was stunned. In joking about a mansion, she had not actually supposed that Mrs. Phelps lived in one, but only thought her to be particular about accommodations. "Caleb." The pit of Elizabeth's stomach grew cold. "Maybe your mother would like to spend the day with just you. I mean, she hasn't seen you in quite a while and—"

Caleb parked the car and put his finger to her lips. "Nonsense. You're just nervous. Of course she wants to meet you."

"I'm from a middle-class family Caleb, not royalty," she said.

"Just be yourself and you'll be fine. You managed to charm me with your middle-class ways," he said, deflecting her comment. "Mother isn't royalty either. Now come on."

As he stepped out of the car, the butler opened Elizabeth's door. "Ms. Chariton is expecting you. Shall I park it in the garage, Mr.

Phelps?" He tilted his head slightly awaiting Caleb's command.

Caleb merely nodded. "We'll be awhile."

"Who's Ms. Chariton?" Elizabeth asked as they mounted the cobblestone steps.

"My mother, of course." He eyed her quizzically.

"Isn't she Mrs. Phelps?"

"She was at one time," he answered as they neared the top of the stairs. "She and Dad divorced when I was little."

Several moments later, Elizabeth found herself seated with Caleb on a loveseat in a living room decorated in Victorian accents. Ornate curtains, made with many yards of expensive fabric, embellished the slender windows.

"If you don't mind my asking," Elizabeth said, lowering her voice, "why did your parents separate?"

Caleb shrugged his shoulders. "Dad held Mother back. She had goals and dreams. She couldn't be stifled at home with us. What do you expect?"

"What kind of goals and dreams?" Elizabeth pressed the issue.

"She was a nurse when she had her second baby."

"You?"

"Yes," Caleb said. "She didn't want to stay home. Dad wanted her to, but she wouldn't give up her job. So, needless to say, she divorced him."

Elizabeth had no reply for Caleb's answer. Who was this woman, anyway? She had money, that was plain to see, but no husband; sons, but no father in the home.

"Caleb!" a feminine voice called from the hallway. Elizabeth turned to see a woman in her early fifties coming toward them. Going to meet her, Caleb held out his arms.

"It's good to see you, Mother." He held her close. Studying the woman, Elizabeth found Caleb's mother to be an attractive woman for her age. Though her thick, chestnut hair had begun to grey, she had styled it in an attractive bun. She wore an ecru skirt with a matching jacket and very high heels.

"This must be Elizabeth," Ms. Chariton said as she came over to the sofa. Elizabeth stood as Caleb extended his hand to her.

"Yes, Mother," he said. "This gorgeous young lady is who I've been endlessly bragging about." Blushing, Elizabeth glanced at Caleb. That had been quite an introduction. She hated to think she had to live up to whatever else he had been telling his mother about her.

"I'm so pleased to meet you, Elizabeth." Ms. Chariton shook

Elizabeth's hand. "My son is not easily enchanted. He has obviously discovered something he loves in you."

"Hey, Caleb!" a voice called from the circular stairwell.

"Jay!" Caleb yelled back.

"My, my." Ms. Chariton covered her ears. "Those boys will never learn not to holler through the house!" Elizabeth smiled. Maybe they would listen if she told them not to holler through the mansion instead.

The man entering the room resembled Caleb, though he was a bit taller and his hair darker. He slapped his brother in greeting, and then eyed Elizabeth. "Who did you bring with you?"

"Jay, meet my girlfriend, Elizabeth. She's my secretary at Poston." Caleb explained.

Jay extended his hand to Elizabeth. "Pleased to meet you," she said. Jay's loud, brash manner annoyed Elizabeth already.

"Your secretary, huh?" Jay said. "That's convenient! I thought Poston was just a place for Japs, but you found a treasure! Think you can find one for me?" He crossed his arms and waited for his brother to reply. Biting her lip, Elizabeth refrained from contradicting not only Jay's slang toward the Japanese, but his vulgar comments regarding her as well.

Caleb hit his brother upside the head. "Find your own."

* * *

Elizabeth stared at the enormous Christmas tree, rays of brilliant white light bouncing off the surface of the red bulbs. A generous stack of presents lay beneath. She was alone in the room, the others retiring for an afternoon nap after a scrumptious Christmas dinner. Elizabeth had never been served by kitchen staff in her entire life. Christmas dinner at the Tyler household had always been a joint effort of the women in the family.

Sipping the hot cider in her teacup, she leaned back and closed her eyes. Christmases at home were so much different than this. Family traveled--aunts, uncles, cousins, and grandparents arrived just before noon, bringing with them delicious, homemade family favorites. After everyone had eaten, her father would read the Christmas story, slowly and reverently.

"Are you asleep or just thinking?" Caleb whispered in her ear. Elizabeth jumped at the sound of his voice.

"I thought you were resting," she said. "I was just thinking, reminiscing about Christmases past."

"Oh?" Caleb sat down next to her and crossed his arms. "Aren't they all pretty much the same?"

Elizabeth shrugged, surprised and hurt by his flippant words. "Not really," she said. "Each is a reminder of family gathering together to celebrate Christ's birth." When he said nothing in return, she continued. "My dad always reads the Christmas story from Luke when everyone has eaten. Do you have a Bible? We could read it together."

"Naw," Caleb said. "I don't know where one would be. Besides, you could probably recite those verses by heart. Why do you need to read them again?" His tone of voice did not merit a reply.

Biting her lip, Elizabeth leaned against the sofa. Did Caleb even believe in the true meaning of Christmas? If Christ had not come into the world, humanity would have been completely lost to sin and disobedience. Did he realize that fact at all?

Sliding his arm around her, Caleb pulled her close to his side. "I'm glad you came with me today," he said close to her ear. With her eyes closed, Elizabeth was still as he caressed her face. Slowly his fingers made a trail down her cheek, across her lips and nose, and down the other cheek. She relaxed her muscles. Caleb always seemed to have this calming effect on her. Even when she was aggravated with him, his touch could neutralize her frustration and excite her heart.

"I love you." Caleb's whisper sent a tingle down her neck. Elizabeth listened to the three words as she had done numerous times in the past six weeks. Each time, though, she had failed to return his endearment. It just didn't seem right or appropriate. She had confessed in her heart that she still loved David. It was impossible for her to sincerely love another simultaneously. Of that she was sure.

* * *

"I'm sorry I'm late, Midori," Elizabeth apologized as she stepped into the elderly woman's apartment.

"You don't have to apologize," Midori said. "I know you have more to do on Christmas Day than visit me. I'm just glad you came."

Elizabeth sniffed. The air smelled of pine. In one corner, Hannah rocked Toyo. The baby's eyes fought closing for a few moments, then finally gave in to sleep. "I think he has had a big day." Hannah gingerly lifted him off her lap and into his bed. A nativity scene was displayed on the small table, surrounded by straw.

"We took the straw from the end of the mattress." Midori pointed to the display. Elizabeth smiled. Such meager decorations Midori had, but what a meaningful way to remember Christ.

"I've brought you each something." Elizabeth directed her words to both women. Reaching into her bag, she pulled out two brightly wrapped packages, handing one to each woman.

"You didn't need to bring us anything." Midori rubbed her fingers across the package's glossy finish.

"You're very dear friends," Elizabeth said, "not to mention much like family. I want to give you a gift for Christmas. Even Christ himself received them from the wise men." She handed an additional package to Hannah. "He can open it when he wakes up." She nodded toward the sleeping baby.

Hannah smiled. Opening their packages, the mother and daughter found brand new Bibles, each with a black leather binding. "Oh, Elizabeth." Midori took Elizabeth by the arm and hugged her. "Thank you for my Bible." As Midori let go of her, Elizabeth saw tears in her eyes.

Guilt over her failure to provide Midori with a Bible sooner washed over Elizabeth. Had she been that preoccupied with David and Caleb and her own concerns? The Word of God meant so much to Midori. A woman of righteous character, that was what Midori was. Her faith led her life, and anything contrary to the Word of God was set aside or eliminated from her life.

Elizabeth turned to Hannah. "It's up to you if you would like to read it." Hannah looked up from gazing at the Book. She stared at Elizabeth.

"I will try," she said simply. Elizabeth smiled and nodded. Hannah was responding. That was good. God was again working on behalf of His children, even at Poston.

"I haven't anything to offer you in return," Midori said, emotion flooding her voice.

"Oh, yes, you do." Elizabeth sat on one of the lumpy mattresses. "I have been craving to hear the Christmas story all day. Will you read it to me now?"

Midori nodded vigorously. "Of course, child. From Luke. Our Christ's most magnificent birth."

CHAPTER SEVENTEEN

"They've done it," Caleb said.

"Done what?" Elizabeth asked without breaking the rhythm of her typing.

"The government created an all-Nisei unit." His eyes scanned the newspaper. Her fingers went numb at the typewriter. A Japanese unit? That might mean that David had enlisted, or was planning to. Closing her eyes for a moment, she prayed for his safety, that God would take care of him and sustain his body, mind, and soul.

"You're quiet." Caleb dropped his hand and the newspaper to his side. He sauntered over to her desk. "What do you think of it?"

Elizabeth placed her hands in her lap, silent. What could she think or say? The only man she had ever loved could be on his way to battle and possible death. What words could be appropriate? Surely she couldn't disclose her feelings and genuine thoughts to Caleb. For all he knew, her former fiancé had all but disappeared. True, David had almost ceased involvement in her life. Scant communication and no geographical contact could only sustain a romance for awhile. "Well?" Caleb crossed his arms, waiting.

Shrugging her shoulders, Elizabeth spoke. "I don't really know what to think. The same young men who are enlisting were those who were uprooted from their homes. They're now serving a government and a nation that once betrayed them."

"It sounds to me like they have more Christian forgiveness than you have," he smirked.

Downcast, Elizabeth studied the floor. Caleb's words may be accurate, but they stung. It seemed he was getting quite good at that lately, criticizing her with a ferocity that paralyzed her thoughts and ideas in an instant.

Caleb walked around to the back of her chair and laid a hand on her shoulder. He began rubbing her arm, then kissed her cheek. Elizabeth cringed. How could he say such hurtful words, then try to make up for it with watered-down affection? He turned her chair to face him, then leaned forward to kiss her lips. Jerking her head away, Elizabeth sought to continue working. "What's up with you?" Caleb demanded.

"I'm not in the mood for your affection." She shoved another piece of paper into the typewriter.

"And why aren't you?"

Elizabeth turned to face him. "Because you say the most hurtful things sometimes."

"Like what?"

"Like I don't know what a butler is, or that I can't forgive others." Her voice broke, but her eyes burned with anger.

Caleb sighed, then knelt on the floor beside her. "I'm sorry, Elizabeth." His voice was low and even. "I didn't mean to hurt you. I just say whatever comes into my head. I need to watch it, I know. Having a woman to care for is a lot different than having a brother. I'm just not used to it." He touched her warm cheek with his finger. "Please don't be upset. We're all stressed out right now. War is ugly."

Elizabeth straightened in her chair and breathed out heavily in an effort to relieve her aggravation. Of course, that was probably it. Caleb wasn't the problem. The war was to blame. That and a series of unfortunate, disheartening circumstances. Right?

He drew her close once more. This time she was able to relax. She felt the beating of his heart. Here was security, sheltering her from the brunt of anything the world threw at her. He was her safeguard.

Caleb broke the silence. "I still love you, even if you get upset with me." He loved her. She had longed to hear those words for so long since David left. Caleb reached into his pocket, drawing out an envelope. "I picked up your mail."

Taking the letter he held out to her, Elizabeth wondered why he would pick up her mail. Was he just trying to do her a favor or was he curious about her letters? Glancing at the handwriting, Elizabeth knew the letter was from David. She had longed to hear from him, but now, things were complicated. Breathing a sigh of relief, she silently thanked God for his safety.

"Aren't you going to read it?" Caleb asked as Elizabeth proceeded to place the envelope in her desk drawer. She gulped. Why did he press her on these issues?

"No-o," she replied as even-toned as possible. "I've got a lot of work to get done this morning. It can wait."

"Is it from a relative or someone?" He reached for the envelope.

"No, don't!" Elizabeth said, more forcefully than she intended.

Caleb stopped and eyed her curiously. "What's the matter? It's just a letter."

"It's private, Caleb." She extended one hand. "Give it back to me."

"What are you hiding?" He tore a corner of the envelope and watched her intently. Biting her lip, Elizabeth resolved not to flinch. What had David written? She half hoped his words were as neutral now as they had been in his last letter. Surely Caleb could find no fault in what looked to be a letter from a friend, even if the friend was male.

A few seconds later, Caleb tossed the letter on the desk. "Looks like a friend of yours enlisted." Elizabeth grabbed the letter and scanned the contents. David's words had been few and unromantic–again. This time it was to her benefit. It read:

Elizabeth,

I have enlisted. I am deployed from here March 3rd. Please keep in contact through Mama. She will have any information about me. Hope all is going well with you.

David

"I'm sorry I suspected you." Caleb walked out of the room without another word. Sighing, Elizabeth propped her elbows on her desk and rubbed her eyes. Why had Caleb reacted like that? She had once told him that she had been engaged before the war. Maybe he was worried the former suitor would take his newfound place. Running her fingers over the words David had written, Elizabeth prayed. Lord, You know how much I still love David. Keep him safe.

A pang of guilt washed over her as she prayed the words. She did love David, yet how could she love him and find comfort in another during his absence? It had been wrong to give in to Caleb, she knew it, yet it seemed she couldn't let go. Caleb had been her security in a time of ravaging war and uncertainty. David's letters were still coarse and in a sense, unloving. He was part of the U.S. Army now, involved in the greatest war in world history. What if he never returned? The thought of being alone was unbearable.

* * *

"I love my Bible very much." Midori stroked the black leather as she spoke. Elizabeth smiled. The gift had been well worth the investment. Midori's thirst for godly wisdom was great.

"What would you like to read today?" Elizabeth flipped through the pages of her own Bible. Hannah was quietly playing with Toyo on the floor. Would she mind hearing the Scriptures read aloud? Elizabeth hoped it wouldn't dispel Hannah's recent openness. Perhaps she was staying on purpose.

"I wish to read of my Lord's suffering and glorious resurrection." Midori paged through to the passage. Obviously, she had thought about her preference beforehand.

"Why do you wish to read that today?" Elizabeth asked. Lately they had been studying Paul's epistles. She had assumed Midori would want to continue with their examination of Ephesians.

Midori looked past Elizabeth toward the door. "Because," she said slowly. "It reminds me of how small my troubles are in comparison to what Jesus has done for me. And because it helps me cling to the promise that He already holds the victory to life's wars." Elizabeth sat silent for a few moments, studying the older woman's countenance. She said the words most reverently, as if Christ Himself stood at the door to her apartment.

Midori's eyes brimmed with tears. "My Lord is near," she said, "even in Poston." Casting her eyes downward, Midori opened her Bible. "May we read Matthew's account?"

Elizabeth nodded. When she had located the passage, she began reading aloud. They followed Jesus through the pages as He dined with His disciples at the Last Supper, and prayed fervently in the garden of Gethsemane. Jesus prayed the will of His Father above His own, although He was part of the Trinity.

Reflecting on the words she had just read, Elizabeth stopped. "What is it, child?" Midori asked.

Elizabeth smoothed out the page as she answered. "I was just thinking about the words of Christ, when He knew He was going to die a horrible death. He gave His will over to His Father, even if it meant sacrificing all He had, including His life."

Midori nodded. "He did it willingly. He had a free will, just like we do. He was probably lonely praying in the garden while the disciples slept." Midori, pausing a moment, looked down at her hands. "He was in every way like us." She took in a deep breath.

"Elizabeth, God's plans for your life far exceed what you dream of even now. The war has scarred you in ways unknown to many others." Midori glanced at Hannah and lowered her voice. "Don't lose the gift God has so graciously given you. You cannot fulfill the extent of His plan outside of the husband He wishes to give you. Don't throw it away because of your fear. Christ's selfless love is ready to take away your fear."

Elizabeth could only stare at Midori, knowing she was referring to Caleb. No doubt she had seen the two of them together and guessed the extent of their relationship to be beyond that of friendship. It was likely she had also been in prayer, asking God to give her words of wisdom when confronting Elizabeth about the relationship. Fidgeting, Elizabeth wondered what she could say. What was appropriate at a time like this? An apology? A promise to break off her relationship?

Instead of waiting for a reply, Midori began reading where Elizabeth had left off. In the verses that followed, Christ was arrested and tried before the Sanhedrin. When questioned, He made no attempt to defend Himself. Before the cock had crowed, Peter denied Christ three times. "Peter is like us in many ways." Midori paused in her reading. "He denied Christ when faced with the possibility of punishment. For us, it is inconvenience. We reject Christ by demanding our own way and proceeding with plans that seem agreeable at the moment."

Instead of further referring to Elizabeth's relationship with Caleb, she pointed a finger at herself. "I have been guilty of that many times," she said. "And so have crucified Christ by my disobedience and sin. Yet He faithfully forgives me and sets me on the path that leads to righteousness." Silence hung in the air for a few moments. "Would you read on?"

The twenty-seventh chapter described Jesus before Pilate. No charge could be made against him, yet he handed Christ over to the people to be crucified. Elizabeth's voice quavered as she read of the soldiers mocking Jesus and leading him away to Golgotha as a man whose identity was covered in blood and the sin of the world.

"No!" a shrill voice rang out. "They cannot crucify Him!"

The two women jerked around to see Hannah, her face ashen.

Rushing over to her daughter, Midori embraced her. "Child, what is wrong?" Hannah's eyes searched her mother's.

"He didn't do anything wrong, Mama," she said in hushed tones, tears streaming down her face. "He healed the sick and cared for the poor. He only did good. I read it."

Elizabeth's hands shook at the scene before her. Had Hannah finally come to the place where she would invite Jesus to be her Savior, too? She had been reading her Bible. Elizabeth smiled as tears welled up in her own eyes. Still, why didn't she expect God to answer her own prayers? As Midori had said, God's love and His care are everlasting.

"He did not die in vain, Hannah." Elizabeth rose from her chair. When she reached the two women, she patted Hannah's shoulder. "Nor did He remain in the grave. He died for us." She pointed to herself, Hannah, and Midori. "And He died for the whole world, because we are sinners and have nothing to offer God as atonement for our sin. We have no sacrifice perfect enough." Hannah stared at Elizabeth with wide eyes. She was silent.

"He became that perfect sacrifice." Elizabeth stroked Hannah's hair. "And He took away the sin that entangled us, making us righteous before God. Though man killed Him, He rose from the grave on the third day, just as it had been prophesied."

"He'll make me whole, then?" Hannah asked, wiping her eyes. "And He'll help me bear my pain?"

Her lip trembling, Elizabeth nodded. She remembered what Midori had said about Hannah's husband being taken from her. What pain she must feel! Perhaps it was an even greater pain than she had experienced, at the loss of David. "Yes, Hannah," she said. "He can help you bear your pain, and make the suffering worthwhile." For a few moments, no one spoke. "Would you like to invite Him into your heart to cleanse your sins and sustain you in the hard times?" Hannah simply nodded.

Elizabeth refrained from leading her in a rote prayer of salvation. "Can you ask Him now?"

"I-I think so." Hannah closed her eyes. A few moments later, she began her prayer. "Lord Jesus," she said, her voice shaking and low. "I'm sorry for the wrong I've done. I've hurt you, even though I didn't mean to. Please make me right before you, and lead me in the righteousness that Mama and Elizabeth have. Come live in my heart. Please take the pain away of being separated from Kiyoshi for so long..." Her voice trailed off as she began crying.

In a few moments, her body convulsed with each sob, as if she were in physical pain.

Wrapping her arms around the young woman, Elizabeth could feel her own pain rising up within her. Being torn from the one she loved most in the world, Elizabeth's heart ached. It ached with a pain and a longing she had tried to ignore by replacing it with something more accessible that met her needs temporarily. What had she created in doing so? More pain? Two broken relationships? Squeezing her eyes shut, she willed herself not to dwell on her loss another moment.

Toyo let out a cry as the tower he was constructing out of building blocks toppled to the wooden floor. Releasing her hold on Hannah, Midori rose to comfort Toyo, taking him in her arms and murmuring soothing words. "It's okay. You did well. Grandma will help you build another." A few moments later, grandmother and grandson were both kneeling before a pile of blocks. Toyo was ready to try again. As Elizabeth watched the child, she wondered how he would react to having a father again, after the war. Would he remember a face that should by now be familiar?

Turning her attention back to Hannah, whose tears had subsided, she wondered if she should share with her the pain she had experienced with David being taken to Manzanar. She felt that the connection would help them both sort through their feelings and cling to the hope of a brighter future. Perhaps it was the answer to Hannah's desperate prayer.

CHAPTER EIGHTEEN

"I'm going to Manzanar," Caleb said. Elizabeth nearly spat out her food, then consciously looked around the restaurant.

"Manzanar?" She breathed deeply, trying to steady her composure. "Why so far?"

"I have to meet with the director there." He wound his spaghetti around his fork. "Are you up to accompanying me?"

Elizabeth's heart began to race. How could she go with Caleb to Manzanar? David would be there for another month before he was deployed to Europe. "When are you going?"

"Next week."

Next week. That was too soon. David would still be there. Taking a sip of water, Elizabeth allowed herself to fantasize about seeing David again. What would his reaction be when he saw her again? Was he in a relationship with someone else? He had every right to be, she reminded herself. She and David weren't engaged and their correspondence had diminished. Could she bear seeing him with another woman?

"Well," Caleb asked, wiping his hands on his napkin, "will you go with me?"

"I should get some things done here." Elizabeth scanned the room for a scant few seconds. "I have a stack of shorthand to get caught up on and transcripts to file and—"

Caleb shrugged. "You can't get much done with me gone, anyway. Let's forget it and get away for awhile, even if it's on business." Looking down at her plate, Elizabeth realized she was no longer hungry. Things weren't supposed to end up like this. "You can present your ideas for camp improvement to the director there," Caleb added.

Elizabeth looked up. If she could get improvements for Manzanar, she would be gaining improvements for David and his family. In her heart, she knew she had to try. "All right," she said. "I'll go, but only if you intend to keep your promise. I demand an audience."

Caleb smiled. "You always were determined." He took her hand in his. "Especially when I was trying to date you. But I won, didn't I?"

* * *

Elizabeth's heart pounded as they neared Manzanar. Normally, it would have felt homey to be back in California, but not today, under these circumstances. They would reach Manzanar in one short hour if the train's speed remained steady. "Your hands are trembling," Caleb commented as he cupped her hands in his. "Are you cold?"

Elizabeth shrugged. "A little, maybe."

Caleb stared. "I don't think that's what's bothering you. I know you better than you think."

Elizabeth's lips tried to form a smile, but failed. It was useless. She couldn't go to Manzanar with one man in hopes of seeing the only man she truly loved. Her eyes welling up with tears, she covered her face with her hands. Caleb wiped the tears away as he took her into his arms.

"Tell me," he said gently. "I've noticed a change in you ever since you got that letter from your friend. Some man. I don't want you entertaining friendships with other men, even if you knew them before you knew me. Not if it does this to you."

Elizabeth pulled away slightly. "What do you mean?"

"Just what I said." Caleb urged her to lay her head down on his chest again. "Some men are wild. You never know what they might do. It's my job to protect you now."

Elizabeth refused to lay her head down. Frustration boiled within her over Caleb's comments. What right had he to tell her with whom she could be friends with? Pulling away completely, she faced the window, concentrating hard on the scenery that flew past.

"Come on, Elizabeth," Caleb coaxed, edging toward her. "Don't take it that way." Elizabeth's shoulders relaxed some at the sound of his words. "I just want you to be safe." Sliding his arm around her shoulder, he leaned a bit closer. "I still love you," he whispered.

Turning her head around, Elizabeth smiled slightly. How could she be frustrated with him one minute, then cave in to his endearments the next?

Forty-five minutes later, the train pulled into the station. Rousing from her nap on Caleb's shoulder, Elizabeth stretched. Now it was time to face her fear. She reminded herself to concentrate on what she was here for—camp improvements--that's all. Parked by the station was an armored car. "That's our ride." Caleb pointed to the vehicle. Elizabeth stared. They were going to be escorted in an armored car? Why? Caleb hurried to explain. "Their security is a lot stricter at Manzanar." David's description of barbed wire fences and watch towers flooded back to her memory. It must be true after all.

After a half-hour's ride, the car pulled into camp. The entrance was much like that of Poston's, with a guard stationed at the gate. Stepping out of the car, Elizabeth looked up at a nearby guard tower. A shiver ran down her spine as she thought of the prisoner of war camps she'd heard about. How could it be possible that these internment camps endured in the United States? The guard in the tower paced back and forth, his eyes plastered to the camp below. What would it be like to think someone could be watching her every move? Elizabeth knew David must feel trapped in a place like this. Maybe that was why he was enlisting, to be free to move around without the constraints of this prison.

A long line stretched out in front of one of the camp's largest buildings. Checking her watch, Elizabeth assumed the building to be the evacuee cafeteria. It looked more like an army mess hall. Elizabeth remembered Midori's descriptions of the distasteful food served at Poston. Caleb took her hand and followed the security guard. As they neared the mess hall, Elizabeth's heart began to race. What if she saw David? What would he do? What would she do? Gripping her hand a bit tighter, Caleb led her past the crowd of evacuees in line for lunch. Elizabeth scanned several faces, but saw none that were familiar.

* * *

Balancing her notebook on one knee, Elizabeth resolved to stay attentive to the meeting at hand. Daydreaming about David would not help anything, especially at a time like this. She glanced around the conference table at the six men present, all were either camps directors or government officials.

"I think the new Nisei unit will help mend relations between the Japanese and Caucasians," the Manzanar project director said. Elizabeth thought he seemed like a congenial man, as he made no slang references to the evacuees and seemed open to her ideas for improving the camps, should they remain open for much longer. "Who knows," he continued, "maybe the camps can close soon."

Caleb shrugged. "Maybe. But much of that decision hinges on developments oversees and the Nisei unit's loyalty and performance."

"I agree with Mr. Phelps," the army sergeant sitting across from him commented. "Recruiting evacuees in the first place seems like a risky business Mr. O'Brion. Why Washington decided on such a plan of action to begin with is beyond me."

"Their plan still might be effective," Mr. O'Brion said, stroking his short white beard. "Japan might come to a truce sooner than anyone expects. And a truce that's been signed by federal courts cannot be reversed."

Elizabeth fidgeted in her chair. If she didn't get a breath of fresh air, she was afraid she wouldn't remain silent about the issue any longer. Quietly excusing herself, she made her way to the back door and stepped into the afternoon sunshine. Closing her eyes, she took in several deep breaths.

"Attention!" Elizabeth jerked out of her reverie at the sound of the militant order. Across the field of deadened grass, a group of Japanese army recruits stood at the attention of a Japanese commanding officer. "Private Mitsuko!"

Elizabeth's heart skipped a beat. Her hands flew to her chest. Had she heard right? Had he just called David? "Yes, Sir!" A recruit stepped forward in response to the command. Squinting at the figure, Elizabeth determined that, yes, it was David. She stared at him as if in a trance. There was her David. As the reality of seeing the one she loved sunk into her soul, her lips began to tremble. Oh, how she had missed him! She longed to run to him and throw her arms around his neck, letting him hold her. They would share of their sorrows and struggles over the past months. And they would be together.

But it could not be. Not now. Not here. David was still under the government's control and she could not interfere. To make herself known could cause trouble for them both. Watching him closely, she memorized his every movement. He was as handsome as ever, she concluded as she studied him. His jaw was set firm as he obeyed orders. Had he changed? Had the severity of the war caused him to become hardened in his heart, even in the slightest measure?

A few minutes later, the sergeant dismissed his troops from their rigorous exercises. Several recruits sauntered off the field, toward the mess hall. Others remained, talking amongst themselves. A group of young women stood at the edge of the field, whispering and looking at the recruits. Elizabeth smiled to herself. Evidently the interest in men in uniform transcended cultures.

"David!" one of them called out. Elizabeth's head jerked in the direction of the female voice. A young woman, set apart from the group, waved at David. Waving back, he excused himself from his friends and walked toward her. The smile on Elizabeth's lips faded instantly. Even from a distance, she could tell David smiled as he greeted the woman. Sliding an arm around her shoulder, they walked in the direction of the mess hall.

Elizabeth's heart sunk. It was true, then. Her greatest fear had become a reality. David had found someone else. His lack of letters and romantic interest must have been his way of telling her he'd found someone else, one of his own. A stab of guilt pierced her heart. Thinking of Caleb, she decided she had done the same thing. Not out of contempt, but out of loneliness and fear. Her body began trembling. All at once, she wished she were back at Poston in her own room, so she could cry and let out all the pain. How could David do this to her? Anger rose within her soul as she contemplated what she had witnessed. At least she hadn't waited in vain for him by turning Caleb down.

"There you are." Elizabeth quickly wiped her eyes before turning to face Caleb. "I was wondering where you went."

"I just needed some air." She waved a hand in front of her face. "All that war talk is nauseating."

"I know." Caleb sat down beside her. "It will all be over soon." He paused a moment before continuing. "You missed an interesting discussion, though."

"Oh?" Elizabeth rested her chin in her hand.

Caleb nodded. "Jon Ono had his trial last week."

Elizabeth's eyes widened. She had nearly forgotten that the man had yet to be sentenced. "What happened?" she asked.

"He pleaded guilty to harassing you."

"Anything else?"

Struggling to keep a straight face, Caleb went on. "He pleaded guilty to breaking into the office last year."

Elizabeth's mouth dropped open. Could it be? After having

been totally convinced of Mr. Collins being the predator, she found the information hard to believe. "Mr. Collins had nothing to do with it then? Why did he resign?"

Caleb held up his hand. "It's not quite that simple. Ono only pleaded guilty to one charge of burglary. He still claims that he had nothing to do with the office being open the day we walked in on their fight. He was sentenced to one year."

Elizabeth sighed. "I don't know what to say." She thought once more of David and glanced across the camp toward the mess hall. There he stood, talking to the same young woman. Elizabeth bit her lip, then spoke again. "I guess I'm glad."

Caleb put his arm around her then. Grasping his fingers, she caressed each one in turn. At least she had someone to hold her. "It's good I was there to protect you," he said, watching her.

Elizabeth nodded firmly. It was wonderful to have someone watching out for her, making her feel secure. What if he hadn't been there to rescue her from Jon Ono's wrath? What would have happened? "Caleb?" she said after a few moments.

"Yes?"

"I love you." The words slid off her tongue easily. She fixed her eyes on his, intent on his reaction. Would he accept the love she had been so reluctant to give?

After an agonizing few moments, Caleb smiled. "I've never heard you say that before." He drew her closer to him. "What makes you say it now?"

Shrugging her shoulders, Elizabeth decided she couldn't let him know that her once fiancé had just rejected her, so now she had love to spare. That kind of explanation just wouldn't do. "I'm just ready to tell you, now."

He gave her shoulder a squeeze before rising to his feet. "At least you can say it now." He chuckled. "Let's get going. We'll need to catch the train soon."

Holding hands, they made their way across camp. Elizabeth's heart began to race as they neared the mess hall where David was waiting in the supper line. He was holding the Japanese woman's hand. Praying David wouldn't look their way, Elizabeth tried to hide her face, pretending to struggle with her windblown curls.

"Miss Tyler!" a voice called. Her heart thumping in her chest, Elizabeth turned to see Mr. O'Brion rushing after them, waving her notebook in front of his bulging belly. Several people in the line stared after him. "You forgot this."

Graciously accepting her notes, Elizabeth tried to hide behind the large man. "Thanks for coming," he said to Caleb. Then he stepped back and went on his way. But he left too soon. Elizabeth could feel eyes on her still. Glancing up, she found David's eyes affixed to her. The ebony pools were just as she remembered them. As the moisture gathered in her own eyes, she could see tears forming in his eyes as well. David took a step forward, then stopped, looking down.

Elizabeth felt a tug on her arm. "Let's go." It was Caleb, leading her away. So close, yet so far away.

* * *

"Who was that guy?" Caleb asked when they had settled themselves on the train.

"Who?" Elizabeth asked.

"That Jap who stared at you just as we were leaving."

She made no comment regarding his slang. His vulgar vocabulary had become all too familiar. She averted his question. "Why do you ask?"

"He seemed quite interested in you." Caleb scooted closer. "I didn't like it. I think he got my message, though."

Elizabeth cringed. Was that what had stopped David from approaching her, when he looked down at the ground? He deserved it, though, she told herself. He was with another woman. How could he possibly love her still? Looking at Caleb, she reminded herself of her confession of love. It was time to move forward with her life. If the future could include Caleb, so much the better. It was more desirable than being alone, differing belief systems or not.

"His name is David." A few moments of silence followed.

"David?" Caleb said finally, almost in a whisper. "You know him, then?"

"Yes," she said in the same hushed tone.

Caleb gripped the seat beside him, his biceps bulging. "He wrote you." Elizabeth said nothing. "You knew him in California?" His voice held an edge of aggravation.

"Yes," she repeated.

"He was a friend?"

Elizabeth's courage began to wane at the intensity with which he asked the question. "We knew each other only a short time." She thought of the year with David that had encompassed both friend and suitor.

"You didn't answer my question," Caleb insisted. He looked at her intently. "Tell me the truth, Elizabeth. Was that who you were engaged to before the war?" His voice calmed down somewhat. Staring back at Caleb, she lowered her eyes and nodded solemnly. Caleb glanced around the train car before giving way to his reaction. "Why didn't you say so before?" he hissed.

When she made no reply, he spoke. "It looked like he found another interest," he taunted. The words stung her heart. Yes, David had found someone else, just as she had. For one fleeting moment, she wondered what the young Japanese woman was like. Was she a Christian? Did she know what a priceless treasure David was?

Looking out the window, Elizabeth sought to hide the tears that flooded her eyes. "I know," she said softly. They fell into silence once more.

"Don't cry." Caleb patted her hand. "I didn't mean to hurt you. I just thought we meant something to each other. I wasn't expecting to run into your ex-fiancé or finding out you had contact with him after you said yes to me."

Turning to face him now, Elizabeth spoke in her defense. "Oh, you and I do mean something to one another." She couldn't let Caleb slip away from her, too. "I don't know what I would do without you. I knew David before I knew you. It hurts still, though. We were separated just months before we were going to get married. But our ties are broken now."

"You still hid it from me that you were corresponding with him," he pointed out. "That's why you got so upset when I brought your mail to you."

Elizabeth nodded. "I'm sorry, Caleb. I should have been honest with you, but I thought you wouldn't understand."

"What do you mean?"

"Him being Japanese and all," she finished.

"That I *don't* understand," Caleb scoffed. Looking down, Elizabeth concentrated on her hands. "I understand that you're mine, though." He enclosed her in his arms.

After a few moments, Elizabeth relaxed in his hold. He was all she had now. It had to work.

CHAPTER NINETEEN

Elizabeth gripped the paper. Caleb would not like this article. Each publication of the evacuee-written newspaper had to be censored by the camp director. If the copy included material controversial to his convictions or taste, he could edit it severely or prohibit its publication altogether.

Scanning the article once more, she thought over its contents. The young Nisei editor condemned the U.S. loyalty questions asked of troops before enlisting. Indeed, they were loaded questions, asking the evacuees to not only give up Japanese loyalty but also the pride they held in their Oriental heritage. Only then were they allowed to pay tribute to their country by joining the armed forces.

Caleb walked out of his office and stopped before reaching her desk. "What's the frown for?" Without a word, Elizabeth handed him the copy. After a few minutes of reading, Caleb tossed the article on her desk. "Cut it."

"Are you sure?" Elizabeth said. "Nisei are American citizens and have the freedom of speech. Nothing in this editorial is slanderous, Caleb. It's true."

"The Japs just want charity from sympathizers like you," Caleb said. "I don't plan to be at odds with the War Relocation Authority by printing such garbage."

Cringing, Elizabeth thought of the government agency controlling the evacuation. In her opinion, the agency that carried out the relocation would do what it could to suffocate the Japanese expressions of civil rights. Still, what could she do about it? Caleb had said to cut it.

"You heard what I said." Caleb walked around the back of her desk chair. He leaned over and kissed her cheek. "I don't want you in trouble either."

Elizabeth relented. "I'll cut it."

* * *

Straining to hear Tadao's speech, Elizabeth leaned forward. She had never been to one of the evacuee talent shows held in the rec center, but at Midori's invitation, she had decided to attend. How she wished she could interpret the beautiful Japanese words spilling off his tongue! As an elder, Tadao was greatly respected among the evacuee community. Elizabeth nudged Midori. "What is he saying?"

Midori smiled at her inquiry, but failed to take her eyes from the speaker, even for one moment. "He speaks of duty and honor to one's country, even in the face of adversity," she interpreted. "The Japanese-American troops, he says, are to be heralded for their courage and acts of forgiveness to the American government."

Elizabeth nodded, listening to Tadao with a new admiration. How he could encourage his race to endlessly forgive the American government and take up arms to defend it was beyond her comprehension. Only Christ could forgive like that. "Why doesn't he speak in English?" she whispered.

"Our native tongue is better received among those elders, Issei, that are still Japanese citizens." After the speaker bowed his head, indicating he was finished, he introduced the next performer.

"Ladies and gentlemen," he said in broken English, "I would like to present to you Hannah Endo."

Hannah stepped onto the platform and positioned herself on center stage. Looking at the young woman, Elizabeth could tell Hannah's heart was meditating on the words of the song she was about to sing. Hannah focused her eyes upward. A few seconds of silence followed before her soprano voice broke the reverie.

She sang in Japanese a song she'd written since her salvation. At first she sang slowly and quietly, but with each stanza gained vocal strength and momentum.

She sang the remaining verses and repeated the first, then bowed her head, just as Tadao had done. The hall fell silent for the first time that night. No one said a word as Hannah stepped off stage and took her seat.

"A lot of us ain't Bible thumpers!" a youth yelled from the back. "You must be part Caucasian or something." A few snickers followed. Hannah said nothing, but looked ahead; ready to listen to

Tadao, now mounting the platform. Elizabeth fidgeted in her seat. What would happen next? Were Hannah's Shinto and Buddhist friends and neighbors ready to hear about Christ?

Finally Tadao spoke. "That concludes our entertainment this evening, friends and relatives." The elderly man stepped off the stage slowly and looked toward Hannah. Soon, others got up from their chairs and made their way to the exit, chattering and socializing as usual.

Elizabeth hugged Hannah. "I'm proud of you, and so is our Lord."

Hannah looked worn. "They do not understand." She shrugged her shoulders. "What am I to do?"

"Keep at it." Elizabeth smiled. "They'll get it. God will make the seed you have planted grow within their spirits."

"Excuse me, ladies." The two women turned to see Tadao standing a few feet from them. What did he want? Was he about to reprimand Hannah for her "culturally inappropriate" selection? When he had their attention, the elderly man cleared his throat once more. He extended his hand to Hannah in one quick motion. She shook it slowly. "Thank you."

Both women glanced at one another. Thank you for what? "I'm afraid I don't understand," Hannah said.

"Your song." Tadao pointed to her. "It is what Japan needs. Grace, freedom, peace. You will tell me more sometime?"

Hannah smiled through the tears that threatened to spill down her cheeks. "Yes," she said. "I will tell you how you can have this grace and freedom and peace to share with Japan."

Elizabeth thought of David's plans to become a missionary. Would he go when the war was over, taking his girlfriend as his young bride? For the first time, her heart ached for Japan's lost souls. Japan needed Jesus. She had the Jesus they needed.

* * *

"Where were you last night?" Caleb asked Elizabeth as they relaxed on his couch the next evening. "I spent an hour looking for you."

"I went to the talent show." He couldn't disapprove of that, could he?

"Why?" He sounded irritated. Why should he object to her going to an evacuee event? She had spent every other night with him this week. "I wanted to spend some time with you," Caleb added.

What was he up to now? He seemed to be more controlling now than any man she had known. Even those men who encouraged their wives to stay home to fulfill the roles of wife and mother seemed less controlling at the moment. Elizabeth sighed involuntarily.

"What was that for?" he asked, his voice growing a bit louder.

"We've spent every other night together this week," she explained. "I just wanted to be there to support Hannah?"

"Hannah?"

Elizabeth nodded. "She's Midori's daughter and has become a very dear friend. She sang last night."

"More *dear* than me?" he asked.

"No, Caleb." Why even try to explain? It seemed he would try to twist anything she said. "My going to the talent show doesn't mean I don't want to spend time with you." It was just as well to smooth things over – again. Even if it meant taking responsibility where it might not be due.

Caleb slid his arm around her, and pulled her to his shoulder. "It's okay." The tension in his voice was gone. "Just tell me where you're going next time. I start to get worried when I can't find you."

Maybe that was it. Was Caleb only trying to protect her? After the incident with Jon Ono, he seemed to stick close by her, especially around other men. The way he had reacted to David staring at her had proven that point. "I couldn't forgive myself if I failed to keep you safe." Surprised at his statement, Elizabeth pulled herself upright.

"Why do you say that?" She looked into the azure eyes. The dim light from the kitchen reflected off them.

Caleb shrugged. "It's a guy thing, I guess." His cheeks reddened slightly at his confession.

"What do you mean?" Elizabeth pushed for an answer.

Caleb was silent for a few moments. "Well," he said slowly. "Since we're together, and your dad isn't here, it's only right for me to do everything I can to ensure your safety. You're a woman; capable of entering a prestigious university and conquering graduate training, yes, but able to physically defend yourself, no. I consider that my job."

Pondering his words, Elizabeth smiled. She liked the way he put it. Mentally capable, yet physically vulnerable. She could accept that. "I kind of like it when you put it that way." Settling herself back into his arms, she relaxed. Maybe he wasn't trying to control her after all. She had begun to wonder, though, with some of his statements, opening her mail from David, and demanding to know what she did with her time.

But now it made sense. He just loved her, that was all, and wanted to keep her safe. It was a comforting thought, knowing she didn't have to constantly look after herself, but could rely on Caleb's protection. Surely that's the way God meant it to be.

Running his hand up and down her arm, Caleb kissed her. "Elizabeth," he whispered.

"Yes." Her eyes closed, she concentrated on his touch.

"You know I love you." His voice remained quiet. Elizabeth only nodded. "I've loved you ever since I caught you visiting that woman, Minordi."

Giggling, Elizabeth opened her eyes. It seemed so long ago.

"You tried to deny me again and again, you know," Caleb said. Again Elizabeth nodded. Because of David, she had turned him down. "But I caught you."

Turning serious, Caleb outlined her profile with his index finger. "I don't want to ever lose you."

He stared at her intently. Adjusting herself on the couch, Elizabeth wondered at his words. Was he hinting at marriage? Her heart began to thud in her chest. What would she say if he proposed? Yes, she had resolved in her heart that she didn't want to be lonely, and she did care deeply for Caleb, but could she honestly pledge her life to him? Again she relaxed against his shoulder. It was something to consider before he asked – if he asked. They hadn't talked of marriage. Maybe Caleb's intentions were not what she had thought.

"After the war," Caleb said, interrupting the silence, "we can concentrate more on us." He looked directly into her eyes. "I want a life for us both, away from this place – together, forever."

CHAPTER TWENTY

The three women looked up as a knock sounded on the apartment door. Enjoying tea, fellowship, and Bible study together, Hannah, Midori, and Elizabeth sat around the table. Midori rose from her chair and opened the door.

"Excuse me," a male voice said. "You have company, I see." Stepping aside, Midori motioned for Tadao to come in.

"Yes, we're having Bible study, but you're welcome to join us," she said with a sweep of her hand. "Come in." The elderly man took off his hat and bowed slightly to Hannah. His gaze paused when he saw Elizabeth. "Here, take this chair." Midori seated herself beside her daughter, then placed a hand on Elizabeth's shoulder. "Elizabeth works here, Tadao, and is a dear friend." Tadao slowly slid into the offered chair.

"I can only stay a minute." He turned toward Hannah. "I only wished to speak with you a moment, if I may."

Hannah glanced at her mother. "Is it something you can share with all of us?" Again, Tadao looked toward Elizabeth. Looking down at her hands, Elizabeth wondered what the Japanese felt like on a daily basis, being scrutinized and judged for their outward appearance, something over which they had no control.

"Why is she here?" He pointed a trembling finger at her torso.

"Whatever do you mean?" Hannah said.

"Does she monitor your Bible study together?"

Jerking her head upright, Elizabeth thought the man must be joking. But his eyes held sincerity. She hurried to explain. "I am only here because I am a Christian and Midori and Hannah have become good friends, Tadao. I assure you my intentions are godly."

The old man's eyes softened. "I am glad. Then we are brother and sister, regardless of race." The women looked at each other, then at Tadao.

"I did it, Hannah." Tadao's eyes were shiny with tears. "I did it. Now I have grace, freedom, and peace, just as you said I would."

Hannah rushed over to Tadao, wrapping her arms around him in a warm embrace. "Christ is in your heart?" He nodded.

Elizabeth sat on the bed, her heart rejoicing in Tadao's salvation. It was amazing. In two weeks' time, Hannah had given her heart to the Lord and led another to His saving grace. Surely God was working, even at Poston.

* * *

"Caleb?" Elizabeth stepped inside his office. "Do you have a minute?"

Caleb's eyes roamed across his desk in one swift motion. Papers and files cluttered the surface. He looked tired. The War Relocation Authority was considering several dates to let evacuees return to their homes, provided they sign an allegiance agreement to the United States.

"You look like you could use some rest." Elizabeth came up beside him. She worked his neck with the tips of her fingers. "Can I do any of that?" She nodded toward his stacks of paper work.

Caleb sighed. "No, not really, but you can work the kinks out of my neck. That feels good." Sliding her arms around his neck, she kissed his forehead. "Did you need something?" he asked.

"Actually," she said, "I need your permission."

"Oh?" Caleb raised an eyebrow and sat upright in his chair. "What for?"

Elizabeth hastened to go on, wishing to get her request out. She had put off this question long enough. "Remember when I spoke with Miss King about her group donating to the children's fund?"

He nodded. "Yes. Didn't they donate yet? I haven't seen a check come through."

Elizabeth bit her lip. "No, they haven't."

"Why not?"

"I told them I would ask you if the children could perform a benefit concert." Noticing the frown on Caleb's face, she rushed on. "Many of them are musically talented and I thought it would be better if they play an active role in the fund-raising, than if we did it all."

"They might be leaving soon," Caleb stated.

"That wouldn't matter. They will still need things when they get home, if they have homes left to go to."

"You want clearance for them." Caleb picked up his paper work. "No-can-do."

"Only for an evening, Caleb," she pleaded. "To the church. You can send security if you like."

"Oh, yeah right," Caleb snorted. "That would look great. A children's choir performing with sentries standing guard on each end of the stage, let alone a church pulpit. Forget it, Elizabeth."

Elizabeth put her hands on her hips. "Why?"

"Because if the WRA hears about it, they'll contact me, and I'll have to refer them to you," he said. "I don't want you in trouble with the law. Remember what we talked about the other night?"

Elizabeth dropped her hands. Yes, she remembered. He was trying to protect her. That was all. Nodding, Elizabeth avoided eye contact.

"Enough said." Taking her hands, he pulled her close to embrace her. "Wait until this war is over, honey. It will be better for both of us."

Elizabeth sighed. It had been stressful living so close to the relocation and everything associated with the world at war. How she longed for it to be over once and for all.

A few moments later, Elizabeth pulled herself away. The office suddenly felt close and stuffy. "I need some fresh air."

Once outside, Elizabeth began walking, in no particular direction. She longed to sort out her thoughts, to distinguish between this reality of war and the muddle in her mind. Approaching the evacuee gardens, she slowed her pace. The beautiful flowers had begun to fade as fall weather threatened to overtake their livelihood. Dead foliage and the chill of colder weather seemed to symbolize death and war and grief. Elizabeth kicked a dead plant. In her mind, the change of seasons signified her experiences with earthly dispute between nations. Each one fought for himself without a thought of common human decency and the value of personhood.

"What's the matter?"

Elizabeth looked across the garden patches to see Hannah busy on her hands and knees, harvesting the remnants of her vegetable crop. "I didn't see you."

"You don't bother me," Hannah said. She glanced at Toyo, who was trying to ingest a clod of dirt. "No, no, Toyo," she chided, taking the earth from him.

"Are you upset about something?" She turned back to Elizabeth.

Elizabeth breathed deeply. "I'm sick of war."

Hannah smiled a sad smile. "Aren't we all?"

"Some more than others."

"Are you the some or the other?"

"The some."

Hannah frowned. "How could that be? You're Caucasian. Caucasians weren't evacuated."

Obviously Midori hadn't shared with her daughter Elizabeth's experience with David. "It's a long story," Elizabeth said. "And a sad one."

"I'm willing to listen." Hannah dusted off her hands. "It won't go any farther than my ears, that I can promise," she assured her.

Elizabeth mentally debated over whether or not to share her experience with Hannah, aware of the pain Hannah felt when she was separated from her husband on that fateful Evacuation Day. Elizabeth took a long, deep breath. "I was engaged about the time the United States joined the war." Hannah nodded, as if waiting for her to go on. That kind of news was common enough. "He is Japanese," Elizabeth added. Hannah's eyes wandered a moment before settling back on Elizabeth.

"He was evacuated?" Hannah asked.

"Yes," Elizabeth said. "We were separated on Evacuation Day."

Neither woman spoke for a few moments. "My husband and I were also separated," Hannah said.

Elizabeth nodded. "I know."

Hannah looked hard at the ground as if searching for a way to recapture that day. "You do not cry when you speak of him."

"No," Elizabeth said. Toyo tugged at Elizabeth's skirts. Taking him in her arms, she held him close, his raven hair pricking her face. "I have no more tears to cry."

"Nor do I," Hannah said. "It seems as if my life with my husband is only a faded dream now."

"Have you heard from him?"

Hannah nodded. "Kiyoshi wrote me shortly after we arrived here, but he gave no return address. His expressions were vague, as if numbed by the crimes of war. As a businessman, he was suspected of feeding Japanese authorities vital information for further attack on the States. Elizabeth, he knew no more than you or I or Toyo."

For the first time in weeks, the fervor Elizabeth had felt against her prejudiced nation came flooding back, its force twisting and pulling at her scarred emotions. "I believe you, Hannah," she said. "As the owner and chief operator of his dry goods store, David's father knew nothing as well, and was taken from his family."

"David?" Hannah asked. "That is his name?"

Elizabeth nodded, a smile forming on her lips. Even the mention of his name filled her heart with pride.

"A strong Bible name, indeed," Hannah said. "You may someday be reunited. Do not lose the love you have for him."

Elizabeth's resolve disseminated upon hearing Hannah's words. She and David could never be reunited. Not with her involved with Caleb and David pursuing a Japanese woman, one of his own kind. At least they wouldn't be harassed by militarist sympathizers and the prejudiced public any longer. "It will never be." Elizabeth turned her face to hide her traitorous tears.

"Of course it will." Hannah patted Elizabeth's shoulder. "We will get out of here soon, I am sure of it. Then you can go home. David will come find you. Men pursue that way, you know." She smiled.

"No. Caleb and I visited Manzanar last week, on business. That is where David was relocated. He was with another woman, Hannah." Looking toward Hannah, Elizabeth saw her smile fade.

"Surely there is some mistake, a misunderstanding between you."

Shaking her head, Elizabeth rushed on to explain. "At first things were fine. We wrote long letters, every sentence filled with endearing phrases. Love was very much alive then. Over time, his letters changed, becoming short and effortless.

"I thought something had changed, that maybe his interest had waned at being separated from me for so long. It didn't seem like him. Then Caleb showed interest in me. Time and again, I tried to evade his advances, but after a while, my strength shook with loneliness. I gave in. David must have, too."

Hannah studied Elizabeth's face. She looked as if she were peering into the very depths of her friend's soul, her eyes still and hard. "You love David still." It was not a question, but a statement. "You are not committed to Caleb, even as much as you would like to think. Elizabeth, you do not love him."

Elizabeth straightened her shoulders, raising her head in defiance. "I care for him," she said. "And caring for him is better than living out my life alone, an antique spinster whose greatest companion is a loveless feline."

Hannah shook her head. "No," she said. "If you are not in God's will by being with Caleb, it would be better to be alone."

Biting her lip, Elizabeth cast her eyes to her lap, her defiance crumbing like the earth she clenched between her fingers. "But what if David loves another and marries another? What would I do?"

"Trust God, my friend," Hannah said. "He won't forget His promise to you, even in spite of the loss of one you love most dearly. His will is greater. Remember the words of Jesus on the night of His betrayal. He prayed the will of the Father above His own will."

Pondering her words, Elizabeth responded, "I understand that. In my heart, I am prepared to follow His divine will, though I know it may be a heavy load and a tiresome journey. But sometimes I am confused."

"Confused?" Hannah said. "How?"

"By the things Caleb says." Elizabeth squinted her eyes, her mind searching her memory for Caleb's exact words. "When we first met, he said that he believed women should have the right and responsibility of becoming whatever they wanted, going to college, having a family if they so wished, but never were they to be smothered by the authority of a man, even their own husbands.

"Lately, though, he has been commenting that I should or shouldn't do something based on his responsibility to protect me. I believe God appointed men to protect, but his logic seems wrong, and his judgments are unlike that of Christ. It makes me doubt God's will for me."

"Has he accepted Christ as his Savior?" Hannah asked.

"No," Elizabeth said quietly.

Hannah shrugged her shoulders. "What can you expect, then? He has no basis for sound doctrine. His own head is his sole determiner of right and wrong. You cannot be subject to his ungodly authority and do the work our Father has appointed for you. Go to the nations, Elizabeth." Hannah's eyes filled with tears. "He is calling."

Shocked at her words, Elizabeth only stared until she was able to speak. "Why do you say that?"

Hannah put her hands to her face, wiping at fresh tears. "I do not know. It was not I speaking, but Christ speaking through me. Just go, that is all I know. Wherever God is calling you, go."

* * *

"Hmm." Caleb shut his office door behind him. He waved an envelope in front of his face. "You have a letter."

Coming over to him, Elizabeth reached for the extended envelope. "Who's it from?" She had become used to Caleb intercepting her mail. Now that he knew her secret of correspondence with David, she had nothing to hide, doubting any further letters would come from a Japanese addressee.

Caleb snatched the letter away. "Who do you know in Tokyo?" He raised an eyebrow. "Relatives?"

"Of course not." Her mind ticked through names of those who could be writing her from Japan. Marie, of course! Did she have news of David? Was he okay? Had his first months in the army been bearable? Was he safe? Alive?

Imagining the worst, she extended one hand, the other propped on her hip. "Give it here, Caleb."

"Who's it from?" Caleb held the letter up to the light. "Nice handwriting," he commented.

Elizabeth hurried to answer him. "It's from a friend."

"What's his name?"

"Her name is Marie," Elizabeth said. "Hand it over."

"Must be pretty important to get you riled up like that." He looked down at her. "Any more secrets I should know about?"

Ignoring his question, Elizabeth raised her voice. "Hand it over now or we're through."

"What are you talking about?"

"Us as in we, a couple," Elizabeth said. "I won't be controlled."

Caleb only stared at her for a few moments, his face blank as if he were trying to digest her words. Slowly handing her the envelope, he ambled to his office, clicking the door shut behind him.

Waiting a few moments to be sure of his absence, Elizabeth stepped outside into the cool afternoon. A gust blew up, wrapping her hair around her neck. Hopefully they would not see another dust storm. Over the past months, the wind had blown for days at a time, making it nearly impossible to go outside.

Slipping her finger underneath the envelope's flap, Elizabeth opened the letter. Yes, it was Marie's writing. Her eyes searched the page briefly before reading its entirety.

Dear Elizabeth,

It has been a long time since I have heard from you. I hope you are well, in body and spirit, and that your work at Poston is proving profitable.

However, I am not writing merely for small talk, though I wish that might be the case. You are aware, I'm sure, that David enlisted and is now serving in the armed forces. Last month, while engaged in the battle of the Vosges mountains in France, many U.S. soldiers were wounded or killed as they relieved the Lost Battalion.

My dear Elizabeth, we have received no news from David since then, and his contemporaries have labeled him as missing in action.

Elizabeth's breath caught in her throat as she read Marie's words. It did not seem feasible. She re-read the daunting message. It was not feasible, yet it was possible—and true. Her heart groaned at the possibility of David in the hands of the enemy, and skipped a beat when she thought of his last remembrance of her as being led away by Caleb.

She shoved the letter into her pocket, her eyes blurring as her body threatened to give in to gravity. Falling to the building's steps, her body shook. The rest of the letter remained unread.

Lord, she silently cried, *help me!* Grey clouds formed at her sight's perimeter, crawling inward. She tried to blink them back, but instead they grew larger, more intense than at first. She couldn't escape.

CHAPTER TWENTY-ONE

Elizabeth batted her eyelids. Shadows danced across her bedroom as she forced her eyes to focus on her dressing table. A searing pain shot through her forehead, and so she closed her eyes once more. "Elizabeth? Are you awake?"

Recognizing Caleb's voice, she reached out her arms, seeking the comfort of his embrace. "Caleb?" Her voice was barely audible. She felt his arms reaching for her, holding her, steadfast and strong.

She licked her dry lips. "What happened?"

"You must have hit your head on the steps." He brushed her hair away from her face. "Did you faint?"

Furrowing her brow, she tried to remember. But it hurt too much to think. "I must have."

"Why?" His eyes searched hers. "Is it something that letter said?"

David! Elizabeth's muddled mind strained to remember Marie's words. David was missing. No one knew where he was or if he was even alive. She sighed deeply, almost groaning at the awful remembrance. Sinking back into her pillow, Elizabeth rubbed her head. "I think I'd better rest some more."

Caleb nodded. "Of course. I'll be right here. Do you need anything?"

"No." She wished to forget reality until her circumstances changed. "No," she repeated.

* * *

"We heard you had an accident." Hannah folded the clothes lying on the bed, her forehead wrinkled in concern.

"Really? Who told you?"

"Caleb," she said. "He seemed quite disturbed yesterday. He feared you had a concussion."

Elizabeth shook her head. "No, just a clumsy fainting fall, that's all. I hit my head on the steps up to the office."

Hannah winced at the words. "Ouch," she said. "Why did you faint?"

Elizabeth cast her gaze to the pile of folded clothes belonging to Toyo. There lay the outfits she had purchased for him all those months ago, giving her and Hannah a chance to get to know one another, and develop an invaluable friendship in hard times. But they were far too small now. She pulled her thoughts back to Hannah's question. "Lately, I've discovered that's how my mind escapes shock. I got a letter from David's sister, Marie. She had been studying in Japan before the war broke out. They haven't let her come home yet."

Elizabeth took in a long breath. "She said David went missing in action at the battle of the Vosges Mountains. They don't know if he's even alive."

Hannah was silent. Returning the skirt she held to the pile of laundry, she put her arms around Elizabeth. "I'm so sorry," she whispered. "Words are not adequate at times like these, but God's power is unlimited. He is the same God who protected Daniel from the lion's den and rescued Shadrach, Meshach, and Abednego from the fiery furnaces those centuries ago. Surely he will protect your beloved now."

Elizabeth nodded. "I am confident He will," she said, surprising even herself at the words. "Somehow I know God's hand is upon David, and that He has work for him to do before he can go home to our Savior. Even if we don't end up together, God has a plan for both of us."

Sitting down, Hannah reached for Elizabeth's hand. "You speak with much confidence," she said, "unlike what I have heard you say before. How is your faith different now? Even when all seems against you?"

"Yesterday, when I was resting, I had a lot of time to think, and to pray," Elizabeth said. "I must have sounded desperate to God. My words were muddled and confused. I had no where else to turn. The thought of losing David to another woman was unbearable enough without thinking that I would never see him again because he had been killed in battle. My mind would not rest. After tossing and turning, my head throbbing from my fall, I gave it up.

"Hannah, I had surrendered to God long before now, or so I thought. But I continually picked up my burdens again, begrudging myself to carry them independently of God. As long as I had someone to lean upon, I didn't need Him. When David and I were together, he would often talk about going to the mission field of Japan. His native land, so he called it. Though I was willing to follow him to the ends of the earth out of a deep love, I didn't sense the calling of God as he did.

"Through knowing you and your family and experiencing living here, with your people, in the midst of your troubles and trials, God has developed within me a longing to help the Japanese know Him, and know His Son. Dependent on my Father, and not on David or Caleb, God has been able to impress His heart upon my will. Now I know I can minister to your people alone, if that be God's will. I have peace that David will follow whatever path God leads him down. If that path includes me, I will be honored. If it does not, I will be honored in knowing a fine, upright, godly man." Tears of joy and peace filled her eyes as she spoke the last words.

Hannah gazed at Elizabeth, her lips turned upward in a smile. "What a peace you have now," she said. After a few moments, the corners of her mouth tugged downward. "What about Caleb?" she asked. "Do you still plan to have a relationship with him?"

Lifting a hand to her face, Elizabeth sighed. "Our relationship is not healthy," she admitted. "We don't seem to get along half the time, and our convictions are diverse."

"Would he allow you to do what you believe God is urging you to do–become a missionary?" Hannah said.

Elizabeth nearly laughed aloud at the thought of Caleb promoting her missionary efforts in Japan. He would unlikely go for the idea of ministry, let alone ministry to the ethnic group he seemed to think beneath him. "Without a doubt, he would not."

Hannah shrugged. "Do you have your answer, then?"

"I hate to hurt him, though. He does care for me, and I have grown fond of him as well." Elizabeth brushed her hair from her eyes. "My contract is up in a month or so, maybe we will just go our separate ways. That would be the easiest course."

Hannah laid a hand on Elizabeth's shoulder. "I will pray for you."

Nodding, Elizabeth looked around the apartment, now being stripped of all its occupants' possessions. Soon it would be empty.

"I can't believe you're leaving," Elizabeth said.

"Yes." Hannah smiled. "Friday will be such a joyful day. When we get on that train, my heart will soar with new freedom. I think I've forgotten what it's like to live a normal life."

Elizabeth cast a sorrowful glance at the suitcase that lay at her feet. "I'm glad you'll be able to get out of here," she said, "but I'll miss you terribly."

"You'll be home with your family soon enough." Hannah put an arm around her friend. "I'll stay in touch. I promise. Maybe sometime we can come to San Francisco, when everything has settled down some more, and see you."

Elizabeth nodded. She would like that, yet it seemed that the last couple of years had been filled with too many sorrowful partings. How she wished she could gather all her friends and loved ones up in one location, never having to say goodbye, ever again.

* * *

The following Friday substantiated Elizabeth's fears of parting. Several more Japanese families from Poston had decided to leave that day. Traversing the corridors of life in company with close friends and extended relatives seemed to be a trademark of the Japanese. All of life's important events were attended by those one held dear.

Caleb lifted the last suitcase from his trunk and walked toward the luggage car. Scanning the cars, Elizabeth wished she was the one traveling today, away from the desolate Arizona desert, heading for home, a place like no other on earth. It had seemed like decades since she had seen her parents. She longed to share her journeys of sorrow, fear, and joy with them, intimately identifying with the belief system they shared. They would rejoice with her in Hannah and Tadao's salvation, while mourning the loss of David in her life. They would understand her, more than anyone else.

"All aboard!" The train master's voice cut into the December wind. Hannah turned to face Elizabeth. "That's us," she said with a weak smile. "I'll miss you," she whispered. "You have given me so much—a friendship, a new trust for the people of this country, an introduction to my Savior. How can I ever thank you?"

Elizabeth smiled. "It was only God, my friend. You have repaid me with your kindness many times over." Midori joined them, Toyo propped on one hip. He had grown into a toddler since their arrival at Poston, and was restless in his grandmother's hold. "Precious little one." Elizabeth cupped the youngster's cheeks in her hands. "I will never forget you." She caressed his cheeks, then patted his head.

Reaching his arms toward her, Toyo looked at Elizabeth. She took him into her arms, glancing about the station. Soon they would have to board. The train master glanced their way, looked at his watch, then looked away. Holding the child close, Elizabeth prayed he might grow up to be a strong man of God. Midori leaned over to hug Elizabeth. "God be with you, my child. Follow His leading. Never underestimate His plans."

The little family moved toward the stairway leading to a passenger car. Midori traveled a little slower, it seemed, than she had in days past. Moving to a pair of empty seats, they sat down, peering out the window and waving as the train blew one final warning whistle before crawling out of the station.

Putting a hand to her mouth, Elizabeth thought of David, waving goodbye on that San Franciscan pavilion over two and a half years ago. Her heart had screamed for him them, as it did now, wanting nothing more than his arms to embrace her.

Elizabeth felt arms encircling her. Caleb. The train picked up speed with every revolution of its wheels, carrying Hannah, Midori, and Toyo farther and farther away. But this time, they were going home. Home to what, no one knew. Was the house empty or was it occupied by neighbors or strangers? No one knew. They would find out when they arrived.

"Are you sad to see them go?" Caleb asked.

Turning her back toward the retreating train, Elizabeth looked at him. "I'll miss their companionship, for sure." She paused. "But I wouldn't exchange their freedom for my comfort."

"They weren't imprisoned, Elizabeth." Caleb walked back to the car. Following him, she said nothing.

* * *

Later that afternoon, Elizabeth wandered about camp, praying and thinking as she went. She pondered her friends' absence and the future that lay ahead, yet to be discovered. Reaching Hannah and Midori's apartment, she gingerly unlatched the door, letting it fall open. The once cramped apartment seemed unusually spacious with no inhabitants. Looking about the single room, her eyes fell upon the lumpy mattress, made of a stiff fabric and filled with straw. A small hole at the end bore evidence to Midori's explanation of where she had found straw for her nativity scene the Christmas before. Elizabeth smiled, tears of joyful remembrance seeping out of her eyes. The room's only window was bare now, the homemade curtains removed and packed away for the homeward journey.

Glancing over the rest of the apartment, Elizabeth noticed something lying on the tiny, circular table. A note lay on it, addressed to her. Unfolding the single page, Elizabeth read.

Dearest Child,

By the time you read this note, I'm sure we'll be out of Arizona and headed for home in the Rockies. My heart aches to be near you still, but I know God's plans have separated us, at least for a time. I have enjoyed you as a friend and as a daughter, Elizabeth. You have treated us well, never considering the cost of your kindness...

Regardless of race or creed, you have loved us, and we have loved you. Thank you for displaying Christ to Hannah. You showed her a sacrificing God who spares nothing for His own. You did not show her a "Caucasian" God as many have done before, but a God of all colors, loving each equally. I believe with all my heart that this is one reason you were placed in Poston. Thank you for being obedient to His call.

Elizabeth stopped reading for a moment, letting Midori's words sink into her soul. God had a purpose in her coming to this desolate place, a place of misery and strife, hardship and pain. Yet good had come of it, a soul had been saved and a wounded heart rejuvenated.

Please accept a gift from this mother as a token of my sincere and deepest appreciation. Dig in the hole in the mattress until you find each piece. May we meet again soon.

Midori

Dig? In the mattress? Each piece of what? Puzzled, Elizabeth made her way to the edge of the single bed, stuffing her hand inside the hole.

"There you are." Caleb came through the doorway. Jerking her hand away from the mattress, Elizabeth rushed to conceal the letter in her hand. "What are you doing?" He looked around the apartment.

Elizabeth bit her lip. "Just reminiscing." She ran her hand along the tabletop. "We had many good times together here."

Caleb frowned. "I didn't know an evacuation camp apartment

could offer such great entertainment." He shrugged. "What did you do, just talk?"

"We talked a lot," she said. "We read the Bible together and prayed together, too."

"Those Japs were Christians?" Caleb snorted. Elizabeth nodded. He jerked his head around, looking from wall to wall, ceiling to floor. "Cramped quarters, huh?" He shoved his hands into the recesses of his coat pockets. "Are you coming to dinner with me?" He headed for the door.

"I'll come in a few minutes," she said.

Caleb shrugged. "Suit yourself."

When the latch had clicked shut, Elizabeth made her way to the mattress once more. What had Midori left for her? The straw was prickly, like the hundreds of needles on a freshly harvested Christmas tree. How could they have slept on such an uncomfortable bed? Elizabeth wiggled her fingers in the mattress. Something was in there, slender and riveted. Pulling it out, she held in her hand Joseph, a piece of the nativity. Dig in the hole in the mattress until you find each piece. Midori had left her nativity scene, a reminder of their Savior's birth. Soon December would melt into the holiday season, bringing relatives, friends, gifts–and Christ.

Elizabeth thought back to the year before, when she had celebrated Christmas with Caleb's family. It had seemed nothing more than an excuse for large portions and holiday treats. Then Midori had read from Luke, graciously and lovingly she savored each word, her tone endearing. How refreshing it had been! Retrieving the last piece of the nativity, Elizabeth rose to her feet. In her hands she held a reminder of that day.

When December had passed, all of Poston would exist only in memory. In a few short weeks, her contract would expire, allowing her to return home. The offices, apartments, rec center, mess hall, all would be part of the past. Even Caleb. What would happen when she went back to San Francisco? What would she do with her time? If David returned, would he marry the girl from Manzanar, bringing her back with him to their neighborhood?

Squeezing her eyes shut, Elizabeth banished the thought from her mind. Allowing that kind of unproductive thinking into her imaginative brain would only cause heartache. The future must be lived. After all, it began now.

CHAPTER TWENTY-TWO

"I'll drive you back." Caleb leaned against the wall, watching Elizabeth clean out her desk. "I don't want you riding the train alone."

Glancing up from her sorting, Elizabeth wished he wouldn't have offered. It would be much easier for her to get on the train, leaving Poston and Caleb behind, all in one shot. "Really, I'll be fine," she said. "I did it once before, I can do it again."

"I insist, Elizabeth." Caleb took a step toward the desk. "It's the only chance we'll have to spend some time together for awhile." Awhile? Was he planning on coming to San Francisco in the future? She certainly hoped not. "I'll miss you terribly, long before you're even home. And besides, I rode the same train you did on part of your trip here, remember?"

It was useless. He was determined to see her to her destination, regardless of her protest. "If you insist."

Over the next few days, in a whirlwind of packing and saying goodbyes, Elizabeth prepared to leave Poston. But all the while, her mind went in circles. She thought about the ride home with Caleb, what it would be like living under her parents' roof again, and the plans she needed to make for the future. A chapter in her life had closed, and a new one was begging to begin, the scenes, settings, and experiences awaiting her entrance.

* * *

Miles of desolate country flew past the car window. Elizabeth sat, gazing out, weary from the hours of travel, and reluctant to muster the strength to carry on a conversation. Her eyes grew heavy, popping open whenever Caleb hit a bump in the road. "Just go to sleep, Elizabeth." Caleb took his eyes off the road for a second. He released one hand from the steering wheel, pulling her toward him to rest against his shoulder.

Elizabeth had no idea how long she slept, waking only when the car slowed to a stop. Was she home already? Caleb opened the door, moving away from her. Squinting her eyes against the sunshine, she decided that it was too early to be in San Francisco, yet. "Where are we?" She asked, sliding off the seat.

"Just crossed into California." Caleb stretched out his arms and legs. "I needed a break." Elizabeth nodded. "Is this a park?" Looking around the landscape, she saw weaving vines overhanging crags, an icy stream trickling down one side of the massive rock. To her left lay a wooden walkway, the steps meandering to the top of one low crag. "It resembles that place we visited near Poston."

"Looks like it, huh?" Caleb followed her gaze. "I didn't see any signs, though. Want to take a walk?" He pointed toward the steps.

"Sure." She followed him up the shallow incline. Breathing heavily, they reached the top step which led to a landing overlooking the stream below. Elizabeth was silent as she caught her breath from the climb.

The soft breeze had formed a stiff wind. "You cold?" Without waiting for her response, Caleb wrapped his arms around her middle, still staring straight ahead. Again, all was silent. Elizabeth fidgeted in Caleb's grasp. For the first time, his arms seemed heavy and constraining, refusing her mobility.

"We should probably get going." She removed herself from his iron hold. Caleb stared at her. Climbing down the first few steps, Elizabeth began to descend the crag. Caleb caught her by the wrist, pulling her back up, into his arms.

"Won't you miss the times we've shared?" he said into her hair. Before she could respond, he firmly pressed his lips against hers, harder than usual, it seemed. David had never kissed her like that. His kisses had been soft and gentle, and few and far between. Not like this. As Caleb swooped in to impress a second dose, Elizabeth stumbled on the step below her. Regaining her balance, she hastily climbed down the steps.

"It will get dark soon." She shielded her eyes from the sinking sun. "We should get on the road."

* * *

The clock struck eleven before they pulled into the Tyler driveway. The house was dark except for a lone light in the living room. Elizabeth remembered her father's reading lamp burning late many nights before, as he was absorbed in the latest business journal or studying his Bible.

Cracking the front door open, Elizabeth peered through. Over the top of his reading glasses, Mr. Tyler spotted her. "Elizabeth!" He rushed to open the door. "Helen, our baby's home!" he called into the bedroom. Not giving her a chance to step past the welcome mat, Elizabeth was covered with kisses and hugs, "I love yous" and "I missed yous."

"And who is this young gentleman?" her father inquired, taking a suitcase from Caleb's arms.

"Dad, Mom," Elizabeth said, "you remember me writing about Caleb?" Her parents nodded. Mr. Tyler helped remove all the luggage from Caleb's grasp.

"Glad to finally meet you," Mr. Tyler said. "You're welcome to the guest room for the night."

"I appreciate the offer," Caleb glanced over his shoulder at the car door that was still open. "But I've already booked a hotel. I'll come by in the morning, though, Elizabeth," he said. Nodding, she wondered at his decline. It didn't seem like him to deny an offer that would keep him close to her.

"Let's put you to bed." Mrs. Tyler guided Elizabeth toward her old bedroom. "You look like you could use some rest. Don't worry about getting up for church in the morning, either."

Elizabeth nodded. Not bothering to even change her clothes, she climbed into bed and fell asleep.

* * *

"Where are your parents?" Caleb asked the next morning.

"Church." Elizabeth moved to sit on the couch. She patted the seat beside her, motioning for him to join her.

"Your dad, too?" He raised an eyebrow as he sat down beside her.

Elizabeth nodded. "Of course, why wouldn't he go?"

Caleb shrugged. "I don't know. Just didn't expect him to, that's all, being a man. You know."

Frowning, Elizabeth thought it ridiculous to assume that masculinity was synonymous with abstaining from corporate worship. Caleb clearly didn't have an accurate interpretation of manhood. "Where did you stay last night?" she asked.

"With a friend," came the quick reply.

"A friend?" she said. "I thought you had hotel reservations."

"Some old college buddies of mine live in San Francisco." He adjusted his position on the couch. "What does it matter to you? I'm here now."

Elizabeth sighed, leaning against the sofa. Such a conversation would go nowhere. She tried to refocus her thoughts. Caleb would be leaving soon. When should she tell him there was no future for their relationship? How should she tell him? Perhaps it was better to wait and explain everything in a letter. No, that would seem cowardly. Caleb, like anyone else, deserved an accurate and truthful explanation, as soon as possible. Taking a deep breath, she mentally chided herself for not explaining the situation at Poston, instead of waiting until Caleb had taken the trouble to drive her home. She hadn't been fair to him.

Just as she opened her mouth, Caleb shattered the silence. "Elizabeth?" He said her name more as a question than as a statement, as if she needed to confirm her presence.

"Yes?" Her heart thumping in her chest, she wondered at her sudden nervousness. Was she frightened to break up with him? Afraid of what he might do?

Caleb slid closer, wrapping his arms around her. Elizabeth closed her eyes for a second. There had been a time when his touch had been life-giving blood itself. Not anymore. It became increasingly difficult for her to succumb to his acts of endearment, however genuine and sincere. "I love you," he whispered, rubbing his cheek against hers.

Biting her lip, she said nothing. Why did he have to be affectionate at a time like this, the exact second in which she had opened her mouth to end it all?

A few minutes later, Caleb slid off the leather couch, letting his knees drop to the carpet. Elizabeth's heart raced faster. Time and again, in the novels she read, the man always knelt when he was about to ask the girl to marry him, and she always said yes. In real life, it couldn't happen that way. She couldn't say yes. "Caleb." The words were almost inaudible. "Please don't–"

He put a finger to her mouth, silencing her request. "Elizabeth Tyler." He looked directly into her eyes. Elizabeth cast her eyes to the floor, averting his gaze. Many times before, she had been unable to resist those eyes, eyes that seemed to reflect his heart's deep love and affection. Turning her head, he latched his eyes onto hers, just like he'd done that day on the train. "Look at me," he said gently. She looked. He looked. For a few agonizing seconds, all that could be heard was the incessant ticking of the grandfather clock.

"Elizabeth," he said over, as if it were a new and wonderful word. "I love you." She could feel her resolve melting with each word he spoke. "I care for you, deeply. I want to protect you, be your security, the love of your life."

Putting his hand into his pocket, he plucked out a velvet box, just like the one that had held her diamond necklace and earrings. The ring sparkled with a brilliance she had never seen before.

"Just for you, my love," Caleb whispered, taking her left hand in his. Elizabeth stiffened her fingers. She couldn't let him do it. It would give him false hope. It would give her false hope as well, and a reason to deny what all sensibility told her concerning the match. It wasn't a match made in heaven.

"Caleb," she said softly.

"Don't answer now." He slipped the ring on her finger in one swift motion. "Think about it."

"But I–" His lips silenced her protest. His kiss was gentler than it had been yesterday. Maybe he had realized his gruffness had not been well received. Elizabeth certainly hoped so. But now what was she to do? With a heavy diamond ring on her finger and the impression of Caleb's kiss on her lips, her heart groaned. Was she about to give in – again?

"Think about it," he repeated. "We'll meet tomorrow." With those words, Caleb stood to his feet. Before he reached the door, he turned her way once more. "I love you." In an instant, he was gone. The growl of the car motor rang in her ears as he drove down East Street. A growing lump gnawed at the pit of her stomach. Tomorrow. She had one day to consider his proposal, her decision determining the fate of the rest of her life. The time seemed inadequate, yet excruciatingly long.

She glanced down at her hand. The diamonds shimmered, reflecting the sunlight from the front window. How could she refuse?

* * *

"It seems to me that you know what you must do, my dear." Mrs. Tyler opened the oven door. Sticking a fork in a loaf of banana bread, she shook her head, closing the door again. "Honestly, I can't visualize you or David with anyone but each other." She crossed her arms and looked at her daughter sitting at the kitchen table.

"That's the whole problem," Elizabeth said. "I have to turn Caleb down this afternoon, knowing that I will never marry."

Mrs. Tyler knit her brow. "David will come home, darling," she soothed. "God will bring him home safely."

"No, no." Elizabeth rose to her feet and gazed out the kitchen window. "We went to Manzanar on business, Caleb and I." She concentrated hard on the bird feeder mounted in the back yard. "I saw him, Mama." Elizabeth stopped for a moment to turn and face her mother. "He was with another woman. They were holding hands, obviously a couple. I won't marry if I can't have David. I could never love anyone else. I tried, just to escape the pain."

"Are you not guilty of having a relationship with someone else as well?" her mother asked in a low tone.

Putting her hands to her face, Elizabeth nodded vigorously. "Yes, and I wish I'd never caved in to his advances."

"Confess it to God, then." Opening the oven door, she set the loaf on the stove top. "You have offended Him as well as David." She walked to the kitchen doorway. "I'll leave you alone with Him."

Elizabeth glanced around the empty kitchen. Now what? She had offended God, her Creator. She had doubted His promise of a life in His will, full and free. His promise of a God-fearing husband seemed only a dream now. He had vowed His ever-presence, knowing the designs He had skillfully woven for her life. Yet she had doubted, and failed Him–miserably.

Trust Me. The words were strong. *Trust Me. My plans for you are beyond your own comprehension. Though you don't always understand your circumstances, I have everything under control and will never leave you without hope.*

"Lord God, I'm sorry." Shaking, Elizabeth covered her eyes. "I have forsaken Your best for my comfort." Tears welled up, threatening to fall on the table. "I was wrong. Please make good come of this situation."

Drying her eyes a few minutes later, Elizabeth glanced at the clock. It was time to go. She had promised Caleb she would meet him in Daytons' Park at noon.

* * *

Elizabeth hastened her step as she neared the park entrance. Not many people had ventured out today. Though the morning fog had cleared, the day remained damp and dreary. Now was the inevitable moment when she would have to be completely honest with Caleb. As she spotted him coming out of the gazebo, she gripped the velvet ring box intently, her fingers turning ghostly white under the pressure.

"You made it." Caleb greeted her with a kiss. "Nice day, huh?"

"It's almost depressing." Elizabeth peered out at the grey sky. At least the weather matched her mood.

"Want to sit?" Caleb motioned toward a bench seat. Nodding, Elizabeth sat down beside him.

Her mind wandered back to the days of their first meeting, when she saw him on the train to Poston, in the cafeteria on her first day at work, and the day he caught her coming from Midori's apartment. It was sad to have to leave him now, turning down the most precious request he could ever make to a woman. A pledge of love for a lifetime.

"What are you thinking?" Caleb pulled her close to him. Elizabeth did not resist his affection, but instead rested her head lightly on his shoulder.

"Just about the times we've shared," she said quietly. How was she to proceed with turning him down?

Caleb cracked a smile. "We've had some rough spots," he said, "but we've persevered, nonetheless. I'm sure we'll have some obstacles along the way, just like everybody else."

Along the way? Was he assuming she had accepted his proposal? "Caleb?" How could she do this? "I have to be honest with you." His eyes searched hers. Turning the box over in her hand, she looked down.

Following her gaze, Caleb's eyes rested on the velvet box. He turned her hand over in his, revealing a bare ring finger. "Elizabeth." His voice turned husky. "You don't mean..." Shaking his head, he indicated that he thought the chance of her refusal to be non-existent.

"I'm afraid it isn't possible, Caleb." Tears gathered in her eyes. "We're very different. We clash. Our hopes, dreams, desires, beliefs, don't coincide. I care for you deeply, but I didn't intend things to happen this way." She paused to wipe away a tear. "Please forgive me, but I can't accept your proposal." She laid the box in his hand.

"Forgive you?" he asked, his voice breaking. "For what? I was the fool who thought you would say yes. That David still has your love, doesn't he? The love that I've wanted for months he's trampled upon and you still won't take it back from him. Now you tell me I can never have it."

Elizabeth bit her lip, but it refused to cease quavering.

She hung her head, knowing she had hurt him more deeply than she cared to imagine.

Caleb sniffed, changing his tone. "I'll be in town for a few days." He stuffed a piece of paper in her hand. "You can reach me here." The pitter-patter of rain drops sounded on the gazebo roof. Caleb ran through the rain, into the January mist, and out of her life.

CHAPTER TWENTY-THREE

Elizabeth unfolded the paper Caleb had given her the day before, as she lay in bed the next morning. Refraining from reading the note, she closed her eyes, grasped the paper in both hands, and tore it once down the middle. Again and again she tore, until the scraps were dime-sized. There, now that temptation was gone.

"Elizabeth," her mother called from outside her room. "Are you awake?" Her voice held an edge of excitement.

Elizabeth opened the door and peered out, the sunshine flooding into the hallway from the bay window in the living room. "Is something wrong?"

Her mother stood still, a smile creeping across her lips. "Mr. and Mrs. Mitsuko are coming home, dear." Her eyes misted over as she hugged her daughter.

Elizabeth's heart jumped in her chest. "When? Is their house ready? What about their store?" The questions tumbled out, one after another.

Mrs. Tyler held up one hand. "First things, first." She laughed. "They are due to arrive on Thursday. That only gives us two days to get things around. The house has been kept up, but will need a good cleaning. I'd like to have things looking like home when they arrive. I'll make them dinner Thursday night, of course. I'll make Mr. Mitsuko's favorite for dessert–rhubarb pie with homemade vanilla ice cream. I even thought–"

"Mother!" Elizabeth said. "Now look who's prattling on!"

Mrs. Tyler shrugged. "I guess I'm just as happy as you are, honey. It's been far too long to be separated from such dear friends."

Elizabeth's smile faded at her mother's words. Yes, it had been too long. Too long to maintain good friendships, too long to cherish a romance. "What about Marie?" She lowered her voice. "And David?"

"Elizabeth, there's something I need to tell you about Marie."

"Surprise!" An excited voice came from the living room. Rushing down the hall, Elizabeth came face-to-face with Marie.

"Marie!" Elizabeth embraced her. "I didn't expect you before your family."

The young woman nodded. "I can see that."

"When did you arrive?" Elizabeth adjusted her bathrobe, her mussed hair tumbling into her eyes.

"Early this morning," Marie said. "Your mom picked me up at the station. We came into Sacramento about midnight."

"You have to tell me about all your adventures in Japan," Elizabeth said. "Both academic and otherwise."

"Otherwise?" Marie shook her head. "Whatever do you mean?"

"Don't be silly," Elizabeth said. "Are there no handsome suitors over there?"

Marie giggled. "Too many. There was one who even–"

"Girls," Mrs. Tyler said. "I hate to interrupt your most exciting conversation, but could you resume while you clean? There's much to be done today."

* * *

Elizabeth scrubbed harder at the spot on the hardwood floor, producing little progress.

"Oh, Elizabeth." Marie came in from the kitchen, mop in hand, a towel draped over her left shoulder. "That spot will never come out."

"You're telling me." Elizabeth tossed the scrub brush back into the tub of hot, sudsy water. "I've been scrubbing at it for five minutes."

"David spilled shoe polish there a few years ago," Marie said. "I think he was getting ready to go on a date with you. It was the night of your very first date, if I remember correctly. He was a wreck."

Elizabeth giggled. Had David been as nervous as she had been? Thinking back, she remembered her own travails dressing that night. Her fingers shaking, she had barely been able to button her blouse, or put her hair back in her favorite silver combs. Luckily, the procedure got easier and less traumatic as time went on. Saying nothing more, Elizabeth picked up her brush and continued cleaning the next section of the floor.

"Elizabeth?" Marie paused in her work a few moments later. Her voice lowered. "Your mother told me about what happened with Caleb, the Poston project director. May I ask, were you really seeing someone else?"

Elizabeth's shoulders slumped. She sighed, fingering the dirty brush. Why did Marie have to ask such a question now? Or at all, for that matter? Turning to face her, Elizabeth decided it was best to get the conversation over with sooner rather than later. "Yes, Marie," she said. "I was. I had given up hope of being reunited with David. Lonely and depressed, I gave in to the persistent requests of Caleb."

She thought back to the times he had asked her out to dinner. "He was charming and smooth, but also a cynical, skeptical, controlling unbeliever, as I later discovered." She paused a moment and looked down at the damp floor.

"I knew better. Such a relationship couldn't glorify God, especially when He had already revealed to me who He had picked out for me," she continued. "Somehow, though, I found it nearly impossible to sever the new ties I had developed and so I continued my relationship with Caleb.

"David's letters become scant. When he did write, his letters seemed stiff and formal. Then he said he was considering enlisting. It was too much for me to handle. At that point, I thought there was a possibility that I would never see him again. Caleb and I visited Manzanar on business. I saw David with another woman, Marie. They were holding hands, obviously a couple. That's when I gave up completely."

"Caleb proposed, though?"

Elizabeth nodded. "Two days ago he proposed. He told me to think it over. Yesterday, I saw him for the last time."

Marie sank into a nearby chair. "I can hardly believe that David could find someone to take the place I know you still occupy in his heart. He will come home, Elizabeth."

"I pray he will," Elizabeth said. "Yet my heart is fearful that he could no longer be mine. I will never love another man. I tried."

* * *

"Everyone get in their places!" Mrs. Tyler whisked through the back door, entering the Mitsuko's kitchen. "The cab is just turning onto Fifth Street." The little party, Mr. and Mrs. Tyler, Elizabeth, and Marie scurried to find hiding places. Elizabeth took in a deep breath as she slid behind Mr. Mitsuko's easy chair. In just a few moments, David's parents would arrive. After having been away from their home for over two years, they were finally returning – hopefully for good. Mr. Tyler flipped off the last lamp and ducked into the hall closet.

All was silent, deathly still. Elizabeth thought of the times she used to play hide and seek with Patti when they were little. The tension between hiding and being found had been tremendous, hearts thudding with breaths shallow and quick.

Finally, headlights shone through the living room window. Drawing nearer the house, the vehicle slowed its speed. It must be them. Thud. A door shut. Thud. A second one shut. A muffled shuffle and the clip-clop of high heels came up the walk.

"Well, dear, I don't know what we'll find," Mr. Mitsuko drove the key into its keyhole, his voice crawling through the cracks around the doorframe.

"It doesn't matter," Mrs. Mitsuko replied. "We're home, that's what counts." Putting her hands to her lips, Elizabeth muffled her sniffles. Why couldn't David be with them? Then everything could be as it was before, as it should be. If only...if only David had not already pledged his heart to another.

The door handle turned, ever so slowly, it seemed, then a head emerged. Mr. Mitsuko stepped through the doorway. A second later, his wife appeared. "I'll get the light," he said.

Before his hand reached the switch, the whole room was ablaze in light, as each stowaway flipped the switch nearest them.

"Surprise!" The welcoming party jumped out of closets and out from behind chairs. The couple looked horrified at first, stunned, then pleasantly surprised, all in the course of one second.

"My goodness!" Mrs. Mitsuko gasped, her hand to her chest. "What a welcome." Her eyes scanned the room, and rested on her daughter. "Marie." She reached out her hands. As mother and daughter embraced, father looked on for several moments, then slowly approached them. They held on to one another, soft sobs emerging from all three.

Elizabeth wondered if she and her family were intruding on the sacred reunion. Maybe the surprise hadn't been such a good idea after all. Glancing at her father, she decided he was thinking the same.

"Elizabeth." Turning around, Elizabeth saw Mrs. Mitsuko standing only a few feet from her.

"Welcome home," Elizabeth said quietly. The older woman

simply extended her arms, just as she had done for Marie. Elizabeth's lip trembled as she accepted the hug.

"My daughter," Mrs. Mitsuko whispered into her hair. "How I have missed you. You and that wonderful head of blonde curls."

Elizabeth laughed through her tears. Unable to say anything in reply, she held on to the woman until Mrs. Mitsuko pulled away. Looking into her eyes, Mrs. Mitsuko put her finger underneath Elizabeth's chin. "Are you feeling well?" she asked.

Shrugging, Elizabeth thought if she tried to speak, her voice would break. How could she tell Mrs. Mitsuko that her heart longed for her son to come home, with everyone now watching them? As if sharing her thoughts, Mrs. Mitsuko glanced at the others. "We will talk later," she whispered.

"Is that rhubarb pie I smell?" Thrusting his nose in the air, Mr. Mitsuko sniffed.

"Yes!" Mrs. Tyler hurried toward the kitchen. "I hope you didn't mind me using your kitchen." The door swung behind her.

Mrs. Mitsuko followed her into the adjoining room, pausing when she had entered. Her hand swept in front of her, capturing the scene before her eyes. "You have put everything exactly where it belongs." For several moments she was quiet as she gazed from one end of the room to the other. "I had forgotten what a luxury my own kitchen is."

Mr. Mitsuko patted his wife on the back. "I'll look forward to you cooking for me again, my dear," he said. He took a deep breath. "But for now, I think dinner is served." Mrs. Mitsuko nodded and smiled. They were finally home.

* * *

Elizabeth breathed heavily. That piece of rhubarb pie had certainly been a grand finale to the superb dinner her mother had fixed, but it wasn't settling too well atop fried chicken, stewed vegetables, and mashed potatoes.

Looking across the room, she watched Mrs. Mitsuko's eyes close as she rocked back and forth in her chair. Elizabeth's parents had gone home for the evening, but at the request of Marie, she had stayed. Marie, sitting on the floor next to her father, talked quietly.

"May I sit with you awhile, Elizabeth?" Mrs. Mitsuko opened her eyes. Elizabeth nodded as she made her way to the sofa.

"You seem disturbed." Mrs. Mitsuko didn't bother with an introduction to lessen the weight of her comment. Glancing at the woman, Elizabeth's eyes fell to the floor.

"Can you share your troubles with me?" she asked, her voice soft and gentle.

Her eyes still downcast, Elizabeth shrugged. "Hmm." Mrs. Mitsuko shifted her weight on the sofa. "Am I right to assume that you are thinking of David?" At the mention of her beloved's name, Elizabeth turned her head.

Their eyes met. "Yes."

"Marie spoke with me this evening about a discussion she had with you yesterday," Mrs. Mitsuko said. Startled by the news, Elizabeth fidgeted in her seat. What did David's mother think of her former relationship with Caleb? "You are concerned about David's safety, no doubt, as are we all."

"As for Joy," Mrs. Mitsuko paused and let out a deep sigh. Biting her lip, Elizabeth knew this Joy must have been the girl she saw with David.

Mrs. Mitsuko went on. "I will have to be honest with you, my dear." Again she sighed heavily, as if the news she bore weighed greatly upon her soul. "I do not know the extent of her relationship with David. Just as you were discouraged, so was he. About a year after the evacuation, he seemed to plummet into a despair I have yet to fully understand. He wondered whether he would ever get out of Manzanar, let alone be able to return home to you, taking you as his bride."

David's bride. That is all she had really longed for these past months. Only to be able to fulfill the promise she made to him on that San Franciscan shore.

"He told me he saw you one day, with a young Caucasian man. We had heard that a meeting of camp leaders was to take place at Manzanar. He told me the night after you came that his worry had been right all along. That you had forgotten him, finding someone else, someone who was Caucasian and acceptable to everyone. Over the next few weeks, before his departure, he began to talk very seriously of Joy. Though she is an accomplished, well-mannered, polite young lady, I could not see the Lord placing them together, regardless of whatever path your own life had taken. Joy is from a Buddhist background.

"Two days before David was deployed to Europe, I spoke with him about my concerns regarding Joy. To this day, I don't know how he left his relationship with her, or whether or not they are engaged. Joy left Manzanar one week after David. I didn't speak with her about their relationship."

Elizabeth let her eyes drop. She wanted to plug her ears and never hear any more about David and this other woman. Especially now, not knowing the status of their current relationship or even of David's safety, for that matter.

"I do not mean to distress you," Mrs. Mitsuko went on, "but only to tell you of the full truth I know." A weak grin crawled across Elizabeth's lips as she processed the sentence structure, reminding her of Midori. Mrs. Mitsuko had told her all she knew herself, as David's mother. What more could Elizabeth ask for?

"Trust God. Do not give up your hope or your love." Mrs. Mitsuko placed a hand on Elizabeth's shoulder. "My son still loves you."

CHAPTER TWENTY-FOUR

Hastening her step, Elizabeth struggled to balance the unwieldy baskets in each hand. A cool breeze laced its fingers around her, sending a shiver down her spine. The darkened sky displayed no stars this night. What sliver of moon hung in the blackness had been covered completely by billowing rain clouds.

The Mitsuko's store was just up ahead. Soon she could put down her load of exotic teas and dry goods. Mr. Mitsuko had insisted on starting up business again, as soon as possible.

Unlatching the door, she stepped inside, grateful to be shielded from the wind. She plopped baskets on the floor and flicked on a lamp. Taking off her sweater, she glanced out the window as a car drove by slowly. After it had passed, she latched the front door. There, now she felt better. Roaming around downtown San Francisco by herself at night had never been a favorite pastime of Elizabeth's. It had been different when she was with David, though. His strength had been enough for both of them. Setting a basket on the counter top, Elizabeth climbed the few steps of a nearby step stool. Looking over the contents of the basket, she reached for a few tins of tea. "Chai goes on the top shelf," Mr. Mitsuko had said.

Reaching up as far as she could, Elizabeth looked down. Through the front window she saw the car had returned, this time crawling even slower past the business. Shuddering at the thought of what intentions the car's inhabitants might have, Elizabeth cautiously began to lower herself from the top step.

The car stopped completely in front of the large front window. Her heart pounding harder and harder in her chest, she froze, waiting. A squeal shrieked from the car, as the driver hammered the gas pedal of his now parked car. Thinking it best that she keep herself concealed, Elizabeth lowered herself even with the counter top, peeking her head above its surface just far enough to see what was going on.

Swinging open the passenger door, a man emerged, puffing on the remnant of a cigar. By the light of the street lamp, Elizabeth could make out the contours of his face, his jaw set firm, lips forming a tight line stretching from cheek to cheek. His broad shoulders and bulging biceps boasted of extreme strength. Tossing the cigar to the pavement and squishing it with the toe of his shoe, the big man tapped on the car's back door. A second later, another man emerged, smaller than the first, yet sturdy and built. His sandy brown hair caught the street lamp's rays. The light traversed across his face at the invitation of his turning head, catching his eyes and displaying their vibrant blue. Straight, white teeth bit his lip.

"Caleb?" Elizabeth breathed. It was half a question, half a statement. What were they doing here? The first man nodded. Both men reached into the car, each of them pulling out a rock the size of a baseball. As a pitcher poises himself to release the ball to an opposing team, each man drew back one arm, and then threw the rocks, one right after the other. Sailing into the window with the force of a catapult, the rocks shattered the front window. Glass fragments slid across the counter top, dropping onto Elizabeth's hunched back.

A moment later, shrieks of delight rose from the car's inhabitants. "Take that, you Jap!" one yelled. It was Caleb's voice. Jap. Had he classified her as such by her refusal of his proposal? The squealing car spun its wheels down the street, black streaks spattering the pavement.

Trembling, Elizabeth rose from her position on the floor. She shook her blouse free of the glass fragments. With each step, glass crunched under her feet. The window had been completely destroyed. Only jagged edges remained in the window pane. Stooping over, she picked up one of the rocks. Upon closer inspection, she spotted something written on it. *The Japs killed my only brother,* it read. Had this reason been the source of the big man's revenge? Picking up the other rock she read, *Elizabeth.*

Had Caleb's revenge been on her account? She sighed. There was nothing she could or should do about that. Caleb had seemed prejudiced before their relationship and falling out. His actions were of his own affair.

Still, feeling the gust and the sprinkling of rain coming from the broken window made her feel somehow responsible. Not for the sake of her previous relationship with Caleb, but for the sake of being Caucasian and American. Numerous reports of vandalism had been reported at the onset of the evacuees' return. This incident would merely become one of those awful statistics.

* * *

"Are you sure it was him?" Marie asked as they swept up the glass the next morning.

Elizabeth nodded. "I'm sure. I could see him from the light of the street lamp."

"Who was he with?"

Shrugging, Elizabeth thought of the friends he had talked of staying with while in San Francisco. "Probably some no good old college buddy, I suppose."

"One of the rocks had your name on it?" Marie asked. She squinted her eyes.

"Yes." She nodded in the direction of the trash can. "It's in there if you want proof." All these questions were making her nervous. Had Caleb any idea the store was owned by David's family, or that she was in there last night? Perhaps he had only seen the Japanese characters on the front window, supposing the owner to be inside.

"Kind of spooky, huh?" Marie emptied the dust pan into the garbage pail, refraining from digging out the culprit's rock.

Shoving her broom up against the wall, Elizabeth sighed. "I don't want to talk about it anymore." She grabbed the trash can, knocking it against the counter in her haste. "I'll get rid of this."

Elizabeth rushed through the storage room and out the back door. She had to be alone, for a few minutes at least. Hoisting the can above her head, she let the remains of the night before fall into the deep, dank bin used by three businesses on the block. The pungent odor of rotting fruit from the produce vendor next door rushed into her nostrils as she bent over the pit. Gagging on her own saliva, Elizabeth stepped back, breathing deeply of the fresh morning air. She sauntered toward the door and sat on the single step.

"I feel like it's all my fault, Lord," she prayed. Why else would Caleb vandalize businesses with which he had no acquaintance of the owner or proprietor? "Why have You allowed this awful thing to happen? I don't understand and I'm worried about David. Please see him home safely." Elizabeth thought of what it would be like to have David back in San Francisco. She would hardly know how to act around him after these three years apart, especially if he was romantically attached to someone else. "How will I ever look him in the eyes and not love him all over again? Lord, as I have prayed before, please don't let me desire what can never be." Her eyes shut tight, Elizabeth sat on the step for a few more moments, not praying and trying not to think. Breathing deeply, she forced herself to her feet. "Grant me Your strength," she said and opened the back door.

* * *

"Is that the last one?" Mrs. Mitsuko opened her front door for Elizabeth.

Trying to catch her breath, Elizabeth set the awkward box down on a nearby chair. "I think so. It was the only one left in the basement."

"Good." Mrs. Mitsuko kneeled beside the box nearest her. "And now we may open these treasures and put them where they belong."

Elizabeth watched as Mrs. Mitsuko cut away the packing string, then gingerly opened the box. Uncovering the contents, she stared into the box for a few moments. "It has been a long time since we packed these away, hasn't it?" she said, mostly in reverie rather than in discussion. She gingerly picked up a teacup and saucer. The intricate designs boasted of Japan's hand-painted china. "Will you help me unpack the others?" She stood, still looking down at the box. "I'll take these to the kitchen."

When the swinging kitchen door had stopped moving, Elizabeth looked down at the boxes surrounding her. Where should she start? Half wondering at the contents, half afraid of unearthing a nearly sacred family heirloom, Elizabeth chose a small unassuming box, its edges torn and damp from the Tyler's basement floor. Cutting away the string, she thought of Mrs. Mitsuko's reaction to the discovery of her treasures, packed away those months ago. Many Japanese families either sold their heirlooms in the urgency of evacuation or had to leave them behind in homes that were soon reclaimed by banks and loan authorities for lack of payment. Some had even been stolen for their market price alone. Thankfully, the Mitsuko's had been able to leave their treasures and the key to their house with Mr. Tyler, who resumed payment while his wife cared for the ornate backyard gardens.

Rearranging the packing to see what lay inside, Elizabeth found two small porcelain dolls, each of them the size of her palm. Each doll's face was painted white with bright makeup accentuating the eyes, cheeks, and mouth. A great mass of black hair was drawn up in a bun, fastened with decorative hair pins. One doll wore a coral colored kimono, the other was outfitted in canary yellow. Studying the toys, Elizabeth thought back to her conversation with Mrs. Mitsuko the night the dolls were packed away, one day before they left San Francisco.

"They were mine when I was little." Mrs. Mitsuko caressed the face of each doll. "In Tokyo, merchants sell hand-made cultural items, mostly to tourists, for very high prices. My family was poor, so I could only dream of possessing such a splendid doll. The one I had at home, though dearly loved and played with, was but a rag doll, faded and torn by years of continued use.

"Every day I would sit on a tree stump not far from the vendor, watching to see who would buy his beautiful dolls, all the while craving one for myself. The day before the merchant was to move to a neighboring city with his toys, an American girl begged her parents to buy her the three dolls remaining on the stand. I watched in fascination as her father, a plump man with jingling pockets, plunked down the money and handed his daughter her new treasures. The girl lagged behind her parents as she passed me.

" 'Haven't you any money?' She looked down at my clothes. Her Japanese was slow, the words holding an English slur. I replied that I did not. Without hesitation, she thrust two of the dolls at me, said, 'They're for you,' then scampered off to catch up with her parents. I will never forget her kindness.

"Elizabeth, I want you to have these dolls when you and David have a daughter of your own. You remind me of that girl who gave them to me."

Reigning in her thoughts to the present, Elizabeth glanced at the kitchen door. No sign of her companion yet. Listening to the tinkling of china, she assumed Mrs. Mitsuko was busy arranging her tea service. She looked down at the dolls she still held in her hands. They had been meant for her daughters, her's and David's. Her lips curled upward as she thought of what their children might have looked like. With almond eyes and dark hair, they would have likely resembled their grandmother more than their mother.

But not now. David was still missing, unheard of and unseen, nonexistent to the world, as far as they knew. How long would it be until news of him reached them? The agony of suspense was almost worse than the worst of news, yet no news, in this case, could be good news. She thought of Mrs. Mitsuko's words the other night after dinner. "My son still loves you," she had said. Was it true? Did David still hold a place for her in his heart?

"Elizabeth!" Mrs. Mitsuko burst through the kitchen door.

"What is it?" Elizabeth imagined a telegram from the government with news of David.

"Come!" The enthusiasm clung to her voice. She motioned toward the kitchen window. "My flowers, they are blooming!"

A smile crept across Elizabeth's lips at her news. At least they could be thankful for the flowers.

CHAPTER TWENTY-FIVE

Elizabeth looked up as she walked down Chenney Lane, the afternoon sunshine spilling over her face and warming the spring blossoms by the roadside. Turning their heads toward the warm rays, violets danced in the breeze. As she approached a brown-sided house, Elizabeth paused, scanning its face for a house number. There, seventeen twenty-one.

Elizabeth took a deep breath, still staring at the structure before her. Marigolds, both yellow and orange, lined the cobblestone walk leading up the front steps. Smiling, Elizabeth decided that, yes, this was Patti's home. Still amazed that her friend could be both a wife and a mother, she held her package closer, nearly squeezing the contents under her arm.

"You found us!" Reeling in her daydream, Elizabeth focused her eyes on Patti, who had just emerged from the front door. When their eyes met, she extended her arms. "It's so good to see you, dear friend."

Elizabeth rushed up the few steps to embrace Patti. It had been a long time.

"How are you?" Elizabeth readjusted her package.

"Very well." Patti's emerald eyes seemed to shine brighter than Elizabeth remembered. "Come in, please. There's someone I want you to meet."

As the two women stepped through the doorframe, Elizabeth sniffed, the aroma of homemade bread filling her nostrils. "Are you baking?" she asked. "It smells wonderful in here."

Patti nodded, but seemed to make light of the comment. "Wait here." She walked down a hallway to the left of the living room.

Elizabeth's eyes scanned the tidy room before her. A landscape mural hung over the sofa, its pastel colors warming the room. A coffee table held a vase filled with freshly cut flowers, a crocheted doily underneath the bouquet. Elizabeth seated herself on the sofa, wondering how Patti's life must have changed during the months she had been at Poston.

Before Elizabeth left for Poston, Patti had started seeing Ben, but was still involved in her work at the library, content to wait for the prince of her dreams, whether he was Ben or someone else, and the heirs that would follow. It seemed that she had reached her goal and come to terms with her dream. Elizabeth remembered her friend's gentle warning about marrying David. She had reminded Elizabeth that there would be obstacles—racial as well as marital. Elizabeth turned her head as Patti returned, cradling a bundle wrapped in a blue blanket.

Seating herself beside her friend, Patti said, "This is our son, Adam." Peering into the folds of the blanket, Elizabeth caught sight of the baby, his fists extended as if in greeting. His lips pursed, he leaned his head to one side, looking at Elizabeth.

"He's beautiful." A longing tugged at her heart. Again she thought of David and the life they could have shared over the past years if the war had not separated them. Maybe by now they, too could have had a child of their own.

Adam started to cry, his little body trembling with sniffles. "Shhh." Patti looked the baby in the eyes. "Mommy's here." She smiled at him, rocking him back and forth. A few seconds later, his sniffles ceased. His eyes kept to his mother, watching her face.

Patti turned to Elizabeth. "Will you stay in San Francisco?" Receiving no reply, she stared at Elizabeth, whose eyes remained glued to the baby. "Are you feeling well?" she asked, placing a hand on Elizabeth's shoulder.

"I'm sorry." Elizabeth turned her head at the sound of Patti's voice. "I didn't hear you."

"Are you feeling well?" Patti shifted Adam's weight, placing him on her shoulder.

Moisture formed in Elizabeth's eyes as she nodded. "Yes, I'll be fine."

"Fine is not good enough for me," Patti said. "You seem disturbed. You're even about to cry. Don't try to hide anything from me, old friend. It simply won't work."

Smiling slightly at Patti's words, Elizabeth thought of how she could explain her feelings to Patti. What was she to say? That she was jealous that Patti hadn't been through the hardship of losing a suitor over the insidious requests of several prejudiced government officials, intent on Japanese reproach? Yet those were the thoughts teeming through her brain. The aggravation at seeing some civilians, such as Patti, completely untouched by the effects of war, when her entire world had changed, irked her beyond words.

"Are you thinking of David?" Patti's tone was soft, such as she had used with Adam a few minutes ago. "How you love him still and wish you could have married?"

Taking in a sharp breath, Elizabeth refused to let her torrents of tears flow. Many times the tears had come, and to no avail, for her circumstances remained unchanged. It would not do to lose control now. "Yes." She replicated Patti's tone, just above a whisper. "I am thinking that and more." She paused, glancing at Patti. Surely she would not be angry if she was completely honest. "I envy the happiness I see in you." Elizabeth dropped her head at her confession.

"Do not be ashamed of your genuine feelings." Patti put a finger under Elizabeth's chin and raised it to its former position.

"You have made a home." Elizabeth gestured toward the expanse of the room they occupied. "It is the very thing I desired, even more than I realized." Pointing at the baby, she continued, "Rightly, you nurture your child. He is content just to be in your arms. You have already captured his heart."

Her own eyes pooling with tears, Patti smiled. "Your heart has matured, I see."

Elizabeth mulled over the words sprung from sincere lips. Had her outlook truly changed that much throughout the war? Thinking back to a conversation she had with Caleb, she remembered his warning of young women marrying, only to find themselves robbed of their energies to pursue their goals, those that really mattered in a selfish life. Giving birth shortly after marriage, a woman should continue pursuing one's personal satisfaction, regardless of the familial cost.

Looking deep into Patti's eyes now, she could discover no symptoms of the kind. Only contentment lived there, coupled with a desire to do her family good all her days on earth. She spoke, her words drawing from some inner wisdom. "God will honor it, Elizabeth."

* * *

Elizabeth turned back to the tea tray sitting on the kitchen table. Muffled voices drifted in from the living room, followed by a burst of laughter. It was good to have the Mitsuko's back, carrying on the tradition of Sunday afternoon fellowship. Yet it was not like it used to be. The house was absent of one special guest, one they all eagerly awaited news of. Elizabeth placed the tea cups on the tray and made her way to join the others.

"We really need someone else to work the night shift," Mr. Mitsuko said as he sipped the steaming liquid Elizabeth had poured into his cup. "Marie expects to finish her studies in town this year. Her load will allow for minimal hours at the store." He paused to sip his tea. "Have anyone in mind?" He turned to Mr. Tyler.

Mr. Tyler shrugged. "Not really, unless Elizabeth hasn't found employment elsewhere. Have you, Beth?" He turned his head toward her.

Elizabeth adjusted her position on the couch. Her father had not called her Beth since she was knee high. She wondered that he decided to use the pet name now. Maybe he feared her going away again and wanted her nearer to home. A job in the Mitsuko's store would ensure her stay in San Francisco, at least for awhile. She groaned inwardly. In hopes of vacating the city, ridding herself of all memories before the war, she had applied at a bookkeeping firm in Tacoma. "I really don't know." She outlined the couch's floral print with her thumb. "I've applied to a company in Washington, but haven't heard back yet."

"Washington?" Mr. Mitsuko's eyes held hers as he stroked his thin, white beard. "Leaving again, are you?"

Elizabeth let her eyes drop to the teacup resting on her lap. "Nothing is certain, yet," she rushed to explain, wishing the wise man wouldn't prod further into her reasons for seeking employment outside the city.

He crossed his arms. "Well, could I hire you temporarily? You can leave anytime a new position is available to you." The room was silent for a few moments as Mr. Mitsuko awaited her answer. She longed to spill her real reason for hesitancy, that she didn't want to be caught in the middle if David came back, engaged to Joy, or worse. In that case, it would be best for her to find work as far away as possible, and to get on with her life.

"It's not exactly a glamorous job." Mrs. Mitsuko directed her words to her husband. "The girl has demonstrated clerical skills. Don't expect her to jump at the opportunity of over-qualification."

Elizabeth smiled. Mrs. Mitsuko always seemed to have her

best interests at heart. If she couldn't accept the job for anyone else, even for herself, maybe she could do it for David's mother. Besides, Mr. Mitsuko had said she could quit at any time. No doubt that included the arrival of their son and possibly new daughter-in-law. "I will accept your offer." She raised her cup to her lips. "But on one condition."

Mr. Mitsuko raised his eyebrows. Perhaps he was not used to negotiating with a woman a third his age. "What is that, my dear?"

"I only work at night." Elizabeth's mind traveled back to the night of the vandalism. Had the men intruded upon private property, they may have harmed any Japanese inhabitants. Strange as it seemed, she was safer than Mr. Mitsuko in the store, at night, by herself.

If he deemed her request odd, he made no reference to it. "Very well," he said. "I'll expect you tomorrow at three."

* * *

The next morning, the sun shone brighter on the beach than it had in a fortnight. Elizabeth breathed deeply of the salty air, closing her eyes and listening to the waves crashing in defiance upon the shore. Scanning the horizon, she decided the ocean was a deeper blue today than it had ever been. She seated herself upon the perimeter of damp sand, setting a small oak box next to her.

Here, upon this very earth was the place where David had proposed. She closed her eyes, seeing once more his jet black hair, his eyes of shining ebony. His tone had been strained before that moment, his gesture rehearsed until he spoke, revealing his intentions toward her. Then all confines had drifted away, as if washed out with the tide. Elizabeth searched her mind for the exact words he had used. "So much has happened," he'd begun. Yes, so much had happened, especially since that time. His words had not been eloquent, nor his ring extravagant. Yet, the meaning had been clear, the symbol of his love unparalleled.

Pulling the box closer, Elizabeth opened her eyes. The tide had receded, leaving damp sand spattered with shells and foliage of the sea in its stead. Dropping her gaze, she released the latch on the box. As if handling a clam's shell, she drew out its contents, a stack of creased, faded parchment. Hands trembling, her eyes scanned the words sprawled out on the top page. It read in part:

You never could imagine how I miss you, my love. I stare up into the darkness at night, wondering about you. Did you look at the stars this night, as I did, and think we see the same cosmos?

...your ring is safe, don't worry."

Elizabeth wondered at these last words. Though she had not asked him where he had put the ring, she had often thought of where it might be. Had he taken it with him to Manzanar? He must have. Where else would it have been safe? Yet at Manzanar there had been Joy, lovely and Japanese. Did her diamond now adorn a stranger's finger? Pushing the ill thought aside, she reached for another letter.

The paper was stiff and crinkled; the moisture of tears stained its surface. Descriptions of camp and life at Manzanar filled the page. Reading the words once more, barbed wire fences, long cafeteria lines, sentries on guard, straw stuffed mattresses, were all resurrected. But this time, Elizabeth's eyes just stared at the words, widening at the descriptions, yet dry, envisioning the portrayal as if through glass, distanced from the pain and overwhelming emotions.

Elizabeth lay back on the sand, her head turned toward the sun, rising steadily to meet the apex of the sky. Closing her eyes, she felt the tickle of the lapping water at her feet. All was silent, save the voices of nature. A clear image of David found its way behind her lids, evoking a smile to play at her lips. My, he was handsome, just as she remembered. But this time, he was not dressed with boyish casualty, but in an army uniform. His arm extended, he bade her come near, pointing far in the distance with his other hand. What was he pointing at? A moment later, she saw it. Her eyes traversing beyond his form, she saw the waters, deep and endless. The sun rose high, just above an island.

Even when the imaginings had faded, Elizabeth lay still, absorbing the sun and the peace that surrounded her. Why the peace came, she didn't know, but soaked in the tranquility nonetheless. The minutes ticked by, maybe an hour, yet nothing changed.

"Elizabeth!" The shrill cry jerked Elizabeth's body as she scampered to put her letters away, out of view of any prying eyes. Scanning the beach for the speaker of her name, she found no one. "Elizabeth!" The voice came again, this time bringing with it familiarity. Several seconds later, Marie appeared over the incline.

"There you are!" She panted, leaning over to catch her breath.

"Your mother said I would find you here."

"What is it?" Elizabeth asked, wondering at the source of her friend's intrusion. "Is something wrong?" Her mind raced. What could have brought Marie all the way out here to find her? Had something dreadful happened? Still panting for air, Marie shook her head, unable to speak.

"What is it, then?" Elizabeth demanded. Surely Marie had not run all the way across the beach front to tell her that her mother's roses had bloomed.

"David," Marie breathed, her hand to her chest. She thrust a paper at Elizabeth. "Read it."

Elizabeth stared at Marie, then stared at the message she now held in her hands. David. News. What did it say? Was he okay? With anxiety unknown to her peace a few moments before, Elizabeth unfolded the paper.

CHAPTER TWENTY-SIX

Tears coursed down Elizabeth's cheeks unchecked, the droplets as salty as the azure ocean water behind her. Could it really be? Her eyes traveled to Marie, who was now calmly staring at her, tears wetting her cheeks as well. Yes, it was true. Elizabeth looked down at the message she still held, allowing herself to reread the scrawled words, the penmanship so familiar.

Dearest Family,

Coming home. Meet me at the train station, 5:00 p.m., Tuesday.

Much Love,
David

Gripping the paper to her heart, Elizabeth closed her eyes, her body shaking. Falling to her knees on the damp sand, she lifted her eyes upward. "Thank You, Father." Her voice barely maintained the volume of a whisper. In an instant, she felt Marie beside her, on her knees as well.

Clasping her hands, Marie prayed. "Lord God, how can we thank You?" Her voice faltered as the words spilled from a grateful heart. A few moments' pause led her to begin again. "You have protected our loved one as he sought to obey You by serving his country. We are ever grateful. See him safely home."

* * *

Tomorrow. David would be home tomorrow. Elizabeth forced herself to concentrate on the woman in front of her. "Will that be all?"

"Yes." The customer dropped a final tin of tea in front of Elizabeth. She studied Elizabeth's face for a few moments, her dark brown roots peeking from beneath a sheath of bleach blonde. "How did you come to work here?" she asked. "I thought the Mitsuko's owned this place."

"Oh, they do," Elizabeth said. "I'm just..." she paused, unsure how to identify herself. What was she to the Mitsuko's now? "...a friend of the family filling in for someone." David's homecoming would determine if she stayed or not.

The shop was quiet the remainder of the night, as the open house for the new coffee shop on West Avenue borrowed all of South Main's customers for the evening. It was just as well. She had been daydreaming a lot ever since she read David's telegram. Right now, she wasn't sure if agreeing to accompany the Mitsuko's to the train station had been such a great idea after all. Maybe it would be best if they went alone, letting David come to her in his own timing. Back and forth her mind went, excited one moment, fearful the next.

Pulling the cash drawer from beneath the counter, Elizabeth decided it was time to go home. Mr. Mitsuko wouldn't mind if she closed a few minutes early if business was slow. They all had a big day tomorrow. Walking to the back room, cash drawer in hand, Elizabeth fumbled in the darkness for the light switch. As she ran her fingers along the wall, the bell sounded on the front door. That was typical. She should have waited until closing time. "I'll be right there," she called. No reply came, but she heard the clomping of feet along the hardwood floor.

In a moment, she returned to the front room. Setting the cash box back in its place, she spotted a man near the door. He faced the window, his shoulders slumping inside his army uniform. "May I help you?" she asked.

The man turned slightly, and the light illuminated his face.

Elizabeth's eyes widened as she stared into the ebony eyes. They stared back at her, nearly boring holes into her soul. "David," she whispered, her voice breaking. He faced her then, not uttering a word. Still staring, his eyes softened as they penetrated her own.

He stepped forward, hesitant at first, but more assured with each step. An instant later, he was at her side, his strong arms encircled around her. Tears of joy began to flow down his cheeks, mingling with Elizabeth's own tears. "Elizabeth," he whispered into her hair. "Elizabeth." Feeling the pounding of his heart against her own, she reached up her hand, stroking his face. Bristling whiskers pricked her hand.

"Are you really in my arms, my love?" After several moments of holding her close, he pulled away to hold her at arms-length. Elizabeth dipped her head slightly. "What is it?"

"You are mine still?" Her mouth suddenly parched. What about Joy? "There isn't another?"

For a moment, David looked down at the floor. "I assume Mother told you about Joy." Elizabeth nodded silently. She longed to give in to her impulse, to embrace him and give in to the strength of his arms. "She and I are no more, Elizabeth," he said. Reaching out his arms once again, he drew her close. "Please forgive my weakness."

A tremor of both relief and guilt darted through Elizabeth's heart. She was guilty as well. Fresh tears of remorse fell to her blouse. "I am to blame as well," she whispered. "Forgive my weakness, too." For several minutes they clung to one another, silent, yet volumes were spoken and discerned.

Cupping her face in his hands, David's lips gently met hers. "I love you." His eyes penetrated her own.

Elizabeth held his gaze as if drawn in by some inescapable force. "I love you, too. I've missed you more than you'll ever know."

"Can we pick up the pieces from where we left off?" he asked.

Elizabeth nodded without hesitation. "I couldn't bear to lose you, ever again."

* * *

"Where are we going?" Elizabeth let David lead her down the beach front the next afternoon.

"I thought we both could use some exercise." Pulling her along, David increased the length of his gait.

"Wait a minute." Elizabeth pulled off her high heels. "You should have told me we would be walking on the beach."

David shrugged. "You ready now?" Elizabeth nodded. "Ready, set-"

She propped her hands on her hips. "What are you doing?"

He nodded down the bench about a hundred yards from where

they stood. "Race you," he said. "Go!"

"Hey!" Elizabeth ran after him. "That wasn't fair!"

Several yards before their destination, David fell to the ground, pulling Elizabeth down with him. Giggling, Elizabeth thought his stunt typical of the man she'd fallen in love with all those months ago. Catching her breath, she realized how much she had missed him, all the fun times and laughter. David leaned on one arm, then quickly sat upright, as if he had touched a hot oven.

"What is it?" Elizabeth's smile faded.

He rotated his shoulder a bit at her question. "Just a little accident."

"David Mitsuko." Elizabeth raised her eyebrows. "Are you hurt?"

David shrugged. "It'll heal up okay, hon," he said. "The doctor said so. No scar or anything."

"Unbutton your shirt. Let me see." She moved toward him.

"It's nothing, Elizabeth, really."

"Let me see."

After studying her expression for a few moments, he unbuttoned the first few buttons. Leaning toward him, Elizabeth brushed back the material to examine the right shoulder. Beginning at the top of the shoulder, jagged cuts wound their way to the top of the chest. "David!" She looked away for a moment. "What happened?"

"It happened relieving the Lost Battalion." He looked down at the wound. "You'll hardly notice it in a little while, I promise."

"It *will* scar, though," Elizabeth said.

"Do you mind?" David asked.

"Mind?" Elizabeth was surprised he would pose such a question. "You're here, alive, well in body and spirit, and you're mine." She lightly massaged the shoulder. "What more could I ask for?" Leaning forward, she kissed the length of the scar. "You were willing to die that I might have freedom."

For a few long, silent minutes they sat, staring out at the ocean, the caps of the waves running toward them. "What do you remember about this place?" David said close to her ear.

Elizabeth smiled. Yesterday, this spot had been her reprieve and solace. A couple of years ago, it had been the setting for his proposal. "I remember you." Her bright eyes peered into his. "And my promise to be your wife."

Digging into his pocket, David retrieved the small Japanese doll with a coral kimono, the one that Elizabeth had unpacked the week before. "What are you doing with that?" Her brow furrowed as he fumbled with the toy.

He tugged at the back of the oriental gown, a boyish grin overtaking his face. "You'll see." Pulling out his pocket knife, he began to cut the seam.

"Don't do that!" Her mouth dropped open as the stitches were severed.

Without a word, David proceeded with unraveling the neat seam. When he'd made a hole the size of a half-dollar, he reached his index finger inside. Retrieving a small wooden box, David clicked open the latch, setting the top to rest on its hinges.

Elizabeth sat and stared, unable to form the words clinging to her tongue. Her ring. *Your ring is safe.* Of course.

"Elizabeth." David's voice was husky as he said her name. Biting her lip, Elizabeth willed her trembling to stop, but to no avail. The tears came, as they had so many times before, but now they were tears of happiness. He leaned closer to her, taking her left hand in his. "We're finally together again." His voice threatened to falter.

He kissed her lightly, then stroked her face. "Will you marry me now?" Unable to swallow or speak, the lump in her throat encroaching, she simply nodded. Yes, she would be his bride. Yes, she would share her life with him. Yes, without a doubt. Yes. She felt the coolness of the ring's metal. This moment was real. As many times as she had dreamed of their reunion, this was the day, the time was now. A single diamond shimmered, as rays of the sun bounced off its surface.

CHAPTER TWENTY-SEVEN

Elizabeth's heart thudded in her chest, threatening to burst with excitement and nervousness. "You'll be fine." Marie squeezed her hand. "I have to go down the aisle first, you know."

Smiling at Marie's encouragement, Elizabeth looked at her soon-to-be sister-in-law. The saffron satin complimented her skin tone, increasing the vibrancy of her black tresses, now carefully pinned and curled.

Elizabeth surveyed herself in the full-length mirror at her side. Reaching out to touch the glass, she felt as if she were a spectator, peering into a long-awaited dream. Only now it was no dream, but actuality. She and David would be married within the hour. Her wedding gown's brilliant white satin sparkled in the overhead light, each sequin serving its purpose. She fingered the gold cross about her neck as she turned from the mirror. Since David's return, she'd worn it faithfully every day.

"What's going on now?" Elizabeth asked. "Can you see?"

Marie opened the nursery–converted into a bridal dressing room–door a crack, peeking her head into the hallway. "He's seating the mothers," she reported a moment later. "Time for me to go."

The seconds dragged on as Elizabeth waited for her father. Closing her eyes, she prayed, "Lord, You are the Author of this day. You alone have brought it into being. May David and I be united as one, just as You have ordained, to Your glory."

Swinging open the nursery door, her father strode into the room. "Are you ready, sweetheart?" Elizabeth gave a single nod, noticing the unshed tears forming in her father's eyes. No doubt this was a turning point for him as well, letting go of a daughter sheltered under his roof for two decades.

"Come." He extended his arm. "Your groom is waiting."

The echoing strains of the organ's reverent chords sounded throughout the sanctuary. Taking a deep breath, Elizabeth took her first step down the long, narrow aisle. Every head turned, and everybody rose, saluting the entrance of the bride. Elizabeth's eyes traveled past the guests, friends, aunts, uncles, cousins, to the altar.

There he stood, staring at her, his navy suit pressed. Her eyes stayed fixed to David's as she walked down the aisle, and her smile beamed ever brighter. Approaching him, her father at her side, she searched his expression. Love, yes love, dwelt in his eyes. For one moment, David averted his gaze, blinked several times, then refocused his eyes on his bride.

"Who permits this woman to be joined to this man in matrimony?" Pastor John asked.

Squeezing her hand, Mr. Tyler replied, "Her mother and I."

The couple grasped each other's hands and stood beneath the wooden cross, high on the church wall. Glancing at the cross, a white cloth draped over its beams, Elizabeth thought of their journey to this place. Their journey had not begun at their first meeting, but when they each had accepted Christ and sought His will for each day of their lives on earth. Christ alone was the reason for this day.

David's eyes were moist, but shed no tears, as he examined her hair, makeup, jewelry, gown. His gaze settled on the golden chain for a moment, his lips curving upward in a smile. *It's all for you, my love.* Elizabeth longed to whisper the words of her vows, words of endearment and love.

"Do you, David, take Elizabeth to be your wife, in the sight of God and of man, until you reach eternity?" Pastor John smiled as he said the words, undoubtedly glad this day had finally come.

Peering deep into Elizabeth's eyes, David responded. "I do."

"And do you, Elizabeth, take David to be your husband, in the sight of God and of man, until you reach eternity?"

Elizabeth's heart leapt at the words directed to her. Grinning wider than before, she formed the words. "I do." Yes, she would be his wife. Yes, she would share her life with him. Yes, without a doubt. Yes. They could overcome the obstacles that would face them in the future. Elizabeth was sure of that now. Just as long as Christ held them together, as one.

ABOUT THE AUTHOR

Contact Raschelle at *raschellewurzer@juno.com* for further information or to schedule an interview or speaking engagement. For the latest news about Raschelle's books, visit her blog at *http://raschellewurzer.blogspot.com/*.

Raschelle Wurzer lives in Northeast Iowa with her husband, Daniel. They have two daughters, Elizabeth Anne and Edith Avery, and are expecting a third child in August 2011. Raschelle holds an Associate of Arts degree in Communication Studies and three writing diplomas. She is a member of the Phi Theta Kappa International Honor Society. When she isn't looking after children or writing, she enjoys cooking, gardening, and getting together with other mom-friends. She anticipates home educating her children as a second-generation home schooler, wishing to inspire life-long, Christ-centered learning.

CPSIA information can be obtained at www.ICGtesting.com
Printed in the USA
LVOW041052081011

249684LV00002B/61/P